# The Shipwreck Secret

### Vanessa Lind

# CHAPTER ONE

## Clatsop Sands, 1888

In the gale, the *Iona* pitches and rolls. Pablo braces against the cool metal walls of the chain locker.

"Ave María, llena eres de gracia," he recites, repeating the Hail Mary. Earlier in the voyage, he would have only mouthed the words, not wanting to give up his hiding place. Now that's the least of his worries. Besides, no one can hear him over the sea's roar.

A rogue wave strikes hard on the ship's beam. The *Iona* shudders, sending shock waves through Pablo's legs and arms. "Dio te salve," he chants in the bravest voice he can muster. The Lord saves thee. He prays this is true. Prays that if her foolish son dies in this storm, his mother back in Manzanillo will never know it.

Beneath the chain locker, he hears the sound of shifting sands, as if he's trapped in a giant hourglass. In Manzanillo, the sand was taken on as ballast. Now its shifting only adds to the ship's unsteadiness. The *Iona* heels to port, thrusting Pablo against the locker's iron wall. The vessel shudders, her deck nearly perpendicular to the waves. Water sloshes past the windlass, drenching Pablo with its frigid spray. The deck levels, but the schooner still leans precariously.

"All hands below!" The second mate yells the command, straining to be heard above the crashing of the wind and the waves.

Pablo clasps his knees to his chest. The crew must be heading below to shovel sand, an attempt to steady the boat. He could help. For a boy of fourteen, he's wiry and strong. In this storm, maybe no one will care that he's stowed away on their ship. He can scarcely believe they haven't spotted him yet, sneaking out between watches to scavenge for food. But there's one man he mistrusts more than the rest, one Pablo suspects would hurl him over the rails and into the sea without a moment's hesitation. So he stays put.

Minutes pass. Maybe hours. Waves pound the deck, drenching him again and again. His abuela used to tell of a hurricane that hit their village when she was a girl. The winds must have been like this, Pablo thinks. He should have known trouble was coming. Last night, the seas were so calm. Eerie calm. He should have jumped ship then, taken his chances in the water.

His plan made sense back in Manzanillo. Hop a schooner bound for San Francisco. Try to find his uncle there. Start over, maybe earn enough wages to send money home to his mama and his abuela. How proud they'd be of him then.

When the *Iona* docked at Manzanillo, he knew she was the one, the ship that would make his dreams come true. Three tall masts and painted all white, the *Iona* was the most gallant schooner he'd ever laid eyes on.

Slipping aboard the night before she sailed, he'd discovered elegance beyond any he could have imagined. Polished mahogany rails, brass fixtures that gleamed in the lamplight, the captain's quarters furnished with plush chairs and a wall of books.

All illusion, he knows now. Once they'd taken to the sea, he overheard the murmuring among the crew. The *Iona* was cursed. When they docked in San Francisco, the chief steward stumbled from the dock and drowned. Rattled, the captain ordered the ship back to sea, and Pablo missed his chance to get off.

From there, it only got worse. The lovely senoritaa dying in the captain's arms. The helmsman steering them off course, swearing he'd seen Miss Emma's ghost. The captain's shrouded body following the pretty lady into the sea.

And now this storm. At sunset last night, the sailors spoke of crossing the bar today. Hanging about the shipyard at home, Pablo learned a good deal of English, but he doesn't know what they mean by the bar. Still, peering out from the chain locker, he could read the worry in their eyes.

Morning brought a breeze that freshened into a gale. By afternoon, the winds were howling, pounding the schooner with waves larger than any Pablo has ever seen. And now, despite the frantic shoveling of the ballast, the ship is still hove to.

The crew scrambles up from the hold. "Top the mast!" The first mate screams the command. From his hiding place, Pablo watches in terror as two men climb the rigging, clinging fast to the ropes. Somehow, they manage to saw away the top of the main mast. With a resounding thud, it crashes down, splintering the deck below.

Pablo crosses himself. Dio mio. He sees clearly the gaping hole the fallen mast has made on the leeward side. Sea water rushes in. The sailors shout back and forth. Three of them make a tarp of the topsail, fastening it as best they can over the hole. Another races about, clearing tangled lines and wreckage that seem to pull the ship even further leeward.

Despite all this effort, the *Iona* is foundering, at the mercy of the wind and waves. The crew climbs the rigging, all but one of them, Pablo sees when he counts them. They perch like birds, awaiting their fate.

In the darkness, Pablo climbs from the chain locker. He crouches into the wind, staying low to the deck, willing himself not to slip off. He slides one foot, then the other, toward a tangle of ropes. A shape forms ahead of him, too small by far to be a man, too large to be a rat.

Pablo drops to all fours. "Queenie," he beckons.

The little white dog scampers toward him. He clutches her tight to his chest, then lunges into the darkness. The ship's timbers groan and crack. It won't be long now.

# CHAPTER TWO

## Josephine ~ 1889

The clock struck midnight, chiming so loudly that Josephine covers her ears. A cheer rang out among the young people gathered in the drawing room of the Sheltons' house, perched on Clatsop Sands near the Columbia River.

"Hip, hip, hooray! Let the New Year begin," Olin Stein said as couples exchanged heartfelt but proper New Year's kisses.

Outside, a violent wind shuddered the house. Jo stirred the chafing dish of deviled crab she'd been tasked with preparing. Olin strode toward her. No, not her. Her friend Amity, who was putting the finishing touches on a chafing dish filled with soon-to-be flaming bananas.

Seeing Olin approach, Amity set down her spoon. Abandoning her dish, she rushed for the window. Olin turned heel and followed, determined, it seemed to claim his own New Year's kiss.

Amity flung open the sash. Sideways rain drenched her instantly.

Shielding his face, Olin backed away. "By Jove, Amity. Whatever are you doing?"

"Letting out the old year's bad luck," Amity shouted over the wind.

The blast of cold air had a chilling effect on the amorous couples, who turned to gape. Amity reached to pull down the sash, but it stuck. As Olin seemed to weigh the virtues of chivalry over dry garments, Jo left her chafing dish and went to the window. Together, she and Amity managed to close it, though not before the front of Jo's frock was thoroughly drenched.

Amity tucked a strand of wind-whipped hair behind her ear. "Bad luck, omens, and curses. You may all thank me for ridding you of them."

"Surely you don't believe such nonsense," Jo said.

Amity glanced pointedly at Olin, who'd turned his attentions to another unattached woman. "Only as it's convenient."

"You mustn't make light of such things." Dorinda Hamilton sashayed toward them, her latest conquest trailing behind.

Jo drew herself up. "I prefer truth over superstition."

"Then you must shun even the luck of a New Year's kiss." Dorinda turned to chuck her gentleman under the chin. "How droll."

Color rose in Jo's face. She opened her mouth to utter a retort, but Amity steered her back toward their chafing dishes. "Mustn't burn our feast," she announced gaily. In an aside to Jo, she added, "Dorinda is just jealous because she knows how sweet Noah is on you."

Their hostess, Clara Shelton, had taken over stirring Jo's crab. "I believe it's done. The yolks have set up. Be a dear, will you, Jo, and set out the saltines."

Jo was happy for any task that kept her from having to interact with Dorinda. They'd been friends when they were young, but now that Jo had taken charge of Astoria's Evening Register, Dorinda seemed intent on taking her down a notch whenever she got the chance. Coming out here on the spit to ring in the New Year might have been a mistake. Between Dorinda's acerbic tongue and a storm to rival all storms, it was going to be a long night.

As she arranged saltines on a platter, Jo's fellow revelers took up plates and began dishing up the midnight chafing dish fare. Besides her deviled crab and Amity's sauteed bananas—crisp-edged but thankfully not burned after their tussle with the window—the menu featured Welsh rarebit, sherried omelet, curried beef, and beignets de pommes.

Laughter and conversation filled the room, punctuated by proclamations of how good each dish tasted.

"I say it's a tossup between the bananas and the crab," Amity said, alluding to the friendly competition that goes along with chafing dish parties.

"I'm too ravenous to care who wins," Jo said. "But I do admit that the dash of sherry you suggested makes the crab superb."

"Mother's secret ingredient," Amity said. "Though you mustn't tell the teetotalers."

Bite by bite, Jo savored the midnight meal. With her belly warm and pleasantly full, her attitude toward the gathering improved. It was rather adventurous, after all, coming all the way out here to ring in the New Year. And now that Dorinda was across the room, head-to-head with her beau, there was no further unpleasantness.

Still, she missed Noah, even knowing his absence was for the best. If not for Noah's gentle prodding, ostensibly connected to the purchase of new equipment for Felch's Canning and Packing, her father might never have been persuaded to travel to California, where she and Noah hoped a side trip to Lake County's mineral springs would ease his gout. And thank heavens they hadn't tried to get home for New Year's. She hated to think of anyone being out at sea in this weather.

"Penny for your thoughts," Amity said.

Jo set down her empty plate. "I'm wondering whether 1889 will be the year you quit breaking hearts and let some lucky man court you."

"If I do, I assure you it won't be Olin Stein," Amity said, keeping her voice low.

"You needn't shun him because he reports for the competing paper," Jo said.

"That has nothing to do with it. Well, maybe a little. But mostly I find him aggressively irksome."

"Can't argue that point," Jo said.

Across the drawing room, Clara stood. In her hand, she held a man's bowler hat. "Let's play the Resolution Game. Violet will pass around paper and pencils, and I'll come around with the hat."

Amity sighed. "Now we must endure attempts at wit by the humorless. I prefer trial by chafing dish."

"It's all in good fun," Jo said.

Chatter ceased as the partygoers considered what to write on their slips of paper. In the quiet, the howling wind sounded even more ominous, rattling the windows. How good it felt to be safe inside a lamplit room, a fire blazing in the hearth.

Jo fingered her pencil. She knew her true resolution, felt it deep in her soul. Taking charge of the Evening Register, she'd committed herself to pursuing the truth, no matter where her investigations might lead. Before coming here tonight, she'd learned from a police officer that money had gone missing from the county safe. The officer had confided that he believed Astoria's police chief, who was not exactly known for his integrity, to be the culprit. It could be a messy situation to report on. Chief Bailey ran in powerful circles. Still, Jo didn't intend to shy from wherever the facts led.

Such serious matters weren't in the spirit of tonight's game, however. Instead, Jo scribbled, *I must never wear my best gloves to bed,* folded her paper, and tossed it into the hat.

Once all the papers were collected, Will Storey volunteered to go first. A surfman at the Point Adams lifesaving station, he was a new addition to the clutch of friends who gathered to socialize.

Will thrust his hand in the hat, stirring the papers and plucking one out. He unfolded it, grinning. "I must perfect my swimming stroke with my ears," he read from the paper.

"Then you'll need ears the size of an elephant's," Olin quipped. A reporter for Astoria's Daily Gazette, he was rarely at a loss for words.

The guests tittered. A pounding at the door startled them into silence.

"Now who could that be at this hour?" Clara scurried toward the door.

"And in this storm," Amity said.

Clara opened the door to a burst of wind stronger even than what Amity had let in through the window. In the doorway stood a figure in a surfman's rain slicker, his wet hair plastered to his forehead. "Will Storey, your services are needed. There's a ship gone aground on the spit."

Will jumped to his feet. "Coming."

Alarm rippling around the room.

"I'll get your coat." Clara started for the anteroom.

"And your boots," Violet said, following.

"I'll come along," said a man Jo recognized as a volunteer firefighter from Astoria.

Olin stepped forward. "As will I."

"What does he think he's doing?" Amity whispered to Jo. "He's never saved anyone's life."

"He's after the story," Jo whispered back. "A firsthand account of the rescue for the morning Gazette. I can't let him scoop the Register."

"If you think the surfmen will let you ride along on a lark, you're sorely mistaken," Amity said. "In case you haven't noticed, there's a wicked storm."

"Where there's a will, there's a way, my mother used to say."

"I doubt your mother would approve of you invoking her wisdom to throw yourself in harm's way."

"I'll be careful."

Clara and Violet returned with boots and rain slickers for Will and the other two men. The guests gathered round as they donned their gear.

With attention diverted, Jo slipped into the anteroom. Amity followed.

"That won't keep you from the rain," she said as Jo fastened her cloak about her shoulders. "Your boots will be sopping wet too."

"What about those poor people aboard the ship? You think they're staying dry?"

"I know you love getting deep into a story. But that shouldn't mean putting yourself in harm's way. Wait till morning. You can interview the survivors."

"And let Olin have the firsthand report," Jo said.

In the drawing room, another man was making a half-hearted plea to be allowed to go along.

"No room in the wagon," Will said.

"There you have it," Amity said. "Even if they were inclined to let you ride along, there's no room."

"Wagons always have room."

Heaving a dramatic sigh, Amity grabbed her cloak from a hook near the door. "I declare, you are the most stubborn woman I've ever known."

"I prefer persistent." Reaching for the door, Jo turned. "What do you think you're doing?"

"I can't let you have all the fun." Amity tossed her cloak over her shoulders. "Not to mention Noah would never speak to me again if I let you go out there alone."

This last point was a weak one. One of the things Jo most liked about Amity's brother was how he trusted her in ventures other men would be quick to shut down, like running a newspaper.

But Amity could be as persistent as Jo when she chose to be, and at any rate, there was no time to argue. Jo flung open the anteroom door. With arms linked, they charged together into the storm.

# Chapter Three

## Josephine ~ 1889

Beneath a tarp, Jo braced herself as best she could against the bumps as the wagon jolted along the rutted dirt road. She and Amity had scrambled beneath the tarp just as the men were emerging through the Sheltons' front door.

She was glad for the cover from the rain, glad for the darkness that kept her from having to witness Amity's discomfort in addition to her own. At least they'd found extra rubber boots and rain slickers under the tarp.

The wagon slowed, then came to a stop. From the scrambling of boots, it sounded as if the men were getting out.

"Now?" Amity whispered.

From outside the wagon, Will lifted the tarp. "What's this?"

Pelted by wind and rain, Jo bolted up. "We're here on behalf of the Evening Register."

"To get a firsthand account." On the pile of boots, Amity stood unsteadily.

"You'll have to wait in the wagon," said the surfman who'd come for Will.

Olin peered over the side of the wagon. "That's right. You'd only get in the way."

"No more than you will." Jo grabbed a slicker and a pair of boots. She put them on. Then, hiking her skirt as far as she dared, she jumped down from the wagon. Amity did the same.

Will and the other surfman exchanged glances. "Got spunk," said the surfman. "I'll give 'em that."

"We'll be of help," Amity said. "Tending to the survivors."

"If there are any survivors," the fourth man said grimly.

Shielding her eyes from the driving rain, Jo looked into the darkness. "Where's the ship?"

"Ran into the jetty," the surfman said. "That's the message we got at the station before the lines went down."

"I thought the jetty was supposed to make things safer," Jo said.

"It will," Olin said. "When it's finished."

"The rest of the Point Adams men are attempting to reach the wreck by boat," the surfman said. "But in this storm, they may not get past the bar."

"You have to go out, but you don't have to come back," Will said, repeating the lifesavers' motto.

"Our instructions are to take the locomotive," the surfman said. "In case they can't get there by water."

"There's a train way out here?" Amity said.

"For building the jetty," Jo said. "It carries the boulders they're using. They set the boulders, then build out the trestle and tracks as they go."

Will pointed into the wind. "Up ahead, we should run into the tracks."

Bracing against the wind, Jo and Amity tromped after Will. Behind them trudged the other three men. In her borrowed boots, Jo struggled to keep her footing. Pummeled by sideways rain, she could barely see. But even as she struggled against the elements, a story was taking shape in her head. Even the venerable Nellie Bly had written nothing so dramatic.

Near the mouth of the Columbia—the treacherous Columbia bar - thousands had died when their ships foundered. She hoped this vessel's occupants had survived. But she knew that even the most experienced crew could be lost in conditions like this. Passengers were at even greater risk when what should have been a pleasant ocean voyage turned into a full-blown disaster.

These were the conditions that had prompted the recent opening of the Point Adams lighthouse and lifesaving station, the second such effort in Oregon. After weeks of practice with signal flags, cannons, breeches buoys, and boat drills, Will and his fellow surfmen would now put their skills to the test.

Grateful as Jo was for the rain slicker, it left her skirt half-exposed to the elements. As she tromped over the grassy dunes, the weight of her soaked frock grew heavier and heavier. Shivering from the cold, she clenched her teeth to keep them from chattering.

Finally, they reached a set of train tracks. Jo fell in line with the others, leaning into the wind as they trudged along them to the west. Just when she thought she couldn't take another step, they came to a hulking locomotive parked on the tracks. Beside it stood a shack.

"Get in the cab," Will said. "I'll wake the engineer and the fireman." He headed for the shack.

"Ladies first." Olin gestured toward the steps leading up to the cab. He offered Amity his hand. Ignoring it, she grabbed the rail and climbed in on her own.

Jo followed. Inside, she let down the slicker's hood, flinging raindrops to the floor.

Amity plopped onto a stool. "Remind me to let you go by yourself next time you come up with a stellar idea like this."

Olin swung himself up and into the cab. "Afraid I'd scoop you, were you?"

"It's a big story," Jo said. "The town deserves multiple perspectives."

"Big enough to make the wires, I hope." Olin tapped the toe of his boot on the floor, a nervous habit.

The surfman climbed up into the cab, followed by Will and the two bleary-eyed men he'd roused from the shack. Jo and the others stepped aside, making room for them.

"Brought a party along, did you?" said the older of the men Will had fetched. He turned his glare on Jo and Amity.

Jo straightened. "We're reporters with the *Evening Register*, sir."

Stone-faced, the man seemed not to hear. He sat down in front of the controls, a complex assortment of pipes, valves, and levers. "Such a night to be out."

The younger man—the fireman, Jo assumed—began loading wood into the tender. As he started up the boiler, the cab began to warm. Jo was tempted to shed her coat. But they'd no doubt be going out again soon.

Studying the gauges, the engineer reached for the throttle. The locomotive chugged slowly forward. "Can't take her too fast. Weather like this, the trestle could be out."

On top of that, fog was rolling in. Huddled together, the group leaned forward as one, peering out the locomotive's front window through the wisps of gray that curled against the night. Soon the fog turned so thick it obscured all but the tracks right in front of them.

Squinting into the night, the engineer squeezed the brake handle, slowing the train to a crawl. All eyes strained ahead. Jo's breath caught in her throat. She wasn't prone to fear, but neither was she keen on plunging with the locomotive into the depths.

As they rounded a corner, Amity pressed toward the window. Ahead, a dim outline took shape, like an apparition forming out of the fog. Crouching close to the tracks, the figure crawled toward them, a bundle of some sort clasped to its chest.

The fireman yanked the whistle cord. Shrill and loud, the warning filled the night.

"It looks like a boy," Jo said, squinting into the dark.

"Carrying some sort of bundle," Amity said.

The engineer came down hard on the brakes. The locomotive jerked to a stop. Amity flung open the door and rushed down the tracks. Jo followed close behind, fighting the wind and rain.

Wide-eyed, the figure gazed up as they approached. In the light from the locomotive, Jo saw the relief that flooded his face. "Angeles," he said, in Spanish. From the time she'd spent in California, Jo knew the word. *Angels.*

Jo and Amity crouched beside him. "We're not angels," Jo said. "We're real people, come to rescue you."

"What's that you've got in your arms?" Amity said.

A thin smile formed on the boy's lips. "Queenie."

The bundle shifted. A dog's face looked up at them, white fur plastered against its skin. Like the boy, the dog was shivering.

Amity touched the boy's shoulder. "Let's get you in where it's warm."

Together, they helped him to his feet. From the direction of the locomotive, Will and the other surfman came running. "You came from the
boat?" Will asked.

The boy nodded.

"What about the others?" the other surfman said.

The boy looked back toward the beach. "No se."

"What about the trestle?" Will said. "Is it damaged?"

The boy looked bewildered.

"The ship." Jo motioned with her hands, the way she'd seen Noah do
with her father's Chinese workers who spoke little English. "It crashed?"
She punched her fist into her palm.

The boy nodded. "Si."

"Where?" Will asked. "How far from here?"

Looking into the fog, the boy's eyes widened. He pointed down the
tracks.

Jo turned to look. A figure stumbled out of the fog. A man, his shirt
torn at the chest, his eyes dazed. "Quarter...mile or so back," he said, in
the manner of a Brit. He swayed, as if the effort of speaking had been too
much.

Grabbing hold of his arm, Amity steadied him. "It's all right. You're
safe now."

"The trestle," Will said. "Is it damaged?"

With some effort, the man nodded. "Up...up ahead."

"How many survivors?" Will asked.

"No...no idea. Call went out for..." His voice faltered.

"Can't these questions wait?" Amity said.

"For...every man... to save himself," the man said.

"We sent a rescue boat," the other surfman said. "Have you seen it?"

"No...rescue." The man's voice sounded weaker.

Coming alongside him, Will gripped his other arm. "Must have turned
around. Let's get these two back to the station, and we'll pick up their
line thrower. And the breeches buoy. Plus every hand we can fit into the
locomotive."

Every hand. Jo intended for that to include her.

She wrapped her arm around the boy's shoulder. The wind at their
backs, they walked into the light beaming from the engine, a beacon in
the storm.

# Chapter Four

## Olivia ~ Present Day

In the tiny back bathroom at Tidewater Books, Olivia adjusts the patch over her eye. How did she let Naomi talk her into this?

She takes a deep breath and exits the bathroom, doing her best imitation of a pirate's swagger.

"Yo ho ho!" Naomi calls out from where she stands, in the center of a group of children sitting cross-legged on the floor.

"Yo ho ho!" the children echo.

Naomi puts her hand to her ear. "I can't hear you."

"Yo ho ho!" the children scream.

"That's better. And look who's here. A pirate, come to read you a story about..." Lowering her voice, Naomi puts her hands on her knees and crouches nearly at eye level. She gazes around the circle from one child to the next. "Buried treasure."

She gestures toward Olivia. To a child, they turn and stare as Olivia strides toward them in her pirate garb. Pulling up a stool, she reaches for the book Naomi has chosen for the bookshop's first-ever children's story time. "The Pirate and the Treasure," she reads from the title page, using the most pirate-y voice she can muster.

Naomi runs her hand through her cropped hair, which this week is dyed purple. She gives Olivia a thumbs-up, then steps back from the circle to ring up a purchase for a woman waiting at the register.

As the children settle into the story, Olivia nearly forgets how ridiculous she looks. It's magical, the way the words and the brightly colored pictures hold their attention. She still feels that way herself sometimes, getting so wrapped up in a book that the world falls away.

She can hardly believe her good fortune, inheriting all these books and a shop for people to find them. There are hassles with owning a bookstore, to be sure. But hardly a day passes without her offering silent thanks to her great-aunt Ingrid for entrusting her with Tidewater Books.

"And the pirate sailed off," she reads, turning to the final page. "Into a sunset painted bright with new adventures."

"But he forgot the gold." A boy from the circle sounds disappointed.

The girl next to him elbows him in the ribs. "He left it on purpose. Weren't you paying attention?"

The boy scowls. "That's dumb."

"Now, now." Briskly, Naomi claps her hands, then holds up another book. "Who wants to hear a story of about a pirate and a cat?"

"Me, me, me," the children squeal, nearly in unison.

Olivia cedes her stool to Naomi, who starts in on the story. As if on cue, Olivia's cat Micki pads in from the back room. Circling the children, she causes enough of a disruption that Naomi has to start the book over after the cat moves on. But it's worth it, seeing the delight on the children's faces. Micki does that with people.

Olivia turns her attention to her grown-up customers. Most are mothers and fathers grateful for twenty minutes of entertainment for their children, so they can browse the shelves uninterrupted. Judging from the volumes they're loading up in their arms, the cash register will get a workout. Naomi was right. Hosting the story time is a good idea, outlandish costumes and all.

One of the mothers is looking for a book on dahlias. Olivia shows her the gardening section in the shop's back room. Searching the shelves for the flower books, she hears bits and pieces of the story. Naomi alternates between a husky pirate's voice and a high-pitched lady's voice. At a well-delivered line about booty, laughter erupts.

Olivia smiles. She can't tell who's having more fun, the children or her assistant.

"This part of the shelf is wildflowers," she tells her customer, gesturing toward the top shelf. "And this part is for, um, other kinds. Not much of a gardener myself, I'm afraid."

The woman laughs. "Who would be, coming from New York City? I'll bet you're glad you got away from all that hubbub."

"A slower pace here for sure," Olivia says, one of a handful of responses she gives when asked about how she's adjusting to small town life in Astoria. It's not that she doesn't miss the city. The shopping. The restaurants. The shows. But she was ready for a change.

Leaving the woman to her browsing, Olivia turns toward the front room. Naomi's talent with voices is amazing. "Deep down in the sea, where the pirate ship sank," she's saying, in a voice that sounds just like a man's.

Except it is a man's voice, Olivia discovers. A wiry, sandy-haired man is standing at the edge of the children's circle. He's about the same height as Olivia and maybe ten years older, with a tan that speaks to a good deal of time spent in the sun.

"You put on your wet suit and your flippers." He gestures as he speaks, putting on imaginary gear. "You strap on your oxygen tanks. Then you climb onto the edge of the boat." As if wearing flippers, he demonstrates.

"And you jump in." He crouches and jumps. "You swim down, down, down."

The children are riveted. "How deep can you go?" a boy asks.

"One hundred feet. Maybe more if you've got the right mix of air in your tank. But you've got to be careful." He looks from one child to the next. "Too deep, and you'll get sick. Maybe even die."

Olivia wonders if she should intervene. She has no idea who this man is, and she's pretty sure the parents didn't bring their children to hear about dying.

Before she can decide, his tone lightens. "And there it is. Stuck in the sand at the bottom of the ocean. A real pirate ship, one that wrecked a long, long time ago. Fish swim in and out through the portholes. Crabs crawl on the decks. And if you're really, really lucky, you'll find treasure."

"Did you ever find a real treasure chest?" a girl asks.

"Maybe." Flashing a smile of perfect white teeth, he winks at Naomi. "But that's a story for another day. This lovely lady has another book to share with you now."

The children pivot toward Naomi, who's holding up a picture book. "The Parrot and the Pirate," she says, and begins to read.

A line is forming at the register. Olivia rings up purchases, glancing now and then at the stranger. He has stepped away from the story circle, but he's watching, listening. As attentive, almost, as the children.

She's running the dahlia woman's credit card when Naomi finishes the story. Applause erupts. Parents saunter over, retrieving their little ones. The pirate-ship man hasn't moved.

"...should've asked earlier," the woman at the register is saying.

"Sorry, what?" Olivia asks, returning her attention.

"My husband wants to build a gazebo. You have any books about that?"

"If we do, they'd be right over here." Slipping from behind the register, Olivia directs her to the construction section.

When Olivia returns, she finds Naomi squatting near the floor, eye to eye with the one child who remains. From the snatches of conversation Olivia can make out, the boy is telling Naomi everything he's ever read about the pirate Blackbeard. Nodding along, Naomi glances at Olivia, who gives her a thumbs-up.

When the boy gets up to leave, Olivia expects him to go over to the man who entertained the children with his diving story. Instead, he goes to the dahlia woman. The rest of the children have already departed with the grown-ups who brought them.

Olivia approaches the stranger. "Quite the story you shared. Sounds as if you've had some deep-sea experience."

"Indeed I have." Up close, there's an intensity in his blue-eyed gaze.

"Now that the commotion has died down, can I help you find anything?"

"I'm interested in shipwrecks."

"So I gathered. Well, we've got a maritime section over here." She leads him to a bookcase. "We get lots of queries about titles related to the sea."

He scans the shelves, top to bottom. "Anything local? On shipwrecks, I mean."

"Those would be in the back."

She leads him to the local history section and pulls out three used books, all of them showing various levels of wear. *"Pacific Shipwrecks,"* she says, reading the titles from the covers. *"Close Encounters with the Columbia Bar. A Maritime History of the Columbia River and Vicinity."*

He flashes another smile. "You know your inventory. And your town, I presume. You must be from one of those fifth-generation families I keep hearing about."

"Not directly." She sets the books on a table near the part of the shop they call the Cozy Nook, armchairs circling a woodstove. In the chairs, two single women are chatting, having taken refuge here when the story hour began. Glancing at Olivia, one of them smiles and taps the corner of her eye.

The eyepatch. Olivia pulls it off and shoves it into her pants pocket.

If the stranger notices, he doesn't let on. He thumbs the pages of the three books. He sets aside two of them and hands her *A Maritime History of the Columbia River and Vicinity.* "This looks promising. Could you set it aside for me?"

"Sure. I'll just need a name."

"Jimmy. Jimmy Stone."

Naomi appears in the doorway that connects the front and back of the bookshop. "You must be the surprise Finn said he was sending over."

"You're a friend of Finn's?" Olivia asks.

"A newish friend," Jimmy says. "Great guy, Finn. With good taste in women." He nods at Naomi. "He said his girlfriend was helping with some sort of pirate thing for kids, and he thought it would be fun for me to say a few words about what it's like to find a pirate ship."

"Sounds exciting," Naomi says. "I hope you find what you're looking for here."

"Already did." Olivia holds up *A Maritime History of the Columbia River and Vicinity.*

Naomi laughs. "I meant the shipwreck."

"Better get going." Jimmy lifts his hand in a wave. "Nice to meet you both."

Olivia watches as he walks out the door. "I had no idea Finn had a friend who investigates shipwrecks," she says.

"He doesn't," Naomi says. "The guy just showed up one day at the dock and said he'd pay Finn to take him out."

"To look for treasure?"

Naomi shrugs. "I guess. Finn doesn't say much about it, except that it's decent money."

"Huh." Olivia stashes her eye patch in the cabinet under the register. "You were marvelous with those kids, by the way. A natural."

"No one listens like a kid. Especially when you're telling a story. And it looked like the parents used their time well. You were busy at the register."

"Exceeded expectations," Olivia says.

"Next month we could do a space theme," Naomi says. "Kids love space stuff. I'll bet we could get the diving shop to let us borrow some gear. A few alterations, and we'd have space suits."

This seems a stretch, but Naomi has a knack for the far-fetched. Olivia is glad she had the good sense to look beyond appearances and hire her as an assistant. She's only a few years younger than Olivia, but with her tattoos and piercings and ever-changing hair coloring, she couldn't look more different. Yet she's diligent and trustworthy and knows the inventory. She has taken Olivia's dream of an espresso bar and made it a reality, and she clearly has a way with children.

And it doesn't hurt that Finn has taken a liking to her. Having brokered an arrangement over what otherwise might have been a contested inheritance of this historic building, Olivia is still feeling her way with Finn Parsons. But they're learning to rely on one another's strengths—hers in managing the shop, his in making what seems like endless repairs to the building.

Olivia plops onto a stool at the espresso bar. "I could use some caffeine before we start planning space suits."

"Me too." Naomi dons her apron over her pirate's coat and slips behind the bar. "Double shot?"

Olivia shakes her head. "I'd be up all night."

Naomi scoops coffee beans into the grinder. "Dark and quiet. That's the best time for reading."

Before she forgets, Olivia grabs a pad of post-it notes. On the top one, she writes *Jimmy Stone*, then sticks it inside the front cover of the shipwreck book. "Good thing that guy mentioned Finn. I was starting to wonder what he was doing here."

Naomi lifts a finger, signaling a wait while the grinder whirrs. When it's finished, she says, "Why's that?"

"Oh, you know. Single guy, hanging out at a kids' story hour."

"You thought he was some sort of pervert? If he was, I doubt he'd be that obvious."

Olivia shrugs. "Maybe an estranged father, looking to nab his child."

Naomi puts her hand on her hip. "You do know where you're getting that, right?"

"News stories. Amber alerts."

"And a certain film for which Astoria is famous. Bad dad looking to steal his son back. Big chase scene at the grade school."

"Oh. Right." Olivia's face grows hot. "Kindergarten Cop." Now that she's an Astoria resident, she's been making a point of watching all the movies that were filmed here, back in the day.

"You don't need Arnold Schwarzenegger looking out for the kids at your story hour. You've got me." Naomi punches the button that starts up the espresso machine.

The overhead lights flicker, then go out. Naomi groans. "Not this again."

"Finn was supposed to come over last night and check out the electrical panel," Olivia says. "Didn't show. You might have to give him up for an evening if we're ever going to have reliable espresso."

"Don't blame me," Naomi says. "He's been out in his boat."

"At night?" Olivia says.

Naomi shrugs. "With that treasure guy, I guess."

"Well, he's going to have to make time for us," Olivia says. "We can't have the circuit tripping every time we fire up this machine."

"I'll remind him next time I see him," Naomi says. "Which he promised would be soon."

"No." Olivia stands. "I'll do it. Finn's been a lot happier since the two of you started dating. No sense letting some faulty wiring get in the way."

# Chapter Five

## Olivia ~ Present Day

F inn isn't answering his phone. So, after Olivia and Naomi close the shop and Naomi heads off to her yoga class, Olivia goes looking for him.

Of the three places she's likely to find Finn—his rented house in Uniontown, the Seaway Tavern, or the dock, tinkering with his boat—the dock seems most likely. From what Naomi says, he hasn't been home much lately. And if he's not at his boat, the Seaway is only a few blocks away.

The dock also gives Olivia an excuse to walk along the river. Even at five o'clock, the sky is bright and the air surprisingly warm. After half a year in Astoria, she still marvels at having landed in such a beautiful place. Picking up the Riverwalk, a patchwork of boardwalks and asphalt trails, she gazes out over the Columbia. Every day, every hour, it seems, the river is changing. She counts the big cargo ships anchored out in the water, emissaries of commerce from across the Pacific. Closer in, a harbor seal dips in and out of the waves, sleek and lithe.

Lapping rhythmically against the shore, the Columbia's gray-green waters are a balm to Olivia's soul. Tensions she didn't know she was carrying ease out of her forehead, her shoulders, her arms. She has survived the bookshop's first big in-store event, involving children, no less. It's not that she doesn't like children. But she's never quite sure how to handle herself around them. They can be so authentic, so transparent, so disarming. Vulnerable in a way that evokes those Kindergarten Cop worries, an irrational but genuine impulse to protect them from harm.

But then Olivia is an only child, her experience with younger children limited. Naomi, on the other hand, comes from a family of eight. Unlike Finn, she's close with her siblings, who all live around here. This is good for Finn, Olivia thinks. When she first met him last spring, he was something of a loner, not so much by choice as by circumstance, an orphan of sorts who'd lost some of the people he'd been closest to growing up and gotten himself estranged from others. As an adult, he came back to Astoria on his own, determined to make a living the way his great-uncles and grandfather had, fishing where the catch has become less and less predictable.

The agreement Olivia and Finn forged with the help of their attorneys prevented a protracted legal battle over which of them would inherit the bookshop and its historic building. Olivia's claim was the stronger of the two. But if there is one thing she has learned from her mother, a high-powered Boston real estate broker, it's that such disputes can turn into legal nightmares. And once Olivia realized Finn's emotional connection with the property, through his great-uncle Sam Shelton, she felt inclined to hammer out a compromise.

In part, that compromise involved deeding Finn an interest in the property, with him taking primary responsibility for maintaining the apartments upstairs and the ground-level retail space, including the bookshop. But judging from the list of maintenance items in her pocket, he may have bitten off more than he can chew. The requests have been piling up, with the bookshop's fuse-blowing at the top of the list.

She turns, leaving the river walk for the marina. She isn't looking forward to prodding Finn. But it has to be done. As her mother has often warned, you let one part of an agreement slip, and pretty soon, the whole thing falls apart.

She finds Finn at the back of his boat, parked at a slip near the end of B dock. The cowling's off the motor, and he's crouched down next to it.

To Olivia's surprise, he's not alone. Tall and slender, the woman next to him sits back on her heels. Blonde highlights gleam in her light brown hair, cropped close to the shoulders and tousled in the wind-swept look that advertisers favor.

In fact, if someone was tasked with doing an ad campaign to promote summer, this woman could star in it. She's wearing cutoffs and a crisp white shirt, sleeveless. Her legs are tanned, her calves muscular. In sum, she's the sort of woman who makes Olivia want to run to a mirror and check her hair and makeup. She thinks of Naomi, twisting away in her yoga class with not a clue that Finn, who has had so little time for her of late, seems to have plenty of time for this white-shirted woman.

Feeling protective, Olivia hastens toward the boat. "Hey, Finn." She steps aboard like she belongs there. "Motor acting up again?"

"If it's not one thing, it's the other." Wrench in hand, he stands. He's got the solid build of a wrestler and gray-blue eyes that mirror the river.

The woman pops up beside him. She tips her head at Olivia and offers a smile. "As I told Finn, a learning opportunity." A British accent. Not something Olivia hears often in Astoria.

"You must be new in town." Olivia thrusts out her hand. "Olivia Crawford. I run the bookshop."

"Jillian Woodhull." Her fingers are slender, her grip strong. "Finn has mentioned the bookshop." She looks up at him. "Some sort of pirate thing going on there, isn't that right?"

"Story hour," Olivia says. "Finn, that surprise you told Naomi about went over great with the kids." A pointed dropping of the girlfriend's name. This is no time to be subtle.

"I figured Jimmy would be great. Not often that kids get to hear from a real live treasure-hunter."

Jillian brushes her hands together, as if she's gotten them dirty. "Enough plugs and sprockets for one day. See you later, Finn." She lifts her hand in a half-wave. "Nice to meet you, Olivia. See you around."

Olivia waits till she's out of earshot, then says to Finn, "Interesting acquaintances you've been making these days."

"Quite the lady, isn't she?" He watches as Jillian saunters away from the dock, then wipes his hands on a rag. "Hey, sorry I haven't been around much. I've been meaning to have a look at that electrical panel."

"Actually, there are a few things that need your attention." Olivia fishes the list from her pocket and hands it to him. "I thought it would help if I wrote them down."

He glances at the paper, then shoves it back at her. "I know all that." He sounds testy. "Just need a chunk of time. Priorities. Isn't that what you're always talking about?"

It comes out as an accusation, borne from the part of Finn she finds hard to navigate, the part that makes her wonder how a man with so many skills can suffer what seems to her such a lack of confidence.

"Naomi says Jimmy has been paying you to take him out in the boat." After seeing Finn shoulder to shoulder with Jillian, it seems wise to mention Naomi again.

"Streak of luck, that I was the one out here when Jimmy came looking. About time something went my way." He reaches into his jeans pocket and pulls out a roll of bills. He snaps off the rubber band holding them together and fans them out for her to see. Twenties, fifties, even a few hundreds.

"That's what he paid you?"

"Yup. And this is just for the past few nights."

"That's good money, all right," she says. The cash makes her suspicious, but she keeps this to herself, wary of offending Finn yet again.

"Just a down payment, Jimmy says. He's going to cut me in on whatever they find so long as I keep it on the down low."

"Keep what on the down low?"

"The shipwreck they're looking for."

"Wow," she says. "I've heard lots of ships have wrecked around here. I never thought they might be valuable."

"Me neither," Finn says. "I mean, I grew up hearing stories about boats that went down, Coast Guard rescues, that sort of thing. It's how the old guys tried to keep us young ones from trying something foolish, I guess. But it wasn't till I met Jimmy that I learned about the big ships that sank back in the day and some of the stuff they had aboard."

"What sort of stuff?"

"You name it, it's down there. Coal. Lumber. Furs. Artifacts." He ticks these off on his fingers. "And gold," he adds with a wink.

"Actual treasure," she says.

He nods. "Jimmy's found it before. He'll find it here."

"I don't get it." She waves her arm, gesturing toward the water. "If there's gold out there, why isn't everyone looking for it?"

He shrugs. "They don't know about it, for one. And even if they did, it's not so easy to get at. Currents break up the wrecks, and the pieces get scattered. Mud and sand cover them up. And in close to the river—that's where most of them are—the water's murky, not to mention cold. Makes finding some of the wrecks in the Atlantic seem like child's play, Jimmy says."

"Sounds risky."

He holds up his hands, palms out. "Hey, I'm just driving the boat."

"Still." She crosses her arms at her chest. "I hope you're weighing risk versus reward. Money isn't everything."

"Now you sound like my mother."

"We make a good team, Finn. I don't want you getting sucked into something dangerous. I may not have lived here long, but I've heard plenty about the hazards of the Columbia River bar." She's not entirely sure what the bar is, but she knows it can be deadly.

"I'm being careful. I watch the weather."

"But you're searching around the bar."

"I didn't say that. Jeez, Olivia. I told you I've got to keep this on the down low if I'm going to get my cut."

The more he tells her, the worse this sounds. "Why the big secret? From what you've said, it's unlikely anybody around here is equipped to get at whatever Jimmy's after."

"Maybe not, but that won't keep them from trying if they find out about it. Some amateur diver goes out thinking he'll beat Jimmy to a find, and likely as not he'll get himself killed. And you know how word spreads these days. People start going off on social media about how Jimmy's looking for the *Iona*, and the professionals will swoop in like vultures."

He pauses, and she sees the worry in his eyes. "Crap. That just slipped out. Olivia, you've got to promise me. Not a word to anyone about that ship I just mentioned."

"One ship's the same as the other to me," she says. "I just need you to find a way to balance this treasure hunting with helping out at the building. The bookshop is going to have a hard time turning a profit this quarter if the power keeps going out."

"Okay, okay," he says. "You forget I slipped up and mentioned that ship, and I'll be over first thing in the morning to work on that panel. Deal?"

"Deal," she says. But between the woman with Finn and his involvement in what seems a shady operation at best, a malfunctioning electrical panel may be the least of her worries. And once a problem presents itself, she's never been one to just let it go.

# Chapter Six

## Olivia ~ Present Day

O livia is the one who suggests sushi that evening. The restaurant is a quiet little place, and now that tourist season is winding down, she and Ethan have it almost to themselves.

Sitting across from him in a booth in the back, she considers how fortunate she is to have him in her life. Not that he's perfect by any means, but she appreciates his easy-going manner, his thoughtful way of probing an issue, and his gentle acceptance of her for who she is, understanding that this isn't a matter she has entirely settled for herself.

He also understands that she's made a big change, departing New York for a little river town on the opposite side of the country to run a business that she's having to learn as she goes. All of which means that as much as she values their relationship, she's glad he seems in no more hurry than she is to get serious.

Over platters of nigiri topped with maguro, spicy tuna, and shrimp tempura, they drink sake and catch up on each other's lives. Ethan tells her about the historic restoration workshops he attended this week in Portland. Some of the architectural details he mentions are well out of her wheelhouse, but others she recognizes from tagging along with her mother on house showings when she was young. With this in common, her mother might even approve of Ethan, a first for any of the men Olivia has dated. And yet, in her zeal to prevent Olivia's marrying badly as she herself had, Steph Crawford would no doubt root up some reason to criticize. Thankfully, she's incredibly busy and three thousand miles away.

Olivia fills Ethan in on the goings-on at the bookshop, including today's story-time success. It feels a minor accomplishment next to the heritage work he's engaged in, but he makes her feel as if running a bookshop is one of the most important jobs in the world. Who knows? Maybe it is. With her books, she can help people escape, the way everyone needs to now and then. Through stories, they can feel what others feel, and there's little in the world more important than that.

It's this last bit, about feeling what others feel, that she tries to keep in mind as she shares her concerns about Finn. "I had no idea he was up to anything out of the ordinary until this guy showed up at our story time and started telling the kids about diving for treasure," she says. "Afterwards, Naomi told me Finn has been taking this guy out in his boat. Which reassured me, since I thought it was a little off for some single guy to saunter in and start engaging with little kids."

"Understandable." His hand brushes hers. "You felt protective. There's plenty of stranger danger in the news."

"You say that so kindly. And to be fair, this guy didn't come off like a total jerk. More like he just wandered in off some sunny beach and checked his surfboard at the door."

"A surfer guy." He raises an eyebrow. "Should I be worried?"

"Naw. I'm more attracted to the beard and chambray type." She plucks his shirt sleeve. "But I still worry about Finn."

"Not sure I've ever heard Finn Parsons and chambray mentioned in the same breath before."

She smiles, then turns serious. "There was a woman with him at the docks, Finn. Supposedly he was showing her how to fix a boat motor. But she didn't strike me as the wrench-toting type."

"There's a wrench-toting type?"

"Okay, I'm generalizing. But appearances aren't always deceiving. I'm afraid her interest in Finn extends beyond mechanics, and I'm worried about Naomi."

"Naomi seems like she's got a good head on her shoulders."

"She does. But if Finn's sneaking around behind her back, I feel like I should say something to her. Or is that better left between the two of them?"

"Hard call," Ethan says.

"And as if that's not enough, Finn showed me this big wad of cash. He says that's how Jimmy's been paying him. For taking him out at night. None of which seems—" With the opening of the restaurant's front door, she breaks off mid-sentence.

In come Finn and Jimmy and Jillian. This is another part of small-town living that Olivia is still getting used to, running into people she knows at every turn. Including those she's only just met.

Ethan lifts his hand in greeting. "Hey, Finn," he says. "How's it going?"

"Going great." Finn saunters over to their table. Jimmy and Jillian follow.

"I had no idea you liked sushi," Olivia says.

"Not sure I do. Never tried it before." Finn juts his thumb at Jimmy. "His idea."

"The ocean air makes me crave it," Jimmy says.

"Fish and chips." Hands in his pockets, Finn shifts side to side. "That's more my style. If I'm gonna eat fish, which I don't usually. But he's the boss."

Olivia sets her mouth in a smile, but inwardly, she cringes at how strong, independent Finn kowtows to this stranger.

"I was just telling Ethan how you had the children mesmerized at the story hour today, Jimmy, talking about diving for treasures at the bottom of the ocean." She figures this will serve as an introduction, since Finn hasn't bothered with any. "And how Jillian is learning to repair motors."

Jimmy laughs. "Only because I suggested it."

Jillian elbows him. "Don't listen to him. He'll take credit for the sun coming up if you let him."

"Anybody diving out in the ocean has earned some bragging rights in my book," Ethan says. "Especially around these parts. Are you a diver, too, Jillian?"

"Marine archaeologist." Jimmy sets his hand on Jillian's shoulder. "Spends half her life on the water."

"How fascinating," Olivia says. "I had no idea."

"We'll leave you to your dinner," Finn says, even though all they've got on their table are empty plates and what's left of a bottle of sake. "Come on, you two. I'm starved."

"Good to meet you," Ethan says.

"See you around." Olivia watches as Finn leads them to a table in the far front corner of the restaurant, out of earshot. Maybe it's her imagination, but once the talk turned toward Jimmy and Jillian, he seemed eager to get away.

Ethan sips his sake. "Feel better now?"

Olivia turns her glass in her hands. "Because Jimmy says she's a marine archaeologist?"

"Because it looks to me like she and Jimmy are pretty chummy."

"I guess. But it seems odd that Jimmy was the one who felt compelled to mention her profession, not her."

"Proud of her, maybe. No harm in that. From what I understand, it's a specialty that requires advanced degrees."

"Then what's she doing in Astoria, hanging out with Finn?"

"Finn's got a boat. And there's a conference in Astoria this weekend, you know. Something about shipwrecks near the Columbia River."

"I didn't know."

"It's an annual event. Maybe she's here for that."

"Are you attending?"

He laughs. "I preserve stuff on land, not sea. Charlotte reminded me about the conference when I was over at the historical society the other day. A friend of hers from college will be speaking."

Sipping what's left of her sake, Olivia considers this. "I suppose this whole thing with Jimmy and Jillian could be above board. Do marine archeologists team up with divers looking for treasure?"

"They might. This friend of Charlotte's could tell you, I'd think. Set your mind at ease about Finn."

Olivia glances at their table. Jimmy's holding a menu up, pointing and evidently explaining something to Finn. The three of them burst out laughing.

"It's probably nothing," she says. But her unease remains.

# Chapter Seven

## Josephine ~ 1889

At the Point Adams lifesaving station, there was a rush of activity. As expected, the boat that had gone out with the other surfmen had been forced to turn around, the bar crossing being far too dangerous to attempt in this storm. With the lighthouse keeper barking orders at Will and the other surfman, Jo and Amity helped the rescued man and boy—and the dog, Queenie—into the upstairs living quarters.

From the closet, Jo grabbed two nightshirts. "Don't know who these belong to. But from the looks of things, it will be awhile before they need them."

She handed one of the nightshirts to Amity, who was holding fast to the man's arm. "You'll feel better once you've toweled off," Amity said. "And once you get beneath a blanket."

From the glazed look in the man's eyes, Jo wasn't sure the words registered. She held the second nightshirt out to the boy. Eying her with what seemed like suspicion, he clutched the dog even tighter.

"I'll hold Queenie." She made a petting motion with her hand. "You get yourself out of those wet clothes before you catch your death."

Reluctantly, the boy handed over the dog, then snatched the nightshirt from Jo's hand. Queenie wriggled, then settled into her arms. Pressing into her chest, the dog stopped quivering.

"You could stand drying off too," she told the dog.

Reaching for a towel, she heard a thud. Turning, she saw that the man in Amity's charge had slumped to the floor. She set down the dog, and it scampered to the boy.

He scooped up the dog. His eyes filled with fear, he backed into a corner of the room. "Maldito," he said. Jo wasn't sure what this meant, but it sounded bad.

Amity knelt beside the man on the floor. "He's so pale. And shivering. We've got to get him dried off and into bed."

"We can't undress him," Jo said. "Maybe the boy will do it."

Amity glanced at the boy huddled in the corner, clutching the dog in his lap. "Unlikely."

"Then we'll have to get one of the surfmen."

"They're busy, in case you haven't noticed. We'll have to do it ourselves."

Amity tugged at one of the man's boots. Coming alongside her, Jo crouched at the man's feet and tugged at the other one. Soaked as it was, it felt as if it was plastered to his foot. She pulled harder. With the sound of a suction broken, the boot came off, the force of it nearly toppling her backward.

Amity's maneuver proved more graceful. They each pulled off a sock.

"His toes are turning blue." Jo glanced up at Amity, who was already wrestling the man's limp arm out of his shirt.

"Then we haven't much time," Amity said.

With some effort, Jo lifted the man's shoulders. Amity peeled off his wet shirt and flung it aside. "Now for his trousers."

"We can't. It's not proper."

Amity unfastened his belt. "This is no time to worry about our morals. We've got to get him warmed up, and fast. Besides, with all the commotion, no one's going to stop to wonder who undressed him. Now help me with these pants."

There was no stopping Amity once she got an idea in her head. Jo went around to the other side of her. "Wedge your knee under his hips." She could scarcely believe she was giving instructions on undressing a stranger. "I'll do the same. Then we should be able to pull them down past...everything."

"Good plan," Amity said.

Jo looked away. "On the count of three," she said.

"One, two, and three," Amity said.

In a single fluid motion, they elevated the man's hips and tugged his waistband past his pelvis to his knees. From there, Amity yanked them all the way off, then grabbed a towel and pitched it toward the man's nether parts.

With a quick glance, Jo saw the towel had found its mark. "You always did have good aim," she said.

"Thanks. Now let's get him into bed."

Fortunately, the beds in the room sat low to the ground. Amity turned down the covers of the nearest one. "You take his feet. I'll get his shoulders."

They got in position. "One, two, and three," Amity repeated. On their separate ends, they heaved him up, only inches from the floor.

"Heavy." Jo let go of his feet.

"Indeed." Amity dropped his shoulders.

In the corner, the boy had taken advantage of their distraction to don the nightshirt. He put down the dog and came over to help.

"The middle." Jo pointed to the man's waist.

The boy nodded. On the count of three, they managed to get the man up and into the bed.

Amity arranged the blankets around him. "His color's better already."

"A little." Outside, the locomotive's whistle blew. Jo eyed the door. "Can you handle things here?"

"Of course." Amity slipped out of her cloak, then pulled a chair beside the sailor's bed. "Go get your story."

Jo caught the boy's eyes. "You cover up and get warm." She gestured at the next bed over, smiling at how quickly he complied. Never mind the language barrier. He understood what it meant to get warm. So did Queenie, apparently. She leaped onto the bed and curled up beside him.

She hurried out the door just as the locomotive was pulling away. She made a dash for it. To her surprise, Olin reached to help her up.

"Thank you," she said, squeezing into the cab.

"Where's Amity?"

"She stayed behind. The boy isn't too bad off, but the man collapsed."

Olin shifted his jaw side to side. Jo couldn't tell which disappointed him more, her being here instead of Amity or his missing part of the rescue drama.

He'd have plenty else to write about, she reckoned. She maneuvered toward the back of the cab, ignoring the skeptical glances from a few of the surfmen. The lighthouse keeper opened his mouth as if he might object to her being allowed aboard, then seemed to think better of it. Now that the locomotive was in motion, it made little sense to stop to drop a female reporter into the night.

A grim silence settled over the group as the locomotive chugged into the fog. The engineer gripped the throttle while the fireman loaded slabs of wood into the boiler. Looking about, Jo spotted the equipment they'd come back for. Close to where she stood was a Lyle gun, resembled a miniature cannon mounted on a wooden platform. From what Will had mentioned previously, the surfmen used it to shoot out a rescue line. Beside the Lyle gun was a breeches buoy, a life ring with a fabric sling seat survivors could sit in as rescuers pulled them over ropes to safety.

The fog grew thicker the closer they got to the ocean. Jo wondered if they'd even find the ship. In these conditions, the shifting sand and pounding waves could quickly obliterate it.

They rounded a curve in the tracks. The engineer pulled back on the throttle. "Here's where we picked up the two survivors," Will told the lighthouse keeper, who had charge of the surfman. "The sailor said it was about a quarter mile more to where the ship went aground."

"He also said the trestle is out," the engineer said.

As the locomotive crawled forward, the darkness shifted. In patches, the fog lifted, revealing a handful of faint stars and a sliver of moon.

"Gap ahead," the keeper yelled.

The engineer squeezed the brakes. Beneath them, the wheels squealed, grinding to a halt. Jo stepped aside as Will and another surfman grabbed the Lyle gun and rolled it toward the door. Leaping out ahead of them, two other surfmen hoisted the contraption to the ground.

Will tossed the breeches buoy out to one of the rescuers. Then he turned to Jo. "I'd have gladly invited you out to observe our drills. It would have been lots safer than this. But you're here now, so I suppose you'll insist on coming along to watch."

"You suppose correctly," she said. Olin was already making his exit.

Will offered his hand, and she stepped down from the cab. "Just make sure you stay out of the way," he warned.

"I shall. Unless I'm needed."

He shot her a look, then hurried to join his fellow surfmen.

"Trestle's smashed, all right," called out a man from the front of the group.

"There's the ship," said his companion. "Looks like the bowsprit broke clean off. And she's leaning heavy to starboard."

"There are men up in the ropes," the first man said. "See that one waving?"

Near the yawning gap in the trestle, the surfmen lit two torches, one on either side of where the tracks fell off into the darkness. Silhouetted against the night sky, the ship leaned precariously to the south. Where the middle mast should have stood, Jo saw only a stump. Beyond the front mast was a jagged edge that dropped into the sand. Judging from the wood scattered about the beach, the bow had been shorn off when the vessel hit the half-finished jetty.

Jo counted four men clinging to the ropes of the foremast. Added to the two they'd rescued on the tracks, that made six, assuming the boy was part of the crew. She had her doubts about that. A skeletal crew for a schooner this size.

The surfmen hurried to position the Lyle gun. Olin stood to one side, furiously jotting notes. Since taking over at the Register, Jo rarely went out without a pencil tucked up her sleeve and a notepad in her purse. She had the pencil with her, but her purse was back at Clara's house. She'd have to rely on her memory.

"Ready," called out one of the surfman once the gun was set. "Aim. Fire."

A boom echoed in the darkness, so loud that Jo covered her ears. A projectile barreled through the sky, a rope trailing behind it, then dropped over the foremast's rigging. The ship swayed side to side, and the rope went taut. Two of the surfmen grabbed it and tugged, securing the doubled hawser.

Another surfman clipped the breeches buoy to the hawser. He pulled the line end over end, the buoy swinging like a pair of shorts on a clothesline. As it neared the mast, the closest of the men climbed over the rigging to reach it. He settled into the breeches, and the surfmen worked the pulley, hoisting him to safety.

A squat, thick-browed man, the sailor stumbled out of the breeches. In the torches' flickering light, his eyes shone with the same sort of terror

Jo had seen in the boy. Falling to his knees, he shook his fisted hand at the ship. "May she rot in hell, that cursed ship, and her captain with her."

On either side, surfmen pulled him to his feet. "Don't go cursing your captain," one said.

"It's bad luck," said the other.

The sailor laughed, unhinged as a maniac. "Bad luck? 'Less you've sailed on the *Iona*, you've got no idea what bad luck is. And there ain't nothing more that can hurt her captain. He's dead."

"Lost in the storm," one of his rescuers said.

The sailor shook his head with the vigor of a dog shaking off rain. "Struck dead in his tracks. Tried to warn him, I did. Tried to warn them all."

Swinging around, he spotted Jo. His finger shaking, he pointed at her. "There she is. The specter. The apparition. Same as I saw the other night. Beware, boys. Might be she's a demon."

First an angel, now a demon. How strangely men responded in the face of fear they were loath to admit.

Jo stepped forward. "I'm no demon," she said. "Only a newspaper reporter who's here to get your story."

He cocked his head, screwing up his eyes as if that might bring clarity. "You won't believe what I have to tell."

"I will so long as you tell the truth." Jo took his hand, his skin rough and calloused. "But first, we need to get you warm and dry."

# CHAPTER EIGHT

## Josephine ~ 1889

The next morning, Jo woke to a shaft of sunlight piercing through a gap in the curtains. Beside her in the bed, Amity was still sleeping. Clad in a spare surfman's nightshirt, Jo got up and padded to the window. When offered the narrow room last night, she and Amity had protested. The other beds had gone to the sailors rescued from the *Iona,* and it felt wrong to take the last one, which by rights should have gone to a surfman. But the keeper had assured them that, worn out as they were, the surfmen would be content in their bunkhouse, and to keep the women over was far easier than hauling them back to Clara's.

Beyond the window, the sky was blue. Trees that last night had thrashed in the wind now stood stock still. From this vantage point, the only evidence of the storm was the mess of twigs, branches, and old man's beard that now littered the ground.

Sometimes a winter storm would blow for days. But not this one. Mother Nature was fickle, people liked to say. Temperamental, like a woman. But Jo thought of storms as nature's way of flexing her muscles, of reminding folks she had power to spare.

Stepping from the window, Jo dressed hurriedly, glad to see that her frock was mostly dry. Then she descended the stairs to the smell of coffee. At the rough-planked dining table sat three of the rescued men, gripping thick porcelain mugs.

"One minute he's next to me on the deck," said a lean, lanky sailor. "Next thing I know, he's gone."

"Went off to take a whizz, probably," said another. His shoulders and chest were broad, and a thick shock of reddish hair topped his head. Like the first man, he spoke with a vaguely British accent.

"There's a lady present." The third man, the one who'd thought Jo was a specter, jabbed the redhead's ribs.

They turned to look. Jo tossed back her shoulders. Better a lady than a ghost.

"Good morning, gentleman. I don't believe we've been properly introduced. I'm Jo Felch, with the Astoria Evening Register."

"A newspaper lady?" the lanky man said.

"Ain't you ever heard of Nellie Bly?" said the redhead. "My sis can't get enough of her stories."

Smoothing her skirt beneath her, Jo took an empty seat. "I don't know that I'll ever have Miss Bly's notoriety, but I pursue the truth as she does. I'd like to provide an accurate account of what happened to your ship. Even if you've already spoken to Mr. Stein."

The third man cocked a bushy eyebrow. "You mean the man that woke me before the crack of dawn, firing off questions?"

"I expect so. He's with the morning paper, so he'll be on his way back to town to file his report of the wreck. My paper comes out in the evening, so we've got time to get the facts straight without having to rouse anyone from their sleep." She slipped her pencil from one sleeve. From her other sleeve, she extracted the folded page she'd torn from the back of the keeper's logbook. "Let's start with your names."

"Douglas Herrington," said the man with the bushy eyebrows. "Helmsman. And that there is Roger." He nodded at the lean man seated across the table from him.

"Roger Conrad." The lanky man had a rough look about him, with the dark eyes of a small animal.

"And I'm Arthur Trill." The man at the end of the table ran his hand through a thick shock of nearly orange hair. "You can put me down as Art."

"As I recall, there was a fourth man rescued from the rigging."

"That would be the first mate, Mr. Perkins," Douglas said.

"Was he in command of the ship? If I heard correctly last night, the captain is dead."

Roger glanced furtively at Douglas. He crossed himself, then looked away.

"A good captain he was, too," Art said. "Not like some."

"Matter of opinion," Douglas said. "You ask me, he never should've brought his wife along."

"Weren't no harm in it." Settling on Jo, Roger's gaze makes her uneasy. "Was a might prettier to look at than the lot of you. Not to mention the ship was hers."

"Don't mean nothing," Art said. "Registered in Mexico. You think they check?"

"And here I thought you was defending Capt'n Watson," Douglas said.

"That ain't nothing against him. All them owners skirt the law, one way or t'other," Art said.

Jo jotted a note. "The captain's wife didn't survive the wreck?"

Roger folded his hands on the table. "Died at sea, God rest her soul."

"Fever took her," Art said. "Dressing for dinner one night, and she collapsed. Two days later, she was dead."

Douglas shook his head. "The curse, I tell you."

"It was the boy," Roger said. "He's the one that brought the fever aboard."

"The cabin boy, you mean," Jo said. "The one with the dog."

"Weren't no cabin boy," Art said. "First we saw of him was last night."

"He was a stowaway?" Jo said.

Art nodded. "Musta hopped on in Manzanillo. Brought the sickness with him."

Jo made a note of this, putting a question mark after the supposed origin of the sickness. "Six of you were rescued last night. If the boy stowed away, that means you were sailing with a crew of five. That seems small for a clipper that size. Did the fever take the rest of your crew, or were they lost in the storm?"

"Two jumped ship in Brazil." Douglas ticked them off with his stubby fingers. "Two more in Mexico."

"And then there was Victor," Art said. "In San Francisco."

"Victor weren't no deserter," Roger said.

"Slipped on the dock, Victor did," Douglas said, explaining to Jo. "Hit his head and drowned."

She jotted this down. She was starting to see why he claimed the *Iona* was cursed.

"And now Bernard," Art said. "Musta got swept off in the storm."

"Might still turn up," Roger said. "He's a tough one, Bernard. Survived many a gale. Knew his way around a ship."

"Even the best make mistakes," Art said.

"Coulda cut loose a lifeboat," Roger said.

"In that gale?" Douglas shook his head. "Lifeboat wouldn'ta stood a chance."

The possibility of a seventh survivor intrigued Jo. She glanced at the clock. Not yet eight. If she walked quickly, she could get out to the wreck and back and still make the trek to town in time for her story to appear in the evening edition. Even if there were no more survivors, she'd be able to get a daytime view of the scene, something that Olin's story would lack.

She tucked her pencil and note-filled paper in her sleeve. Standing, she reached for her cape, hung to dry on a coat hook. "Thank you for your time, gentlemen. Now if you'll excuse me, I've a bit more information to gather before I write up my story."

"You'll print our names in the paper?" Douglas asked.

"I'd advise against that," a man said from the stairs.

Jo turned to see the man she and Amity had surreptitiously undressed. His voice sounded much stronger than he had last night. Standing upright and with his full wits about him, he looked a far cry stronger, too, his shoulders squared, his dark hair tousled, his eyes an arresting shade of green.

"I shan't compromise anyone's integrity. We only print the facts."

"Admirable." He descended to the floor. "But we'll be having the court of inquiry to contend with. Casual remarks made beforehand might be misconstrued."

"Gus would know," Roger said to Jo. "He's wrecked before."

"Trying not to make a habit of it," Gus said. "Though in my defense, I could hardly have been held responsible."

"And what about this time?" Jo said.

He laughed. "Unlikely. Second mate's got charge of next to nothing. Boatswain's locker, that's about it."

"Barks the orders, he does." In Art's tone, Jo detected a hint of derision.

"When the orders are appropriate."

"And when they're not?" Jo asked.

"Called it straight with Bernard," Roger said.

Gus rubbed his stubbled chin. "Any sign of him?"

"Not yet," Roger said morosely.

With more questions than answers, Jo slipped out the door. The morning air was brisk. Though the sun had shone brightly past the curtains only a short time ago, a bank of clouds had moved in, covering it up. Rain might follow, Jo knew, but hopefully it would be nothing like the torrents that had fallen last night.

She started off on foot toward the ocean. The going was easier by far than the trek they'd made last night, breeching the distance between the wagon and the train. She stepped quickly, hoping to get beyond view of the keeper, who would no doubt object to her venturing out on her own.

Once before, while visiting Clara, she'd walked part of the jetty so she could write up a firsthand account of the construction for the newspaper. In the interests of saving ships and lives, Congress had appropriated funds for the project a few years back. The goal was to lessen the impact of the Columbia bar, where river currents collided with the ocean's pounding waves, resulting in a treacherous underwater sandbar that had caused many a shipwreck. Bar pilots came from Astoria to guide ships over the bar and along the river's most recently sounded channels. But not every ship waited for a bar pilot, and even with an experienced pilot, crossings could be hazardous.

When finished, the jetty would shift the currents and the sands, lessening the bar's dangers. But building into the ocean what was essentially an earthen wall able to withstand the brutal pounding of the waves, was no small feat. For transporting fifty-ton boulders to bolster the jetty, crews had to lay railroad tracks. Now, after last night's wreck, it seemed a portion of the trestle would have to be repaired.

The *Iona* joined hundreds of other vessels with the dubious distinction of having succumbed to the hazards of a stretch of ocean known as the Graveyard of the Pacific. Almost as much as salmon and logging, shipwrecks were part of the fabric of life here.

Jo had grown up hearing stories of wrecks. When she was young, her father had taken her to see them, for wherever a ship went aground, locals gathered. Some aided in the rescue. Others were simply curious. And a good number more came out to see what treasures they might salvage from the wreck before the insurers and the contracted salvors descended.

As Jo's father explained it, the legality of such pillaging rested on a sort of "finders keepers" provision that applied after a ship was abandoned. It was for this reason, Jo supposed, that a man she now assumed to be Mr. Perkins, the ship's first mate, had wanted to remain with the ship after he'd been rescued last night. But he'd injured his arm, and when the keeper objected to him staying, he'd been in no condition to argue. Besides, as the keeper pointed out, in its present location, no one could reach the wrecked ship except by water, and last night's conditions were sufficient to warn off even the greediest salvors.

But looking down the tracks, Jo saw that Mother Nature had other ideas. Sometime during the night, the combined effects of wind and tide must have broken the *Iona* loose and carried her inland. Instead of being grounded on the far side of the broken trestle, the ship now rested on the near side of the gap, easily reachable from shore.

Veering from the tracks, Jo set off over the dunes toward the wreck. Wet sand clung to her boots. As she neared the ship, she saw the first mate, Howard Perkins. His injured arm in a sling, he waved the fist of his good arm at several people who were carrying items away from the *Iona*.

"Away with you!" Perkins yelled. "All of you, away! And beware. This vessel is cursed. Whatever you take from her will curse you too."

With fear in her eyes, a woman tossed aside the books she'd been clutching. They landed with a thud in the sand. "Come along, George," she said to the man beside her, who held a mantle clock in his arms. "Ain't nothing here worth a curse."

With what looked like some reluctance, the man set down the clock. Another man let go of two shirts. The shirts tumbled in the wind, then came to rest in the sand near Jo's feet.

The treasure seekers began to disperse. Undaunted, some held onto the items they'd recovered from the ship. How much more had been taken, Jo wondered, before the first mate arrived.

The sun peeked through the clouds. Shielding his eyes, Perkins surveyed the scene. "My satchel," he yelled. "Which one of you good-for-nothing thieves has got my satchel?"

He might as well have spoken to the wind. Without turning, the treasure seekers trekked toward their carts. They tossed their booty in the back of their carts, then climbed in and, with a flick of the reins, headed south on the stretch of sandy beach the locals used as a highway.

Perkins descended the ship's ladder. "Vultures," he muttered as his feet hit the sand. "Knew I should've kept watch last night."

"You couldn't have known the ship would break free and drift inland," Jo said.

He squinted at her. "And you are?"

"Jo Felch. With the *Astoria Evening Register*."

"A girl reporter. Taking the world by storm, or so I hear. Amazing how things change when one's at sea. And not necessarily for the better."

He likely meant this as a jab, but she chose to ignore it. "I'm curious as to what you think caused the *Iona* to falter."

His gaze sharpened. "That will be for the court of inquiry to decide. But if you're insinuating there was some fault in leadership, I assure you, you'll find none."

"I meant to imply nothing of the sort, sir, only that—"

At a cry from down the beach, she stopped short. At the water's edge, two salvors had climbed down from their carts and were gesturing at what looked like a hunk of driftwood.

Perkins marched toward them. Lifting her skirts, Jo hurried after him. Drawing close to the men, she saw not a slab of wood but a man lying prone on the sand, his face bloated and his shirt tattered.

Perkins leaned over the body, inspecting it. Then he looked up at the men who'd gestured them over. "See what I mean? This ship's cursed. Now off with you."

One man backed away. The other glared at Perkins, defiant. With the toe of his boot, he lifted what remained of the man's shirt, exposing a gaping wound in the man's chest.

"Ain't cursed," the man said. "Someone's killed him."

# Chapter Nine

## Olivia ~ Present Day

A marine layer rolls in overnight, fog settling in over the river and town, a reminder that winter is just around the corner. This will be Olivia's first storm season in Astoria. Having heard plenty from locals about how the winds will howl and the rains will beat down, she's rather looking forward to it, so long as she's nestled indoors with her books.

As promised, Finn shows up first thing in the morning to investigate the bookshop's electrical problem.

"How was your sushi last night?" she asks.

"Not bad. Except the eel. Not a fan of anything that swims like a snake. You got one of those for me?" He points at the steaming coffee mug in her hand.

"Sure thing."

He pulls up a stool, and she fires up the espresso machine. It whirs to life but then shuts off. The lights go out too. "Rats," Olivia says. "It's erratic like that. Runs for a cup or two, then goes on the fritz."

Finn reaches for his toolbox. "All right, then. Work first, then coffee."

Olivia follows him to the back room. He shuts off the main power, then removes the electrical panel's cover. "Looks up to snuff," he says, inspecting the breakers.

"Better be," she says. "I paid that electrician an arm and a leg."

"Maybe there's a problem with the outlet." He tromps back to the front, crouches down near where the machine's plugged in, and touches the cover. "Shouldn't be this warm."

"The electrician wanted to replace it," she says. "But the estimate was so high already, and when he tested it, it was working fine."

Finn pulls the plug on the machine. "I'll pick up a new outlet and swing by tomorrow to install it. That should do the trick."

"Sorry about your coffee," she says, looking guiltily at the last swig in her mug.

He nudges the brim of his hat. "Just as well. I could use some shuteye."

"Up late last night?"

"Pretty much all night."

"In the boat? With this fog?"

"Yup. The fog's a plus. Folks can't see where we are."

"Other people are out there in the middle of the night?"

He shrugs. "Could be."

"I know it's none of my business, Finn. But none of this sounds legitimate."

The hard set of his jaw tells her she's pushing too far. "Jillian's a freaking maritime archeologist," he says, so loud that his voice echoes off the ceiling. "It doesn't get more legit than that."

"Okay, okay." Olivia holds up her hands in a gesture of surrender. "I just don't get all the secrecy."

"I explained all of that." His voice drops a notch. "More than I should have."

There are so many things she'd like to say, so many questions she wants to ask. But after all these months, she's still getting to know Finn, and she doesn't want to jeopardize the working relationship they've established.

"I swear, I won't mention the details to anyone."

"You better not." Returning to the back room, he flips a breaker, and the lights come back on. Grabbing his toolbox, he heads for the door.

"See you tomorrow," she says in her cheeriest voice.

"Sure thing," he says, but he doesn't sound happy about it.

When he's gone, she pulls a book from the shelf under the register. It's the hardcover book Jimmy asked her to hold for him. It's missing the flap jacket, and the corners of the front cover are worn, but the title is clearly visible: *A Maritime History of the Columbia River and Vicinity.*

She flips through the pages, the type set in an old-fashioned font, to the index. There it is, tucked between entries for the *Iberia* and *islets.* The ship Jimmy and Jillian are looking for. The reason Finn's so distracted. The *Iona,* page 238.

Olivia flips to the page. In the middle of the text is a black-and-white photo of what Olivia, with her limited maritime knowledge, would call an old-fashioned sailing vessel. It's a beauty, with multiple rectangular sails unfurled over three tall masts. Painted white and with multiple windows, the *Iona*'s hull looks like an oversized version of the boats Olivia has seen at Cape Cod. She imagines it's nicely furnished too.

Under the photo is a caption. *The schooner Iona, Captain Nicholas Watson, from Manzanillo, Mexico, for the Columbia in ballast, was wrecked in January, 1889, off Clatsop Sands. All but one of the crew got off safely, and they made their way to Astoria.*

Grabbing a yellow pad and pen from the drawer under the register, she jots down the information in the caption: *Capt. Nicholas Watson, Manzanillo to Columbia, January 1889, Clatsop Sands.* She scans the rest of the page but finds nothing else about the *Iona.*

Just to be sure, she checks the page before and the page after. But all she finds are profiles of another captain and mention of two other wrecks, one of them going into much more detail than what the caption gives on the *Iona.* She checks the index again. No, that's it. One page listed.

Beneath what she has written on the notepad, she draws a line, then lists a few of the thoughts that are swirling in her mind. Last on her list is why Jimmy would want a book that contains only a single photo and caption about the ship he's after.

The bell on the door jangles. Naomi comes in. "Lost in thought already?" She tosses her jacket over the coat hook near the door.

Olivia stuffs the notepad back in the drawer. "Someone could steal that, you know."

Naomi laughs. "You can take the girl out of the city, but you can't take the city out of the girl. Did Finn come by this morning? He told me last night he would."

"I thought he was out on the water all night."

"We ate at the sushi place. With Jimmy and Jillian. You should hear the stories those two tell. Quite the life they have, chasing shipwrecks."

"Ethan and I were there too. We'd finished eating when those three came in. You must have joined them after we left."

"Right. I had yoga, remember?"

"Finn didn't tell you about us being there?"

"Nope." She grabs a mug and starts for the espresso machine.

"No coffee today," Olivia says. "Made a cup for myself, but when I tried to make some for Finn, the electricity wigged out again. He thinks it's the outlet. Said he'll come by tomorrow and install a new one."

"Ugh. I'll make a sign for the machine and then grab a cup of java down the block, if that's okay with you."

"Sure thing. Better if we're both firing on all cylinders."

Grabbing a sheet of blank paper from the printer, Naomi pens *Out of Order* in big, loopy letters with pink, green, and purple markers. She illustrates with a sad-faced cartoon lady holding an empty mug upside down. *Check back tomorrow,* she adds at the bottom. "Finn had better come through," she says as she tapes up the sign.

"Does it bother you, him going out nights in his boat? Seems dangerous."

She shrugs. "Finn's like a cat. Nine lives, and depending on how you count them, he's only gone through two or three so far."

"It just all seems so...clandestine."

"Has to be. There can be a lot of competition over shipwrecks, apparently. Especially if there are valuables to be found."

"Like gold?"

"Uh huh. Jimmy's found it before, on other wrecks."

"What about Jillian? I didn't think archeologists went looking for treasure."

Naomi puts her hand on her hip, feigning exasperation. "Don't tell me you never saw Raiders of the Lost Ark? The ark was covered in gold."

"Right. And some kind of demon came out of it."

"I doubt there's a demon at the bottom of the ocean."

"I still think an archeologist would be more interested in artifacts."

"A ship could have both, you know. Gold and cool old stuff that's been sitting at the bottom of the ocean for ages."

Olivia leaves it at that. No sense putting Naomi in a position where she feels she has to defend Finn and his friends.

Still, Olivia is elated when Ethan phones later in the day and says Charlotte from the historical society has invited the two of them to dinner to meet her friend Glen Foster, the marine archeologist.

"I figured you'd have questions for him," Ethan says.

"Do I ever," she says. She just has to figure out how she can pump him for information without mentioning the *Iona*. Or gold.

# Chapter Ten

**Olivia ~ Present Day**

Charlotte Tilson lives high on one of Astoria's hills in a beautifully restored Craftsman home overlooking the Columbia. From where Olivia sits at her dining room table, she counts the big cargo ships anchored in the water. Five of them tonight. Even as dusk falls, they're easy to see, the fog having dispersed early in the afternoon.

"Boston cream pie." Like a butler in a movie, Charlotte comes from the kitchen with a pie plate raised on one flattened hand. "In honor of our Bostonian turned Astorian via New York City."

"I'm not sure I've ever had Boston cream pie," Olivia says.

"Well, don't I feel misled." Charlotte sets the pie on the table. "I guess that's what comes from trusting in a name."

The first time they met, Olivia found Charlotte intimidating. She's young and blond, tiny and yet also curvaceous, with striking green eyes. As it turns out, she's also whip-smart and a whiz at research.

With their mutual interest in history, Olivia figured she and Ethan were a couple. Now she knows their relationship is strictly professional. Charlotte is seeing a man from Portland, and Ethan has eyes only for Olivia.

Now that she has gotten to know Charlotte, Olivia counts her among her friends. At the archives, she immerses herself in her work, resurrecting bits of the past. Outside of work, she's lively and fun and adventurous. She's also great at cooking, a skill Olivia would like to develop herself.

"Whether it's from Boston or not, that pie looks delicious." Olivia pats her belly. "I believe I left just enough room."

"Nothing better for the cook than an appreciative audience," Charlotte says as she plates the pie.

"I've got to say, I never saw this domestic side of you in college." Her friend Glen has his fork poised for action.

"Something about a small town and an old house." Charlotte hands him a slice of pie. "Good food makes memories."

Memories have been a theme of the evening. Charlotte and Glen have shared some fun incidents from their college days, shenanigans suggesting that Glen's serious scholarly demeanor, amplified by his wire-rimmed glasses and receding hairline, was likely acquired after he graduated. Ever the gracious hostess, Charlotte has insisted Ethan and Olivia share a few of their more outrageous collegiate exploits too.

Now that they've all had a good laugh over those and are diving into dessert, Olivia wants to learn more about Glen's work. "Until recently, I'd never heard of marine archeology," she says. "What made you decide to pursue it, Glen?"

"In high school, a buddy of mine was always coming up with wild ideas of things we should try. One of them was scuba. When I was growing up, my parents always had us kids tromping along on some adventure or another, and this buddy convinced me there was a whole other world to explore beneath the waves. He was right. One dive, and I was hooked."

"Glen's been after me to get certified for years," Charlotte says. "He says the earth's best museum is underwater."

"I've toyed with it too," Ethan says. "Love the idea of going underwater and touching pieces of the past."

"You should do it," Glen says. "There's a dive shop right here in Astoria where you can learn."

"How about you, Olivia?" Charlotte says. "You in?"

"Isn't the water awfully dark and cold here?" Olivia says. "And hazardous?"

"Not the easiest conditions, I'll admit," Glen says. "Current rips through like a banshee. You can pretty much only go out at slack tide.

And you're right about the darkness. Lots of mud near the water's surface, so when you get down to the bottom, you're relying on a flashlight to help you feel your way."

"We should make a field trip to the Caribbean," Charlotte says. "Clear waters. And warm."

"Anybody can dive down there," Ethan says. "I like the idea of a challenge close to home."

"I'm with you," Glen says. "One of my first big dives after I got certified was with an older guy who'd been on one of the early teams to explore a wreck a few miles north of here. A tricky dive, but it was rewarding."

"Which ship was it?" Olivia asks.

"The *Isabella,*" Glen says. "A Hudson Bay Company supply ship bound for Fort Vancouver to drop off trading goods and pick up a load of furs. She ran aground trying to cross the bar back in 1830."

"I hear people talk about the Columbia bar, how treacherous it is," Olivia says. "But I don't really know what it is."

"Silt and sand, isn't it, Glen?" Ethan says. "Washed out to sea by the river."

"Right," Glen says. "Between the currents and tides, it's a sort of collision zone between river and sea. It's constantly shifting, which is why bar pilots have always made a steady living out here, guiding ships to and from the river."

"That's how George Flavel could afford to build his big mansion," Charlotte says. Even Olivia knows the Flavel House, an Astoria landmark. "He ran a piloting business."

"Nothing to mess around with, the Columbia bar," Glen says. "Cross it in a small boat, and it's like riding a roller coaster, up and down the waves."

"Sounds terrifying," Olivia says.

"It's better than it used to be, with the jetties," Charlotte says. "Those were massive government projects, especially back in the late 1800s.

"Even so, plenty of ships have wrecked," Ethan says.

"Two thousand or so, by some counts," Glen says. "There's a reason people call it the Graveyard of the Pacific."

Olivia shifts in her seat. None of this is making her feel better about Finn's venture. "You get paid to look for shipwrecks," she says to Glen. "Is that because people are looking for treasure?"

"Never confuse a nautical archeologist with a treasure hunter," Glen says sternly. "Two entirely different beasts. People like me explore and survey wrecks for the purpose of conservation and study. These days, if someone's going to develop waterfront property that might be of historical value, they've got to bring in a marine archeologist to make sure the construction won't disturb any historical artifacts."

"So you're not after gold?" Olivia says.

Glen laughs. "If I had a dollar for every person who's asked about treasure at the bottom of the sea, I'd be a rich man."

"But gold has been found in shipwrecks, hasn't it?" Olivia says. "Or is that only pirate ships?"

Charlotte grins. "Olivia just hosted a pirate story time at her bookshop. That's why she's got treasure on her mind."

"Gold has been recovered, and not just from pirate ships," Glen says. "Not as much as the stories and legends let on, but a few ships have gone down with some pretty valuable cargo. A famous one is the wreck of the *Central America*, a steamer that sank on its way from Havana to New York with nearly ten tons of gold on board."

Ethan smiles. "That's some serious booty."

"But no pirates," Glen says. "The gold was fresh from the California Gold Rush."

"That would be the 1850s," Charlotte says. "Before the Transcontinental Railroad, so overland travel was sketchy. To get from San Francisco to New York, you'd have to sail around South America."

"Right," Glen says. "Although there was a sort of shortcut. You could change ships at Panama."

"But that was before the canal," Ethan said.

"Yes. They'd haul passengers and cargo across the isthmus of Panama, then load everything onto a steamer on the other side," Glen says. "The *Central America* ran the Atlantic part of that route. Got caught in a hurricane off the Carolinas. Hundreds lost their lives, not to mention the gold. Something like 700 million dollars' worth today."

Ethan gives a low whistle. "For that kind of money, I might take up treasure hunting myself. Where did you say we can sign up for that diving class?"

They all laugh.

"The real treasure is the wreck itself, for its historical value," Glen says. "We marine archeologists fight like hell to see that it's preserved. Though I'm afraid all too often, we lose."

"It's hard enough getting government money to preserve a historic building." As head of the Astoria Preservation Society, Ethan knows this all too well. "I can't imagine trying to get it for a structure people can't see."

"Not to mention that we have to compete with treasure hunters. Even if there's no gold, there are often artifacts they can sell."

Charlotte tips her head, a quizzical look. "I thought there were laws protecting shipwrecks."

"There are," Glen says. "State and Federal. In Oregon, there's a permitting process. But people find ways around it. And enforcement is difficult. It's a big ocean out there."

"Still, they must get caught sometimes," Olivia says.

"Oh, some have gotten in trouble, all right. Paid some hefty fines, even served time in jail. Depends on the infraction and who's bringing the case."

Finn has no idea what he's gotten into, Olivia thinks. She wishes she could ask Glen if he's heard of the *Iona*, but that would betray Finn's trust, and she has nothing firm to prove that what he and Jimmy and Jillian are up to is anything but above board.

"I'm curious what you marine types do at a shipwreck conference," Charlotte says. "Don your wet suits and oxygen tanks and go for a swim?"

"Sounds like more fun than some of the presentations. But for the record, beyond a depth of a hundred feet or so, depending on the mix of air in the tanks, there's only so much a human diver can explore directly in these parts. For deeper wrecks, we rely on technology like ROVs and side scan sonar."

"ROVs?" Olivia says.

"Remote operated vehicles. Sort of like an underwater robot tethered by a cable to a boat. From the deck, we can maneuver the ROV around the wreck and take photos using its camera. That's how the gold from the *Central America* was recovered."

"Making someone very wealthy," Charlotte says.

"That's where it gets complicated," Glen says. "A treasure hunter spearheaded the whole effort. He and his team had the backing of investors. But with a shipwreck, there can be conflicting claims under maritime law. If the ship has been abandoned, salvage rights apply. In the most basic terms, it's a case of finders-keepers."

"By definition, I'd think all wrecks are abandoned," Ethan says.

"Not necessarily. And keep in mind that ships and their contents are typically insured. The insurers will have paid out claims after a wreck. If the wreck is later recovered and anything of value is found, they'll typically go to court to recover at least a portion of what they paid out."

"No matter how much time has passed, the insurance companies can still recover on the loss?" Olivia says.

"If they can prove the ship wasn't abandoned. A bunch of insurers got together after the *Central America* was located and staked their claim to the gold. But the courts ruled the ship was abandoned and that the treasure hunters, who to be fair went to some trouble and expense to conduct their salvage operations, were entitled to whatever they found."

"So someone did get very rich," Charlotte says.

"Yes and no. The guy who spearheaded the discovery reneged on his deal with his investors. He took the money and ran. Was in hiding for years. When the US Marshals finally found him, he turned over 500 gold coins and said that was all he had."

"Did he bury the rest of it somewhere?" Ethan says. "I feel like we're back to the pirates."

"In a way, we are. Last I heard, this guy was still locked up in prison, refusing to tell what happened to the fortune he pulled out of the ocean. Meanwhile, our archeological expeditions go unfunded."

Charlotte gathers up the empty pie plates. "You work with a foundation, don't you, Glen?"

"That's right. Pretty much get by with sophisticated versions of passing the hat."

"There's a quilt shop here that raffles off specialty quilts to benefit nonprofits," Charlotte says. "Ethan's group made off with a pretty big haul a while back."

"With help from Olivia." Under the table, Ethan squeezes her hand. "She displayed the quilt and sold raffle tickets at her bookshop."

"I'll bet Vi would be happy to help out your group," Olivia says. "She's always on the lookout for worthy projects. And with the conference here, there's a local connection. Want me to ask?"

"Definitely," Glen says. "Every little bit helps. And about those diving lessons—I'd be happy to take you all over to the dive shop and introduce you to the owner. He's got a ton of experience in these parts."

"Count me in," Charlotte says. "It seems like the ultimate adventure."

"It is," Glen says. "With any luck, you'll soon be diving wrecks yourselves. Fair warning, though. It can be addicting. Every wreck has a story to tell. When you're down there, you can feel the history all around, whether it's in the bones or the artifacts or just the silent hull of a ship that once sailed proudly over the seven seas."

"I'm sold," Ethan says. "You too, Olivia?"

She shivers at the thought of trying to navigate beneath the waves while relying on a tank for air. But she has never liked disappointing people, especially her friends.

"Put me down as a definite maybe."

# Chapter Eleven

## Josephine ~ 1889

B ack at the newspaper office, Jo read over the two articles she'd typed up—one about the wreck of the *Iona* and the rescue of her crew, the other about the man's body that had washed up on shore. Dramatic stories, both of them. She hoped she'd done them justice. She wanted readers to feel as if they'd been there with her. She wanted them to hear from the survivors even as they tried to piece together what had gone wrong.

By recounting astutely observed details, she hoped to distinguish her reporting from Olin's. She knew he'd be fuming when he discovered she was first to report on the murder of Bernard Ainsworth, the sailor who'd gone missing last night.

Not that she took any pleasure in recounting an unnatural death. The last time she'd written up a murder, the victim was Cecil Wisener, the publisher who'd gotten her started in the news business. Perhaps sensing he was in danger, he'd bequeathed her the *Register*. As the newspaper's new publisher, she had assumed a role that while not unheard of for a woman was not exactly common either.

The position was a gift she'd have done anything not to have received. Yet she'd accepted it with gratitude, cherishing the opportunity to indulge her inquisitiveness while fulfilling the solid purpose of keeping her community informed and, where possible, seeing that justice was served.

Cecil would have been the first to point out that she'd done everything she could to get justice for him. She wished she'd been able to do more. But Astoria's police chief, Jedediah Bailey, was notoriously corrupt, the money missing from the safe being only the most recent of the scandals that plagued his office, and he'd done little to help.

"Finished with your stories?" The typesetter, Nan, came alongside Jo's desk.

When Jo first started at the paper, Nan had worked sullenly, as if she couldn't wait to get done. Jo couldn't blame her. In her introduction to the newspaper business, Jo had done a bit of typesetting herself, a task that was tedious at best.

But slowly, Nan had come out of her shell, due in no small part to Amity's gentle but persistent cajoling. Amity had seen an intelligence in Nan and thought she should be given more responsibilities. And she'd been right. Once Nan perceived that her perspective was valued, she'd begun sharing her thoughts when asked—and sometimes, even when she wasn't.

"They'll have to do for now." Jo handed her the typed pages. "Though I'm afraid there are still a lot of unanswered questions."

Scanning the pages, Nan gave a low whistle. "A man stabbed. You think he was murdered?"

"That's the most likely explanation, unless he fell on his own knife, like Brutus."

Nan looked puzzled.

"Shakespeare, *Julius Caesar*. One character kills himself by falling on his own sword."

"Seems there'd be easier ways to go than that, if that was his aim."

"Agreed. But I don't think it was. From the looks of his hands, he was trying just as hard as the rest of the crew to save himself."

"You examined the body?"

"Briefly. I had to feign disinterest, of course. But aside from the wound, it was his hands that drew my attention. Early this morning, I spoke with the surviving sailors. Their palms were chafed, no doubt from clinging to the rigging. This man's hands looked the same. He also had a big knot on his forehead, like he'd fallen. Plus he was stabbed. Someone wanted him dead."

"You say here the crew is here in Astoria, waiting for the court of inquiry to convene. You think one of them is a murderer?"

"It's possible. Strange things happen at sea. You hear it all the time. Sailors get stir-crazy, grate on one another's nerves. Maybe one of the men snapped."

"During a gale, when they're all fighting for their lives?"

Nan had a point. She thought of the men she'd met. Art. Douglas. Roger. Gus. And the boy, whose name she'd learned was Pablo. Even Howard Perkins, the mate in charge of the vessel, could not be above suspicion.

"There will be a court of inquiry," Jo said. "Perhaps they'll rule on what happened."

"We've covered those proceedings before. They determine who's at fault in a wreck and who gets what's left. Never heard of them dealing with a murder."

"Sadly, I doubt Chief Bailey will expend much effort investigating an incident that occurred at sea among a group of strangers who are just passing through."

"So the murderer gets away with it. Goes on to kill again." Nan gave Jo a pointed look. "Unless someone takes it upon herself to investigate."

The door banged open. Amity rushed into the office. "Jo, you've got to do something. They've arrested that poor boy."

"The stowaway?"

She nodded. "Pablo. Gus says Chief Bailey is holding him on suspicion of murdering that sailor."

"Based on what evidence?" Jo said.

"I have no idea. But when was the last time Bailey worried about evidence? Arresting that boy, he'll make it seem as if he has solved the case."

"While conveniently turning attention from the tax money that's gone missing from his safe," Nan said.

"Pablo can't be a day over fourteen," Amity said. "And he's so far from home."

"Without having paid for his passage," Jo pointed out.

Amity's eyes flashed. "That doesn't make him a murderer. First the storm, and now he's locked up in jail. He must be terrified."

Jo reached for her wrap. "Chief Bailey wouldn't talk to me earlier. Perhaps he'll have something to say to me now."

"You've got to persuade him to release Pablo," Amity said. "Gus says he'll keep an eye on him while the investigation plays out."

"Gus again?" Jo fastened the clasps of her cape. "It sounds as if the two of you are becoming fast friends."

Amity's cheeks colored. "He's grateful, that's all. Says we saved his life last night."

"And now he wants to save an orphan who might be a murderer."

"You saw how frightened the boy was last night. Do you truly think he's capable of murder?"

"Appearances can be deceiving," Jo said. "And people are capable of more than we'd ever dream."

Jo knew this all too well. Her hand on the doorknob, she turned. "Where's he staying?"

"I told you. The jail."

"Your new friend, I mean. Gus."

"At the Occident. The looters took everything he had with him. All he's got now are the clothes on his back and a few coins in his pocket. At least Mr. Perkins secured him a room on credit. There were no beds left at the boardinghouse where the rest of the crew is staying."

"Not Jim Turpin's boardinghouse, I hope." Turpin was one of Astoria's most notorious shanghaiers. Jo had little use for him.

"They're at the sailors' rest home," Amity said. "The one the church ladies run."

"Good."

On her way to the police station, Jo considered how best to approach the police chief. She hoped to come away with more information than she had earlier. As for the boy's release, she wasn't so sure. Maybe jail was the best place for him. It wasn't as if he had lots of options. At least there he'd have a place to sleep, and he'd be fed.

She was glad to see that Bob Melbourne was manning the desk at the station. He was the officer who'd tipped her off to the money missing from the safe. He'd slipped her an unsigned note that mentioned the money. *Please make no mention of how you came to know of this,* it said.

"Good day, Miss Felch." Of all the officers, Melbourne had the cheeriest disposition, though today, his smile seemed forced. "I hope you weathered our latest storm without incident."

"I'm no worse for the wear. Is Chief Bailey in? I tried to catch him earlier to get a comment on the wreck of the *Iona* and the man whose body washed up on Clatsop Sands. But he claimed he was too busy to see me."

Melbourne drummed his fingers on the desktop. "Chief's been a little...out of sorts lately."

"I won't take but a moment of his time."

Melbourne stroked his chin. "Well, you could try him at the jail. He went to check on our prisoner."

"The child, you mean. Another matter I'd like to look into."

"Now, Miss Felch. You know the Chief won't like you poking around in that too."

"Perhaps not. But I intend to get the boy's perspective all the same."

"That boy hasn't said boo since we first brought him in. Don't think he speaks a lick of English."

"We'll see. Perhaps he's just being prudent. A wise choice under the circumstances. Good day, Officer Melbourne."

The jailhouse was down the block from the police station. Turrets flanked the entryway, as if the building aspired to something greater than the detention of common criminals. Jo had been inside once before, visiting Cecil's wife, Stella. She'd failed Stella, who'd been shipped off to the mental asylum in Salem. Someday, she hoped to see her freed from there, though she knew the odds were against it.

Entering the jail, she heard Chief Bailey shouting. "Hand it over! Now. Or I swear I'll shoot."

He was standing in the entrance to a cell, a gap-toothed guard at his side. Huddled in a far corner of the cell was Pablo. In his thin arms, he clutched Queenie. Nearing the cell, Jo saw that the little white dog was quaking.

"Boy and dog shot in Astoria jail," she said. "Now that would be a headline."

Bailey turned, his dark eyes flashing. "You again."

"Happy New Year, Chief Bailey. I hope you've resolved something more purposeful than terrorizing a child arrested without evidence."

Lit by a single window high on the wall, Bailey's balding forehead gleamed. "You don't know what evidence I do or don't have."

"Then perhaps you can enlighten me." She withdrew her pad and pencil from her purse. "I'm all ears."

"He's a stowaway."

"So I hear. That doesn't make him a murderer. If there's no evidence to report, perhaps you can tell me who has accused him."

"Don't reveal my sources," the chief growled. "Not to the likes of you. Now if you'll excuse me, I've got work to do."

"Perhaps a more mundane topic will suit. I've been thinking it's high time we did an accounting of the county's finances. It's your department that collects property taxes, is it not?"

He glared at her. "I'm not a bookkeeper, Miss Felch." He turned to the guard. "Get that dog out of here. Now."

The guard started into the cell. Furiously, the dog began to yap.

"That dog has been traumatized," Jo said. "Its owner died at sea. So did the ship's captain. So did the ship's steward. Not to mention the murdered man whose body washed up on Clatsop Sands this morning. Doesn't that series of deaths strike you as strange, Chief Bailey?"

"Who knows?" said Baily. "Maybe the kid killed them all."

"The child was a stowaway. Until the storm, no one on the crew had ever seen him before."

"Only proves his kind is sneaky."

"Anyone on that ship could have been responsible for those deaths," Jo said. "Although I can't help but wonder about your jurisdiction in this matter."

"Body washed up here," Bailey said. "That makes it my business."

"And yet the murder, assuming one occurred, must have happened at sea." She paused, thinking of the Portland newswoman she admired. "I wonder what Melvina Lockwood will have to say about your locking up a child with neither cause nor evidence. She has a keen interest in matters of child welfare, you know."

"Even if he weren't a murderer, this boy has nowhere to go. He's a vagrant. We can't have him wandering our streets. And I suggest you leave Melvina Lockwood out of this. She's a troublemaker. She'd best not come poking around here. It's bad enough that I have to deal with the likes of you. Newspapering is men's work."

Jo drew herself up. She hadn't meant to get involved with the boy and his troubles. But if Bailey insisted on using him as a scapegoat, the truth about what had happened on the *Iona* might never be known. And she had resolved to pursue the truth, no matter the cost. She couldn't stand idly by while Bailey made a token arrest without an actual investigation. Especially not the arrest of a child with only a little dog to cling to.

In the cell, the guard tried to wrestle Queenie from the boy's arms. "Ow!" He drew back his hand. "Damned thing bit me."

Jo pushed past Bailey, entering the cell. "We can't have that. A vicious animal for you good lawmen to contend with on top of everything else."

She reached for Queenie. Pablo loosened his grip, and the dog wriggled into Jo's arms.

This told her everything she needed to know about the boy's character. Much as he cared for the dog, he was willing to let go if it meant saving it.

She extended her hand to him. He clasped it, and she pulled him to his feet. With the dog in her arms, she led Pablo from the cell, marching him toward Bailey. "I understand how busy you are, Chief Bailey. Keeping Astoria's streets safe is no small task. So allow me to rid you of what is on the one hand an annoyance and on the other a potential source of attention you may not wish to suffer. I shall look after this boy. And this dog. If your department comes up with actual evidence against the child—sources who'll go on the record and stand up under cross-examination—I'll be more than willing to surrender him into your custody."

Bailey laughed. "Listen to your lawyer-talk. On top of jilting Warren Hatch, it sounds like you intend to compete with him."

"Mr. Hatch and I came to a mutual agreement," Jo said of the attorney to whom she'd been engaged. "Not that it's any of your business. And now, if you'll excuse me, I need to get going."

Tugging Pablo by the hand, she headed for the door. Bailey made no move to stop her, furthering her suspicion that he'd been holding the child without cause.

Jo's father had entrusted her with their household while he was away in California. Soon, he and Noah would be home. She hoped he wouldn't mind that their household now included a stowaway and a dog.

# CHAPTER TWELVE

## Josephine ~ 1889

Jo ushered the boy inside her father's Italianate mansion that overlooked the Columbia River. "I know you don't say much," she said. "But I have a feeling you understand more than you let on."

Pablo glanced away, then looked back at her and nodded.

"Fair enough. I won't press you to speak. Not until you've gotten comfortable here. For now, this will be home. But you are not to leave the house unless you're with me or someone I trust. If you do, I won't be able to keep the police from throwing you back in jail. You don't want that, do you?"

He shook his head. "El perro?" He pointed at the dog in her arms. "Can stay?"

"Yes, the dog can stay too." Looking down, she saw Queenie had fallen asleep. Gently, she nudged the dog awake, then set her down on the carpet runner. Queenie looked around, taking in her new surroundings, then scampered down the hall.

The boy ran after her, scooping her into his arms.

Coming out of the kitchen, the Felches' maid, Effie, nearly collided with the two of them. "What's this?"

"Houseguests," Jo said. "From the *Iona*. Pablo and Queenie."

As she studied them, Effie's gaze softened. "Hyvyyden tähden," she said, a Finnish expression she used to express wonderment. "I thought it was a cargo ship that wrecked."

"It was. Queenie belonged to the captain's wife. She took sick at sea and died. Pablo was a stowaway. Chief Bailey had him locked up in jail. One of the sailors was stabbed, and Pablo was apparently the most convenient person to arrest for the crime, seeing as how he speaks little English and has no one to defend him."

Effie lifted an eyebrow. "You convinced Chief Bailey to release him?"

"For the time being. I told him we'd keep the boy here until such time as he produces actual evidence against him. The child was petrified, locked up in jail. So was the dog."

"No wonder they look so bedraggled. You did right to bring them here, Miss Jo." Effie set her hand on the boy's shoulder. "Let's get the two of you cleaned up, shall we? And some food in you. Goodness knows you could stand some meat on your bones."

Pablo looked up at her, eyes shining with gratitude. "Gracias, Senora."

"He understands more than he speaks," Jo said.

"Don't I know about that, coming here from Finland without speaking a word of English. Come along, child. We've just enough time to get you washed up before supper."

She steered Pablo toward the kitchen. Jo started for the stairs. Behind her, the front door opened. Turning, she saw Amity entering, arm in arm with Gus Leighton, the *Iona*'s second mate.

"Presses are rolling," Amity said. "I knew you'd probably want to write up more about the ship and the murder, so I asked Gus if he'd come have a word with you."

"Mr. Leighton and I spoke this morning." Jo cherished Amity's friendship, but sometimes her enthusiasm got the best of her. "He warned his men not to give their names for my story. He warned their remarks could be used against them in a court of inquiry."

"That was before Bernard's body turned up," Gus said.

"You have something to say about the circumstances of his death?"

"I know a thing or two." A glance passed between him and Amity. "And your associate here can be quite persuasive."

"I bribed him with an offer of tea," Amity said. "Where's Effie?"

"Busy."

"Then I'll get the tea. Come along to the library, Gus." She tugged his arm, and they proceeded down the hall. Unsure what she was getting into, Jo trailed after them.

In the library, Amity arranged three chairs around a circular table. "Make yourself at home, Gus. And don't be put off by Jo's questions. It's only her profession that makes her nosy."

Jo shot her a look. "I doubt anyone has ever accused Olin Stein of being nosy."

"I'm only teasing. Don't get your feathers ruffled." Amity bustled from the room. With what seemed an unnecessary gesture, given how few people were in the house, she shut the library's double doors behind her.

Jo took a chair. "You've certainly captured my friend's attention."

"Amity is utterly charming. But I don't mean to impose, Miss Felch. If you'd prefer, I can be on my way, with no hard feelings."

"Feelings have nothing to do with it," she said, though this was not entirely true. "And let's dispense with the formalities, shall we? Under the circumstances, they hardly seem appropriate." Circumstances that included her having seen far more of his physical attributes than she'd have chosen.

He folded his hands on the table in front of him. "Very well, Jo. What would you like to know about the *Iona*?"

She took her pen and notepad from her purse. "The vessel is registered in Mexico. Iron-hulled, three masts. I know that much. Up till now, I presume she's been a reliable schooner?"

"She's been in a few scrapes. But the same could be said of many a ship. And I won't hold her wrecking last night against her. That storm was fierce."

"You seem compelled to defend the vessel. Have you sailed with her from the start?"

"Not from the start. I first sailed with the British Navy. Later I shipped out on the *Astral*, then on the *Copenhagen*. Folks like to judge a ship, same as they judge other people. Can't say that I favor one over the other, as long as they get to where they're headed."

The knob of one of the double doors rattled. Gus leaped to his feet and opened the doors. Amity stood in the hallway, a silver tea tray wobbling in her hand.

Gus reached to steady the tray. "May I be of assistance?"

"You certainly may." She handed it over to him. "I don't know how Effie juggles it all."

He set the tray on the table, arranging the tea pot, the creamer, the sugar bowl, the porcelain saucers and cups, and a plate of Effie's spoon cookies much as the maid would have done.

"Aren't these British men delightful?" Taking her seat, Amity poured the tea. "If I didn't know better, I'd guess Gus has experience as a butler somewhere in his storied past."

"A second mate is known as the sailors' waiter." Setting aside the empty tray, Gus sat back down. "No other officer gets so little respect. Bunks in a cabin but eats at second table, making whatever meals he can from what's left by the captain and the first mate."

"You must covet a higher rank," Jo said.

"The position has made me resourceful." His green-eyed gaze seemed meant to disarm her. "And should I want another, I wouldn't let anyone stand in my way."

This seemed a strange point to make in the aftermath of a murder. "I understand the captain's wife was traveling with the *Iona*," she said.

"Along with her little dog." Amity reached for a cookie. "Which is getting a bath in the kitchen sink as we speak."

"How kind of you to have taken in little Queenie," Gus said. "She's been quite forlorn since Emma died."

"Jo has rescued Pablo as well," Amity said. "He, too, is getting a bath, Effie tells me."

Gus tipped his chin to one side. "You ladies are quite compassionate, taking them in. I was worried about Pablo being in jail."

Jo glanced sideways at Amity, wishing she'd had the sense not to broadcast this development. But she supposed the whole town would know soon enough.

"Our chief of police has an unfortunate habit of incarcerating the folks who are least able to defend themselves. It seems he prefers an easy solution over a thorough investigation."

"How unfortunate," Gus said. "I'd like to know what happened to Bernard."

"I'm curious what you make of the circumstances surrounding his death. Did you see or hear anything unusual before the call to abandon ship?"

His lips twisted in a smile. "On a ship that's foundering, there's precious little time to pay attention to such things."

"Jo knows that firsthand," Amity said. "Several years ago, she was aboard a northbound steamer that went aground."

Jo shot her a look. "A traumatic experience, to say the least. The strain of it was too much for my mother. She was already suffering from an illness. She died not long after we were rescued."

"I'm sorry for your loss," Gus said. "It's tragic to lose one's mother under any circumstances."

"Indeed. Which brings me back to the captain's wife. Had they any children back home?"

He shook his head. "Emma was quite young, you see. Nineteen, I believe, when she and the captain met."

"And no one objected to him bringing her aboard the ship?"

"How could they? The *Iona* belonged to her."

"A nineteen-year-old woman owned the schooner?"

"She came from money. Raised with every advantage. Educated in Paris. An accomplished swimmer, quick at tennis, good with horses. Fine-looking too."

"Sounds like quite the catch," Jo said.

"Captain Watson, he had a way with women," Gus said. "Quite the dashing Scottish gent. I expect he swept her clean off her feet. Not that her remaining family approved. Fourteen years between them, and then she goes and buys the ship he's been sailing."

"They thought it a poor investment?" Jo asked.

"More like they thought her decision rash. The ship itself was a glory to behold. Sailed like a clipper. Emma had her painted all in white, then had the captain's quarters made over like a pleasure yacht. Polished mahogany, white ceilings trimmed in gold. At sea, they had nearly every luxury they'd have enjoyed on shore. Books, music, food. And from the attention they gave each other, you'd have thought no one else was aboard. Nary a care in the world for those two."

"Surely the captain had his worries with running the ship."

"Not especially. Howard ran things."

"The first mate, you mean," Jo said.

"Right. And a good crew needs little supervision."

"But the *Iona* lost some sailors, didn't she? Owing to the curse, from what I'm told."

He laughed sharply. "Surely in this day and age you don't believe in such things."

"What I believe is irrelevant. The sailors I spoke with seem convinced."

"Men of the sea are a superstitious lot."

"Still, something must have put the idea in their heads." Amity said.

"An old woman peddling apples, if you can believe it. Came aboard while we were docked in Melbourne. Captain sent me to escort her off. She wouldn't budge. Screamed all sorts of abuses at me. Finally, Perkins came along to see what all the fuss was about. Between the two of us, we got her to the dock. She cursed us all. Captain, crew, ship. That's the sort of thing that will spook a sailor. Any misfortune that befell us, there were whispers about the old hag and her curse."

"What sorts of misfortunes did befall you?" Jo asked.

"Foul weather. Dismastings. Grounding on the Heads coming back into Liverpool, though that can scarcely be blamed on the old apple woman. The court ruled it to be the fault of a drunken pilot charged with bringing us in." He sipped his tea, then set his cup back down.

"And how do you expect the court of inquiry to rule in the wreck of the *Iona*?"

"Simple enough. Abandoned due to weather. Every man for himself."

"What about Bernard Ainsworth? Will the court consider his murder?"

"Hard to say. Bernard didn't do himself any favors." Gus pushed back his chair and stood. "Thank you for the tea. But if I'm not mistaken, I smell a beef roasting, and I don't want to overstay my welcome."

"Oh, but you must join us for dinner," Amity said.

"It's kind of you to offer. But I really must be going. Perkins will be wondering where I've made off to."

"You no longer need to answer to him," Amity said. "Now that you've left the ship."

A half-smile. "If only Perkins saw it that way. Good evening, ladies."

He crossed the room, his boots thudding on the floor, and let himself out.

"Fine fellow, isn't he?" Amity peered over at Jo's notepad. "He gave you plenty to write about."

"Only one man's perspective." Jo set aside her notes. "Though you seem quite taken with him."

"There's nothing wrong with extending a kind hand to a shipwrecked stranger."

"Except that you generally go out of your way to hold men at arm's length."

"Because all the men around here are so...ordinary. Gus is different. He's traveled the world. He can hold up his part of a conversation. He has opinions on things but respects my thoughts equally."

"That's all well and good," Jo said. "But you're forgetting one thing. He could be a murderer."

# CHAPTER THIRTEEN

### Josephine ~ 1889

A bath, a fresh set of clothes that Effie hastily altered from a pair of pants and shirt that no longer fit Jo's father, and Pablo looked respectable enough that even Jedediah Bailey would have a hard time turning the town against him.

Not that he wouldn't try. Despite a dearth of evidence, Jo worried Bailey would attempt to arrest the boy again. Yes, there had been a murderer aboard the *Iona*, but Jo was certain it wasn't him. Pablo was too young, too slight of figure to have stabbed a grown man to death. Besides, what motive would he have had? He'd wanted only to remain unseen.

Until more was known, she hoped Amity would refrain from spending more time with Gus. True, he'd been forthcoming on some matters. But he'd said little about Bernard's murder.

Jo vowed to learn more. Upon waking the next morning, she decided she'd interview the other survivors of the wreck. Even if she learned nothing worth publishing, she might at least set her mind at ease about Gus. She'd start with a visit to the boarding house, where she could question the seamen separately and see how their stories lined up.

When she went downstairs for breakfast, Effie informed her that Pablo was sleeping in, with Queenie curled up beside him on the bed. Insisting they shouldn't be awakened—not after the ordeal they'd been through—she asked if Jo would look after them while she ran to the market.

After a breakfast of muffins and a soft-boiled egg, Jo retreated to the library with her coffee and began a list of questions for the sailors. She hoped they'd say more than Gus had about Bernard Ainsworth not having done himself any favors. And wondered, too, about how Gus and Howard Perkins got along. Had Perkins secured Gus a room at his hotel as an act of generosity, or did he want to keep an eye on the second mate's comings and goings?

As she jotted this last question, Pablo and the dog came downstairs. His hair tousled, the boy poked his head through the library doorway, grinning sheepishly. "Good morning, Miss Felch," he said in slow, careful English.

"Good morning, Pablo. I trust you slept well."

He considered this a moment, then nodded. Beside him, Queenie let out a little whine.

"There are muffins in the kitchen." She pointed that direction. "And a basket of fruit. Help yourself." Rising from her seat, she scooped up Queenie. "I'll take the dog out for a little walk." She moved two fingers back and forth in a gesture that simulated walking.

"Gracias, senorita Jo." If he'd had any doubts about trusting her, they seemed to have dissipated.

She saw Pablo to the kitchen, then went out through the back door and set Queenie down in the yard. The dog scampered toward the rhododendron hedge and squatted, relieving herself. With a glance back at Jo, she trotted along the hedge, sniffing as she went. Likely it had been a while since the dog had had grass to sniff, Jo thought.

Out of the corner of her eye, Jo saw movement. She whirled around. On the boardwalk stood a dark-haired man, tall and lean, gazing up at the Felch mansion.

"Roger," she called out, recognizing the sailor. "Roger Conrad."

As if he hadn't heard, he started off toward the river. She hurried toward him, Queenie trotting at her feet.

"Looking for someone?" Jo asked, catching up with him.

He slowed his pace. "Just admiring the architecture. Quite the fancy place you've got. Didn't realize there was so much money in the news business."

She hadn't said it was her house. She'd told none of the sailors. Only Gus knew.

"There's money in fish." She fell in step beside Conrad. "My father owns a cannery."

"Well, then. That explains it. Our little stowaway must be having the time of his life."

Who had told him Pablo was staying there? Or had he only assumed it because of Queenie? Either way, she didn't like the way he looked at the dog.

She scooped Queenie into her arms. "I trust you're comfortable at the boardinghouse."

"As comfortable as I can be without so much as a change of clothes. Quite the welcome folks here gave us, filching everything we owned off that ship."

"I expect the court of inquiry will sort that out."

"They don't bother themselves with the small stuff." He took a rolled cigarette from his pocket and lit it with a match. "The big money. That's all they care about."

"The insurance value of the ship."

"Yup." He took a drag on his cigarette.

"I've heard of ships being run aground on purpose. To collect from the insurance."

"Happens." He blew smoke at the sky. "Coffin ships, they call 'em."

"But you don't think that's what happened to the Iona."

"Captain and Mrs. Watson, they loved that ship. Like a big old yacht for them to ride around on, with all of us to do their bidding. Hauled cargo, too, so there was always money for them to truck with the rich folks when we went into port."

"That must have been upsetting, them living the good life while the crew looked after everything."

He shrugged. "No different from crewing a passenger ship, 'cept we only had the captain and his wife to contend with."

"Until they died. It was the fever that took Mrs. Watson, wasn't it?"

"Yup. Went just like that." He snapped his fingers. "Shame. Quite the beauty, she was."

"And then the captain died too. I suppose he caught the fever from her."

"Maybe." He dropped the cigarette and snuffed it out with the toe of his boot.

"There seems some difference of opinion regarding the captain among you and your mates."

"Ain't much we all agree on." As they came to the river, he shoved his hands in his pockets. "Now if you'll excuse me, Miss Felch, I'll be on my way."

"Of course," she said. "Good day, Mr. Conrad."

He turned from her, walking briskly away. Headed back to the boarding house, she supposed. She wished she knew why he'd stopped to stare at her house. Not an interest in architecture, she was certain. He'd not so much as glanced at Dorinda's house next door, though it was built in the same style.

In her arms, Queenie squirmed. She set the dog down. It raced away from her up the sidewalk. "Queenie!" she yelled.

The dog froze a moment, then scampered off again. Jo chased after her. Reaching the backyard of her house, Queenie finally slowed. Jo lifted her up, looking her in the eye. "No running off like that."

Queenie twisted, flopping onto her back in the crook of Jo's arm, exposing her belly for a scratch that Jo delivered. She wasn't sure, but she thought Queenie smiled.

Entering the house, Jo heard the telephone jangle. Racing to answer, she saw Pablo staring quizzically at the source of the noise.

Picking up, she heard a familiar voice. "Jo? It's Clara. Can you hear me?"

"Yes." Jo raised her voice. Telephone service in the area wasn't especially reliable, and connections were scratchy.

"I'm at the cannery office. A situation has come up..." Clara's next few words were garbled. "Man from that ship. Father is away, so I'm left to deal with it. I figured you'd know..." More static. "Knew you'd know what to do."

At times like this, Jo couldn't help but curse Mr. Bell's infernal, unreliable apparatus. She glanced at the clock. If she left now, she could catch the ten o'clock ferry to Point Adams.

"I'll be there," she said.

"Come again?" Clara said.

"Next ferry," Jo yelled.

The line went dead. Jo considered calling back, then decided it would only be a waste of time. Amity could handle things at the newspaper office for a few hours. But what to do about Pablo? Effie was still at the market.

"Get your coat," she told the boy, plucking at the sleeve of her own wrap. "We're going on a boat ride."

# Chapter Fourteen

## Olivia ~ Present Day

After talking with Glen, Olivia is more skeptical than ever about Finn's involvement with Jimmy and Jillian. They seem friendly enough, but from what Glen says, treasure hunters and marine archeologists are at odds with each other. Yet here's Jimmy, who has all but said he's a treasure hunter, working alongside Jillian, who claims to be a marine archeologist.

She also can't figure out why the two of them seem so convinced they'll find gold. Not when according to the book Jimmy had her set aside, the *Iona* was sailing in ballast.

She's pretty sure Finn hasn't thought through any of this, hasn't asked the questions she's asking. To him, treasure hunting is a grand adventure, not to mention a handy source of cash in the off-season. If he's getting mixed up with the wrong people, she doesn't want him to land in jail or end up on the wrong side of a lawsuit.

But before she presses her luck trying to get him to listen to reason, she needs to arm herself with facts. So, the day after Charlotte's dinner, she asks Naomi if she'll mind the shop while she runs an errand or two.

Naomi is happy to take charge. It's a slow morning, and Finn hasn't come back yet to install the new electrical outlet, so she doesn't have to deal with both coffee and books.

Olivia's first stop is the quilt shop next door. The owner, Vi Waterford, looks up from the fabric she's arranging on the cutting table. "Howdy, neighbor," she says. "I was just thinking of running over to your place to grab an Americano."

"No coffee today," Olivia says. "The machine has been tripping breakers. Finn thinks the outlet's gone bad. He's supposed to be coming by today to replace it."

"Ah. One of mine went bad at the house too. Had no idea that was even possible." Vi's house is a magnificent Victorian on the hill, built by cannery owner Lewis Felch.

"I just hope it's not some more extensive problem," Olivia says. "I didn't realize all the expenses that come with an old building."

"You're making good improvements," Vi says. "And from what I see of people coming and going, you're getting more business every day. A couple of my quilting moms were in here raving about that story time you hosted. Said their kiddos were already asking about the next one."

"Naomi gets the credit for that. She's always coming up with ideas. A lot like you in that respect."

Vi laughs. "Naomi's a good deal more colorful than I am." She touches her white locks, cropped close to her head. "Although I suppose I could give purple a try."

"Don't mess with a good thing," Olivia says. "That's my advice. Say, I remember you were trying to figure out what to do for the next quilting circle. Did you come up with anything?"

"Not yet. Might have to do a repeat. We've donated to pretty much every nonprofit in town."

"A friend of Charlotte's is here for a shipwreck conference. He's into marine archeology. Like Ethan's preservation work, only underwater. He runs a foundation that hosts this Astoria conference every year. Says they're pretty strapped for cash."

"Marine archeology. I've got just the ticket." Vi opens a drawer beneath the cutting table, takes out a swatch of fabric, and hands it to Olivia. The fabric is clearly old, the colors faded, and yet the mix of reds, blues, and golds is still striking. A border of curlicues and botanicals surrounds the image of a three-masted sailing ship.

"It's perfect, all right. Where'd you get it?"

"Salvaged it from an old quilt I found in my attic," Vi says. "Figured in this town, I'd find a use for it sooner or later. We'll make it the central medallion, then put little star and nine-patch square all around it. What do you think?"

"Um...sure." Olivia lacks the quilting skill to make a genuine assessment. Still, she enjoys being part of Vi's Saturday morning quilting circle. She has met some fascinating people, including old-timers who share intriguing tidbits from local history. "Glen will be thrilled."

"I am too. One thing to check off my list. I don't suppose you'd care to stick around and help me check off a few more."

Olivia laughs. "I'd love to, but I've got a list of my own."

She sets off, leaving Vi to her cutting. If nothing else goes as planned this morning, at least she's gotten the wheels in motion for Glen and his foundation.

Her next stop is the Astor Library. Margaret Allen, the head librarian, looks up from her desk as Olivia enters. She's a small, middle-aged woman with close-clipped brown hair and friendly eyes. "How's the book business?" she asks, her usual greeting.

"Not bad, considering that tourist season is winding down. The story time was a big hit."

"I hope you'll do more," Margaret says. "Our youth librarian is stretched thin, and parents around here are always clamoring for more kids' activities."

"Naomi's already scheming over a theme for the next one," Olivia says. "In the meantime, I've got a bit of local history to research. I don't suppose you're familiar with a ship that wrecked around here back in 1888?" She hesitates, then decides it won't hurt to drop the name with Margaret, who knows nothing of Finn's current pursuit. "It was called the *Iona.*"

"Never heard of it. But of course lots of ships went down around here. Hard to keep track of them all. Normally, I'd send you over to check the shipwreck books in the local section. But a guy came in the other day and put all those titles on hold."

She gestures toward a stack of books on the shelf behind her. From the spines, Olivia reads the titles. *Lewis and Dryden's Marine History of the Pacific Northwest. Columbia Crossings.* And the same book she's holding for Jimmy back at the shop, *A Maritime History of the Columbia River and Vicinity.*

"Could I have a look at them?" Olivia asks.

"I don't know why not. Just can't check them out." Margaret hands the stack to Olivia. The post-it note on the top book says *Jimmy Stone.*

"I wonder why he put them on hold," she says, hoping she doesn't sound overly curious.

"Said he'd forgotten his library card. I offered to look up his account using his phone number, but he said he was in a hurry."

"I know the feeling," Olivia says, though she can't imagine why Jimmy Stone, who doesn't live here, would have an account at the Astor Library.

She opens the top book, *Lewis and Dryden's Marine History of the Pacific Northwest.* The copyright date is 1895, but this must be a reproduction, since it's available for checkout.

"The definitive book on nineteenth century maritime activity in the region," Margaret says.

Olivia flips through the book, noting the old-fashioned type font and numerous black and white portraits of seafaring men. "No index," she says.

"Not uncommon in those days," Margaret says. "But there's a list of names in the back, isn't there?"

"Right. In a section titled *Marine Men Engaged in Waters of the Northwest.*" Olivia scans the alphabetized list. In the W's, she finds the entry she's looking for.

Watson, Captain Nicholas K., was born in Aberdeen, Scotland in 1855. Beginning his marine service in 1875, he earned a reputation as a skilled navigator. He joined England's naval reserve, attaining the rank of lieutenant. He made his first voyage to the Pacific Coast in 1881 on the ship *Empress of the Waves.* Afterwards, he took command first of the *Umpqua* and then the *Iona,* running routes around Cape Horn to Australia and between the Columbia River and Mexico. He died at sea aboard the *Iona* in 1888 while en route to Oregon.

She closes the book and hands it back to Margaret. "There was a gold rush in Australia, wasn't there? In the 1800s?"

"Not long after the California rush," Margaret says. "Want me to check the dates?"

"No, that's all right. I was just thinking about all the ships that must have carried gold from there back to wherever the miners came from."

"Would've been a fair amount of it," Margaret says. "Before airplanes, the oceans were even busier than they are today."

Olivia opens *Columbia Crossing*. It's an older book, too, with a copyright date of 1963. From the Table of Contents, she sees that it's a chronological account of maritime activity in the region, beginning with Pacific trade routes in the sixteenth century. Scanning the pages, she sees few mentions of specific ships except where they're used as extended examples to illustrate a historical point.

But the book does have an index, and she finds the *Iona* listed there. The single page referenced is part of a chapter titled "Pleasure and Purpose." Two paragraphs are devoted to the *Iona:*

*In vessels with more expansive officers' quarters, it was not uncommon for a ship's captain to bring his wife and even his children and pets on extended sea voyages. There were also instances where a ship was registered in a wife's name, either because she had provided the funds for purchase or because untoward circumstances precluded registration in the captain's name. One example is the* Iona, *a fully rigged, iron-hulled vessel built by C.J. Potsfield and Sons of Liverpool in 1876.*

*Constructed to sail like a clipper, the* Iona *was used first for emigrant voyages between England and Australia but was eventually converted to carry cargo. Under the command of Captain Nicholas Watson, the vessel benefited from a female touch. Painted white and outfitted like a pleasure yacht, the* Iona *was said to be among the gayest of ships ever to dock in San Francisco. Watson's wife reportedly made many happy voyages aboard the schooner, with stops at port brightened by the couple's welcome into the homes of wealthy patrons. But their idyllic life at sea was cut short with Emma's death, and the heartbroken captain soon followed her into the grave.*

Nothing about gold, but the details are fascinating all the same. Olivia closes the book and hands it back to Margaret. "Such tragedy aboard some of those ships. There's an account of a captain's wife dying at sea, and her husband dying shortly after."

"A testament to their love," Margaret says. "That's how it was with my grandparents. Married fifty-nine years. When Grandpa passed, Grandma followed a few months later. Too hard to go on without him, I guess."

"I've heard of others like that." Olivia returns the third book to Margaret. "I've already looked at this one. We have it at the bookshop. I'll check the newspaper records."

"You know the drill." Margaret returns the books to the shelf labeled *Holds*.

The local history section is to the right of the circulation desk. The library's microfiche collection of old newspapers is indexed in an old-fashioned card catalog like the one Olivia vaguely remembers from her grade school library. By the time she got to second grade, a bank of computers had replaced the card catalog.

She finds the card catalog here rather charming. But there's little cross indexing, and mostly, the search terms are the names of prominent people. She finds nothing listed under *Iona*. She finds a couple of cards under Watson, but no Captain Nicholas Watson. That makes sense, she supposes, since he wasn't from around here, and since he died at sea before the *Iona* wrecked.

No matter. She knows the date of the wreck, December 31, 1888. What a way to end the year, she thinks as she retrieves the microfilm reel.

From researching an earlier mystery, one her great-aunt Ingrid left her to solve, she knows Astoria had two newspapers during the late 1800s. She's partial to the Evening Register, in no small part because its publisher, Josephine Felch, was at the center of her aunt's project. Before she did that research, Olivia hadn't realized Victorian women were in the news business. And Josephine's reports were thorough. Olivia hopes she can locate her account of the wreck. Most of the Register's editions have survived, but Margaret has warned in the past that some issues are missing.

With the wreck occurring on the last day of 1888, Olivia loads the 1889 film into the machine. Sure enough, there's coverage on January 1. *Iona Wrecks on Clatsop Sands,* the headline reads.

*The year ended badly for the three-masted schooner* Iona, *which wrecked on Clatsop Sands during last night's storm.*

*The new year had just been rung in when the surfmen at the Point Adams Lifesaving Station were forced to venture out to attempt a rescue amid the wind, rain, and fog. A rescue party went out by boat but was forced to turn back, the bar proving too hazardous to cross in such conditions.*

*The land effort, going over the dunes to the tracks, proved more successful. The jetty's locomotive was powered up, and the engineer took the surfmen as far as he could. To the dismay of the rescuers, the* Iona *had taken out a section of the trestle, and so they had to cover the remaining distance on foot.*

*Undaunted, the* Iona*'s rescuers forged on. They discovered the once-proud vessel lodged in the sands, leaning heavily to starboard. Her bowsprit had broken clean off, as had a large section of her middle mast.*

*To save themselves, four of her crew had taken to the rigging. The ship's second mate, Gus Leighton, was rescued while making his way along the train tracks. In his company was a boy, said to have been a stowaway. By torchlight, the Point Adams men deployed the breeches buoy, transporting the remaining sailors safely from the rigging to shore.*

*Registered in Mexico, the vessel was sailing with a diminished crew, four of her men having previously deserted. Another reportedly slipped on a San Francisco dock and was drowned. In addition, the* Iona*'s captain and his wife had recently succumbed while at sea, leaving the vessel in the charge of the first mate, Mr. Howard Perkins.*

*After spending the night at the Point Adams station, the survivors were transported to Astoria, where a court of inquiry is expected to convene as soon as the relevant parties can be brought down.*

Olivia reads through the article a second time, taking this all in. In any report on a shipwreck and the ensuing rescue efforts, there was bound to be some drama. But the details in Josephine's paper make the scene especially vivid. Olivia can picture the rescuers trudging through wind and rain to save the poor souls clinging to the ship's rigging.

What bad luck those men had endured. Four of their crew deserting. A fifth man dying from a fall. The captain and his wife dying at sea. Then the wreck. All the more reason the *Iona*'s remains should now rest undisturbed at the bottom of the ocean.

Olivia is about to turn off the machine when she notices a second headline and a briefer story with the headline *Seaman Found Dead.*

*When treasure-hunters descended on the wreck of the Iona this morning, two of them discovered the body of one of her sailors, which had washed ashore during the night. His shipmates identified the man as Bernard Ainsworth.*

*Although the first impulse was to attribute Ainsworth's death to the storm, a wound to his chest makes this unlikely. The unfortunate sailor's remains have been transported to the county coroner for further examination.*

"Oh my," Olivia says aloud.

"Found what you were after?" Margaret asks from her desk.

"And then some," Olivia says.

# Chapter Fifteen

## Olivia ~ Present Day

Armed with the information she has learned at the library, Olivia heads for the docks. Finn's boat is there, but there's no sign of Finn himself. He has likely been out all night with Jimmy and Jillian, so maybe he's still in bed.

Olivia checks her watch. Nearly noon. She could go to Finn's house, remind him that without the espresso machine, they're missing out on sales. But if she wakes him, he won't be in much of a mood to listen to anything she has to say. Better to wait, she decides.

Turning to leave, she nearly runs headlong into a bearded man she recognizes as one of Finn's fishing buddies.

"I don't suppose you've seen Finn this morning?" she asks.

"Up at the warehouse." Sliding past her, he gestures vaguely toward shore.

"Thanks," she calls after him.

Every building around the marina looks like some sort of warehouse. She tries the door of one with peeling blue paint. The door is locked. But at the red building next door, the overhead door is open.

She pokes her head inside the opening, blinking as her eyes adjust to the dim light. Overhead, weak fluorescents buzz, illuminating boats in various stages of disrepair. The space smells of saltwater, diesel, and a hint of mold.

Finn is in one corner, tossing crab pots atop one another. He looks over as she approaches. "Headed your way, soon as I finish up here." He doesn't sound angry, just tired.

"Thanks. I didn't figure you'd forgotten, but I was out anyway, so I thought I'd come by. Out all night again?"

"Pretty much." He lifts his ball cap and wipes his forehead with the back of his shirtsleeve.

"Sounds grueling. At least with the conference this weekend, you should get a break."

"Conference?" He tosses another crab pot on the stack. The way he's arranging them, it looks as if he's building a wall.

"The shipwreck conference. A gathering of marine archeologists. Charlotte has a friend from college who's attending. I figured Jillian would be there for sure."

"Not this weekend. They caught a ride to Coos Bay to see some friends this weekend."

Strange that Jillian would choose to go out of town during a conference of her peers, Olivia thinks.

"Too bad," she says aloud. "I could have introduced Jillian to Charlotte's friend. But I suppose they already know each other. Marine archeology seems like a pretty specialized field."

"Probably." Finn hoists another crab pot to the rim of his wall.

"Crabbing season coming up?"

"Not till December."

Olivia edges close, peering over the top of the stacked pots. On the other side, she sees what looks like a small torpedo lying on the cement floor. A light is mounted on one end, along with some sort of mechanical arm.

"What's that?"

Finn looks around as if someone might be listening. "ROV." He keeps his voice soft, though they're the only ones in the warehouse. "Remotely Operated Vehicle. It belongs to Jimmy. Cost him a pretty penny, so we figured we'd better lock it up when we're not out in the boat. Don't want people snooping around and getting ideas."

"How does it work?" This question, she knows, is impossible for Finn to resist. The only thing he loves better than tinkering with all things mechanical is explaining how they work.

"Have a look." He gestures for her to follow him around the crab-pot wall, where they stand in front of the ROV. "Divers can only go so deep," he says. "Hundred feet or so, maybe more if they've got the right mix of air."

"So I've heard," Olivia says, remembering what Jimmy told the kids at the bookshop.

"When you need to find something deeper, you send this puppy down, tethered with a cable to the boat. Thrusters propel it through the water. From the boat, you use a sort of joystick to move the ROV whatever direction you want. It takes pictures, shoots video."

"I can see how that would be helpful. But I don't see how you know where to start looking, with all the ocean out there."

"If ships stayed where they wrecked, you could just check the records. Pretty much every wreck is documented in some way or another, Jillian says. But a lot of them get moved around by the wind and the waves. So Jillian is using some sort of computer modeling to show where the *Iona* might have ended up."

"And the modeling is accurate?" she asks. "You've located the ship?"

"I'd tell you, but then I'd have to kill you." Shock must show in her face because he follows with, "Sorry, bad joke. Jimmy says we're close. It'd go a lot quicker if we had side sonar and a magnetometer. Expensive, but the returns will be worth it, Jimmy says. This isn't his first treasure hunt, you know."

Maybe not, she thinks. But if he's so experienced, why doesn't he already have all the equipment he needs?

"Charlotte's friend mentioned something curious," Olivia says. "About treasure hunters and marine archeologists being at odds with each other. It's interesting that Jimmy and Jillian get on so well."

"Power of attraction, I guess. She's a looker. Smart too."

"What makes them so sure there was gold on this ship?"

He shrugs. "Got their reasons."

She lets this go. If she tells him the ship was in ballast, he'll know she's been snooping around. And there's a more important point to make.

"According to Charlotte's friend, there are all sorts of legalities in-volved with exploring shipwrecks," she says. "Especially if there's any-thing of value to be found. Whatever that might be, the companies that insured the ship back in the day could lay claim to it."

From the set of Finn's jaw, she can tell he doesn't like her pointing this out. "Pretty sure Jimmy and Jillian know a lot more about that than you do," he says.

"Right. And they must know all about the applicable laws, state and federal, that protect shipwrecks. About the permits that are required to do what they're doing."

"They're professionals," Finn snaps. "Of course they know about the permits."

She draws a fortifying breath. "I just don't want you to end up in jail because you've gotten mixed up in something shady. Or on the wrong end of a lawsuit. It's happened before with treasure hunters."

"What I do and why I do it are no business of yours."

"That's not entirely correct, Finn. I'm concerned for your sake, obviously. But you also own a valuable piece of real estate, in the bookshop building. Co-own, I should say."

He folds his arms at his chest. "And that building has a lot of deferred maintenance. You know it and so do I. Unless you're making a lot more money selling books than I think you are, we could use an infusion of cash. I'm willing to stay up nights, take a few risks, to make that happen."

She wants to reassure him that they've got this, that the building is holding its own for the present and that the bookshop is turning a profit. They've got units rented out, and they can raise the rates if they need to. But she can see he's done talking.

# Chapter Sixteen

### Josephine ~ 1889

Steering Pablo by the elbow, Jo got off the ferry at the Point Adams pier. He'd been reluctant to come along, relenting only when Jo made clear that Queenie could come too. Once they'd boarded the ferry, he'd been calmer than Jo had expected given the harrowing experience he'd been through. Even so, she'd seen the relief on his face when the ferry turned toward shore.

To the north of the dock was the Point Adams lighthouse and life-saving station. Ahead were the tracks she'd followed to get to the wreck. To the south was the Fish Rock Packing Company, belonging to Clara's father. Aside from a small contingent of soldiers at nearby Fort Stevens, the cannery was the main reason the ferry stopped at Point Adams.

Now the jetty project was adding to the traffic along this part of the river. Only a skeleton crew, including the locomotive's engineer and fireman, stayed over for the winter. But come spring, when construction started up again, the rest of the workers would return to make repairs, starting with the portion of the trestle taken out when the *Iona* rammed into it.

Then the pile-driving machine would resume sinking timbers that workers would anchor together with crossbeams as they extended the train tracks. On the sandy ocean bottom, they would deposit brushwood bound with wire, to be topped with huge boulders from a quarry farther up the river. Section by section, workers would extend the jetty into the ocean, taming the waters that were so treacherous to seafarers.

Turning from the pier, Jo glimpsed the remains of the *Iona* in the distance, along with the section of the jetty she'd breached. As she started toward the cannery, the boy and the dog trotting alongside her, she wondered why Clara had summoned her. The two of them had been classmates in Astoria before Clara's father moved his family to be closer to his work.

If Clara was disappointed to live a half-hour ferry ride from Astoria, she didn't show it. She hosted parties like the chafing dish affair she'd put on for New Year's and invited her friends, offering rooms where they could spend the night. And as one of the few women living out here, Jo suspected she got a good deal of attention from between the Fort Stevens soldiers, the surfmen at the life-saving station, and the construction workers in season.

The trek to Clara's house was far easier than it had been New Year's Eve, when Jo and her friends had battled the wind and rain in the dark. The path had even dried out a bit.

As they walked, Jo asked "What do you think of Mr. Gus, Pablo?"

The boy shrugged.

"Did you see who killed Mr. Bernard?"

He looked at her blankly. That didn't mean he hadn't understood, only that he wasn't talking. Likely he had his reasons. She only wished she knew what they were.

Arriving at Clara's house, Jo lifted the knocker and banged it against the door. Scarcely a moment passed before the door swung open.

Clara clasped her hands together. "You came. I was so hoping you would. But with that blasted telephone, I could make out only half of what you said."

"It was the same on my end. I'll need you to explain all over again."

Clara glanced at Pablo. "Is this the stowaway?"

"Yes, this is Pablo. Chief Bailey got it in his head that he's the one who stabbed that sailor. I don't believe it for a minute. So, I suppose you could say I sprung him from jail. Now he's staying with us. But I promised to make sure he was supervised, and we were the only ones home when you called, so I brought him along."

"He speaks English?"

"A little. But he understands more than he lets on, I think."

Petting the dog, Pablo acted as if all of this went over his head.

"Maybe he can play outside or something." Clara took her cape from the chair by the door and flung it over her shoulders. "While we get this situation sorted out."

"A situation you want me to report on?"

"Quite the opposite." Clara stepped outside, shutting the door behind her. "I hope you'll tell me how to keep this out of the papers. Of all the times for Father to be away. And Mother has taken to bed with one of her headaches. So that leaves me to handle this."

They started toward the cannery buildings, Pablo and the dog trailing behind. "If it's something newsworthy, I can't promise not to report on it, you know."

"I wouldn't call it newsworthy. But it reflects poorly on Father's business. And unfairly, I might add. He keeps a watchman on at the cannery during the offseason. I suspect your father does too."

"Of course. Equipment, business records, inventory. There's a lot he wants protected. He worries about vagrants too. And hoodlums. Anyone who might start a fire and burn the place down, taking half the town with it. But you can't possibly have hoodlums out here, not with all the soldiers and surfmen."

"Father still wants a watchman. And he's been reliable, up till now." Clara stopped at the door of a large cannery building.

Jo turned to the boy. "Pablo, I need you to stay outside with Queenie. There are...no dogs allowed inside. Understand?"

He nodded vigorously. "Si, Senorita Jo."

Jo followed Clara inside. The warehouse had the same dusty smell as her father's storage buildings. As her eyes adjusted to the dim light, Clara led her around stacked cases of last season's salmon to a back room. There stood a large man with a blockish head and a crooked nose.

"Jo, this is Hank, Father's watchman. He's caught an intruder."

Hank had a pistol he pointed at a man seated before him in a straight-backed chair, his hands tied with a rope behind his back. Though his captive wore a cap, it only partially concealed his bright hair.

"Arthur Trill," Jo said. "What are you doing here?"

"You know him?" Clara said.

"He crewed with the *Iona*."

"Caught him snooping around," Hank growled.

Defiance shone in the sailor's eyes. "Didn't take nothing."

"Have you summoned the sheriff?" Jo said.

"Under the circumstances, I didn't think that was wise," Clara said. "And he seems to be telling the truth. Nothing appears to be missing. Nothing belonging to Father, anyhow. In the off-season, this part of the warehouse is empty."

It wasn't empty now. Jumbled about the floor were plates, glasses, bottles, cups, pots, and pans, as if the contents of a kitchen had been gathered and spilled there. Next to these were items that looked as if they'd come from a lady's dressing room—combs, brushes, pots of face cream, bottled perfume, silk gowns. In a separate pile were men's breeches, topcoats, and cufflinks, plus two gold watches on chains. In another area, Jo spotted an assortment of ship parts.

She met Hank's eyes. "This all came from the *Iona*, didn't it?"

He glanced away. "Crew abandoned ship. Folks like me deserve a crack at it, same as the wreckers."

"I don't know that the law would see it that way," Jo said.

"Which is why I hesitate to call in the sheriff," Clara said. "Hank has been a trustworthy watchman. I suspect Father would hate to lose him based on a point of law."

"You got all this off the vessel yourself?" Jo said.

"Me and a few other folks. And we didn't nab everything, not by a long shot. The way she was creaking and moaning, we grabbed what we could and got off quick."

Arthur offered a crooked smile. "That'd be the ghost, same as what Doug saw. Ship's cursed, you know."

Hank's face paled. He eyed the piles on the floor.

"And you let your friends stash their loot here," Jo said.

"Just till the dust settles."

"I checked with the keeper at Point Adams," Clara said. "Not about the particulars, but just inquiring as to who has legal claim to the belongings left aboard the ship. He says that's for the underwriter's agent to decide on behalf of the insurers. He's coming down from Portland, the keeper said, to check out the prospects for refloating the ship. And to determine what will become of its contents."

"Ain't nothing here he'd care about," Hank said.

"You don't know that," Arthur said.

"What made you come looking here?" Jo asked.

"Folks flap their lips," Arthur said.

"Where?"

"Astor Saloon."

So much for the church ladies who ran the boardinghouse. But to be fair, it wasn't easy keeping sailors out of the local saloons, especially when they'd been through an ordeal like these men had.

"And you came looking for what, exactly?" Jo said.

"My trunk. Ain't got but the clothes on my back."

"This is a long way to come in hopes of finding a clean shirt," Jo said. "Not to mention breaking and entering."

"And I don't see any trunks," Clara said.

"Some fellas took stuff home," Hank said. "Stuff they thought wouldn't be missed."

"You see how it's complicated," Clara said, turning to Jo. "I thought of trying to track down the underwriter's agent, but if there are illegalities, I don't want that coming back on Father, since this is all stored in his warehouse."

"I could make some inquiries," Jo said. "In a general sense, about who under the circumstances has claim to the contents once the crew abandoned ship."

"Can't fault us that," Arthur said.

"We're not here to determine fault," Jo said. "We're just trying to figure out what to do about all...this." She gestured at the piles. "One thing's for certain. Someone needs to get it out of here so Clara's father doesn't get mixed up in this mess. It either goes back to the ship or it goes home with the people who've claimed it."

"Stole it," Arthur said.

Jo ignored his remark. "As for you, Hank, I expect you now know better than to take liberties with the property you're paid to protect. Now I suggest you turn that gun away and allow Mr. Trill to be on his way."

"He broke in. And it weren't no shirt he was after," Hank said.

"Hank," Clara said. "Do as she says."

With a grimace, the watchman holstered his gun and untied the ropes. Art jumped up from the chair.

"Senorita!" Pablo burst into the warehouse. "El perro!"

Jo hurried toward him. But Arthur got there first. He took the boy by the shoulders and shook him. "This is your fault. All of it."

She stepped between them. "I'll not have you blaming the boy. Your ship wrecked in a storm. He had nothing to do with it."

"He knows." Arthur brushed his hands together as if they were dirty. "He knows."

Jo put her arm around Pablo's shoulder. "He knows precious little. He's a child. A child in a foreign land. Leave him alone."

Arthur glared at her, then turned and went out. "Tell your friend Roger to leave the boy alone too," Jo called after him.

She crouched beside Pablo. "Now, what's this about Queenie?"

Grabbing her hand, the boy tugged her toward the door. Stepping into the daylight, Jo blinked, surveying the field where she'd left the two of them playing.

"Gone." Pablo's eyes brimmed with tears.

"What's this?" Clara came alongside them.

"Queenie's run off." Jo scanned the horizon. "I've a good idea where she's gone."

Holding Pablo by the hand, she started off across the spit, following a narrow path.

"The wreck?" Clara asked, falling in step behind them.

"Exactly. Queenie's owner died aboard the *Iona*. I've heard tales of dogs that still sought out their owners after they died. One went for years to the cemetery to lie beside its owner's grave. And that ship would be the closest thing Emma had to a grave."

Arriving at the beach, Jo thought the *Iona* looked even more forlorn than she remembered. Above the sound of the waves, she heard the dog's faint yapping. Pablo must have heard it, too. He ran toward the ship.

"Wait!" Running after him, Jo grabbed him by the shoulder and turned him around. "We need to make sure it's safe before anyone goes aboard. You wait here. I'll check the ladder."

From the far side of the wreck, an older, mustached man strode toward them. With one hand, he held his bowler hat to his head, bolstering it against the brisk wind that came off the ocean. "That vessel has endured a good deal of stress. I don't advise anyone to go up there."

"But the boy's dog is on the vessel," Clara said.

The man cocked his head. "I thought I heard yapping. What would possess a dog to climb aboard?"

"The dog sailed with the *Iona*," Jo said. "As did the boy. Now if you'll excuse me, I'm going to try to coax Queenie down."

She started for the wreck, the agent marching after her. "I'm warning you, those timbers are unstable. Should any harm befall you, the ship's owners will not be held responsible."

"And who would those owners be?" Jo reached the hull, Clara and Pablo following close behind. She tugged on a rung of the ladder that went up the side. It would hold some weight, she suspected, but not much.

"None of your concern," the underwriter said. "After a wreck, we take over on behalf of the insured. If we can, we'll refloat the vessel for salvage. If we can't, we'll recover whatever we can safely get at and pay out the remaining value."

Cautiously, she started up the ladder. "People were carting things off of here yesterday."

The agent shook his head. "Gets worse with every wreck. Between the pilferers and the ships run aground intentionally, my firm's going to get run out of business. Spread the word, will you? That anyone caught with stolen goods will face prosecution."

From the ladder, Jo exchanged glances with Clara. "We'll let folks know," Clara said. "Do you want things returned to the ship?"

"Inadvisable. You can see how hard it is for your friend, climbing up there. Couldn't do it at all with a load of pilfered goods in your arms."

Jo held back from saying that she'd like to see him try this in a skirt. Reaching the deck's railing at last, she called to Queenie. "Here, girl. Come on. I'll help you down."

"Jo's doing swimmingly," Clara said. "Though I see your point about the hazards of returning items to the ship. We'll advise folks to surrender whatever they've recovered to the nearest law enforcement agency."

"Anonymously," Jo called over her shoulder. "I'll post a notice in the paper."

"Just make sure there's no cost to our company," the underwriter said.

Queenie hadn't budged. "Come on, girl," Jo coaxed. "I know you miss Emma. But she's gone now."

Queenie cocked her head, then took a tentative step forward.

"That's Emma's dog?" the agent said.

"So I'm told," Jo said. "There now. That's a good girl," she said as the dog inched toward her. "I'll help you down."

Tail wagging, the dog came forward. Leaping into Jo's arms, she threw her momentarily off-balance.

"Careful!" Clara said.

"I warned her," the agent said.

With Queenie tucked in the crook of her arm, Jo backed down the ladder. Kicking back the hem of her skirt, she felt with her foot for each rung. Relief washed over her when her feet finally hit solid ground. She handed the squirming dog over to Pablo, who was waiting with outstretched arms.

"Gracias, senorita." He grinned ear to ear. "Muchas gracias."

Jo dusted off her trembling fingers. If only every matter associated with this wreck could be so readily solved.

# CHAPTER SEVENTEEN

## Josephine ~ 1889

"I was getting worried about you," Amity said when Jo finally arrived at the newspaper office that afternoon.

"Sorry." Jo hurried over for a look at the page one layout. Nan had already set the other pages, she saw. "Clara called. At her father's cannery, the watchman apprehended an intruder. Her father is out of town, so Clara was left to deal with it. She called and asked me to help."

"Should've called the sheriff," Nan said.

"She would have, except that the watchman and his friends were using an empty room at the warehouse to stash items they'd taken from the ship. Clara's father is fond of the watchman, so she thought it best not to involve the authorities. As it turned out, the intruder was Arthur Trill, the red-haired man from the ship."

"Can you blame him? He probably just wanted his belongings back. Seems like those beachcombers are getting cheekier with every wreck. Didn't you say Mr. Perkins had to chase them off the ship yesterday?"

"He did. They were hauling things off right and left. And now we know where at least some of them went."

"Poor Gus. All those months at sea, and now that he's finally in port, he's got nothing to his name."

"The underwriter's agent was out at the *Iona* today, making his assessment. I told him we'd post a notice in the paper saying that any items taken from the ship are to be turned over immediately to an officer of the law, no questions asked."

"You think Bailey will go along with that? He seems to enjoy punishing petty criminals."

*As a diversion from his own crimes,* Jo thought, but she refrained from saying this out loud. Better to gather her evidence before she made accusations.

"I'm headed over to the police station to tell Bailey about the notice. The layout looks good, Amity."

"Nan helped," Amity said.

Nodding her approval, Jo pointed at an auction notice on page one. "This auction isn't scheduled till next week. Let's replace this notice with one about the items taken from the *Iona*. Can you write that up, Amity? I trust you to get the wording right."

"I'll write something up," Amity said. "But after that, I've got to get going. I promised Gus I'd help him pick out some new clothes. Then he's taking me to dinner for my troubles."

"I thought you said he had no money," Jo said.

"He doesn't. But he's such a friendly guy, people around town are letting him buy on credit. He's going to stick around for a while, take whatever work he can get, so he can pay everyone back. He says he's done with the sailing life."

"I should think they'd all be done with the sailing life after that wreck," Nan said. The page one layout in hand, she went to her bench and started setting type for the articles that Jo had approved.

"Be careful," Jo said to Amity once Nan was out of earshot.

"Careful about what?"

"About getting involved with a stranger."

Amity laughed. "You sound like Mother. I'm a big girl, Jo. I can take care of myself. Gus is a fascinating man. Not at all like the boys around here. He studied medicine, then left his family home in the English countryside to see the world. I could listen to his stories all day."

*But are they true?* Jo wondered as she set out for the police station.

For someone who'd always prided herself on her good judgment, Amity seemed to have taken leave of her senses. After all the men she'd turned away, her interest in Gus was a puzzle. A puzzle among several

other puzzles. The misfortunes that had befallen the *Iona*. The talk of
a curse. The agitated sailors.

As she entered the station, Jo saw that the *Iona*'s first mate, Howard
Perkins, was speaking with Bob Melbourne. Not speaking, actually.
Shouting.

"Enough with the runaround," Perkins said. "You tell your
chief—"

"Tell me what?" Bailey came in from the back hallway.

"Sir, this is the man who had charge of the *Iona* when she ran
aground," Melbourne said. "I told him you were not to be disturbed,
but he insists he must have a word with you."

Perkins' face relaxed. He extended his hand to Bailey. His arm, Jo
noticed, was no longer in a sling.

"First Officer Howard Perkins," he said, his voice considerably
calmer now. "I need to speak with you about the items that were stolen
from the *Iona*. Among them, my belongings, and those of my crew."

"Welcome to Astoria." Bailey's tone was sarcastic. "This town has
more than its share of thieves. Keeps us hopping. But I'm afraid that
wreck is out of my jurisdiction. You need to speak with the sheriff."

"I've been to see him already," Perkins said. "He refuses to intervene. Says it's a matter between us and the underwriters and whatever
salvage measures they elect to take."

Bailey rubbed his chin. "He's got a point."

"But it's outright thievery." Perkins was becoming agitated again.

Jo stepped forward. "Then why not assign your crew to stand watch
over the ship? They seem to have plenty of time on their hands."

Perkins scowled. "You again. The girl reporter."

"As it happens, I just came from the wreck. The underwriter's agent
was there, making his assessment."

"Precious little left to assess," Perkins grumbled.

"It does appear the beachcombers overstepped, going aboard the
vessel instead of waiting for the boat to break apart. I told the underwriter's agent we'd run a notice in the paper stating that all items
taken from the *Iona* are to be immediately surrendered to the nearest
law enforcement agency."

Bailey snorted a laugh. "No self-respecting thief is going to march
in here and turn over what he's taken."

"I suppose that depends on how valuable the cargo was. Perhaps Mr. Perkins can enlighten us on that."

"No cargo," Perkins said. "We were sailing in ballast, heading for Portland to pick up a load of timber."

"All this fuss over your sailors' personal belongings?" Bailey said. "Those can't be worth much. Apologies, Mr. Perkins, but if your sailors are like all the other ones that come through here, they've squandered their wages on women and whiskey and have precious little to show for their work."

"We officers hold to higher standards," Perkins said.

"Meaning your concern is for your own belongings, Mr. Perkins?" Jo said. "And those of Gus Leighton?"

"Leighton's no better than the men beneath him. Lots of years at sea, and not much better off than when he began."

"Yesterday morning, you seemed eager to recover some sort of satchel," Jo said.

Perkins squared his shoulders. "There's quite a lot I'm eager to recover. Captain Watson and his wife, they traveled in style. The cabin they kept could have stood up to any drawing room in this town."

"But the Watsons are gone now, aren't they? Dead of fever, I'm told."

"Emma died of fever." Perkins glanced away, then returned his gaze. "Captain followed days after. If you ask me, he died of a broken heart."

"They must have been deeply in love," Jo said.

Bailey drummed his fingers. "If it's a novel you aim to write up, Miss Felch, I suggest you use your own office to do your research. We've police business to take care of here."

"Apologies, Chief Bailey." Jo offered her sweetest smile. "I'm a hopeless romantic. How difficult it must have been for you, Mr. Perkins, taking charge of the *Iona* under those circumstances."

"You have no idea."

"I hope the notice in the paper will prompt the return of at least some of your belongings. That is, if Chief Bailey agrees to the station as a drop-off point."

Bailey shrugged. "No harm in it, I suppose."

Jo wondered whether it was Perkins' mention of valuables that made the chief so amenable. Perkins had best check in regularly, or the best of the returned items might well disappear before he got to them.

"Then it's settled," she said. "We'll run the notice. With any luck, Mr. Perkins, you'll soon have your satchel back."

Curious, Jo thought as she left the station, this business about seamen and their money. Arthur had patronized the Astor Saloon and purchased passage over to Point Adams. Somehow he'd had the money for that.

Yet according to Amity, Gus was scrounging around town, relying on Howard Perkins for his hotel room and on his charm to establish credit with local business owners. And Jo had caught Roger checking out her house and Art breaking into the Sheltons' warehouse.

Aside from Perkins, only the helmsman, Douglas Herrington, had done nothing to rouse her suspicions—nothing that she knew of, at least. A chat with him was in order.

She turned toward the river. Seafarers' Rest was a rambling gray two-story house, presentable without being pretentious. To Jo's knowledge, it was the only sailors' boardinghouse in Astoria that was out of reach of shanghaiers.

Arriving at her destination, she rapped on the door.

Fannie Thornton, the widow who owned the boardinghouse, greeted her. "Why, you're the Felch girl. Running the Register, and doing a fine job of it, no matter what people say about a lady taking charge. Come in, come in." She ushered Jo inside. "I suppose you've come about my boys from the *Iona*. Quite the ordeal they've endured. Mr. Herrington was telling me all about it last night, while the others were out for a stroll." She leaned close. "He says the ship was cursed."

"So I've heard. Is Mr. Herrington in? I was hoping for a word with him."

"Oh, yes. Sticks close, that one does. That business with the ship's got him rattled. You have a seat here in the parlor, and I'll fetch him for you."

Moments later, she returned with the helmsman. His gaze darted about the parlor before landing on Jo. "Didn't expect to see you again so soon, Miss."

"I have a few more questions if you don't mind. You seem to have strong opinions about the *Iona*."

He raised a bushy eyebrow. "This for the paper?"

"Not at present. And in any case, I won't use your name, if that's what you're worried about."

"Right. No names." He hesitated a moment, then sat across from her.

"I'll fetch tea if you like," Mrs. Thornton said brightly.

"That's kind of you, but I don't expect we'll be long," Jo said.

"If you change your minds, I'll be in the kitchen," she said.

Douglas watched as she retreated from the parlor. "A good woman, that one. Reminds me of my Mary, God rest her soul. Does what she can to make us comfortable here. Not that those other louts appreciate it." He turned to face Jo. "I hear you sprang the boy out of jail."

"The police chief has entrusted Pablo to my care until he can produce evidence that warrants the boy being locked up."

Douglas shook his head. "I know it don't look good, him being a stowaway and all, but that boy didn't kill nobody."

"What makes you so sure?"

"Trying to stay hid, weren't he? It don't make sense he'd do something that'd draw attention."

"Maybe Bernard found his hiding place."

"Kid had to have been scared out of his wits in that storm. Even if Bernard found him out, there'd have been no point in killing him. Didn't have to be a seaman to know that ship was foundering. And the kid ain't the strength to have taken on Bernard."

"Even with a knife?"

"Ain't heard of the kid having no knife. Have you?"

"I have not." Effie had said the boy's pockets were stuffed with odds and ends, a fact she'd discovered when washing his clothes. But she'd said nothing about a knife. "Who do you think killed Bernard?"

Douglas worried his thumbs one over the other. "Bernard, he was a bit too eager to do the captain's bidding."

"I should think that's a good trait in a seaman."

"Depends." He twisted in his seat, then hiked up his shirt tail, revealing thick red welts striping his back.

Jo stifled a gasp. "The captain had you flogged?"

He let down his shirttail and turned back around to face her. "He did. Bernard was the one who carried out his order. Gus refused."

This seemed a point in Gus's favor, refusing to flog a man. Yet she knew rebellions like that were ill-tolerated aboard ships. "What offense had you made?" she asked.

Douglas glanced toward the doorway. For a moment, she thought he might get up and leave without answering her question.

"Seen a ghost," he said at last, his voice noticeably softer than before. "Emma's ghost, all wispy-like, hovering out over the water. Rattled me something fierce. Woulda rattled anyone. Before I knew it, we was off course. Come up close to land, just like that." He snapped his thick fingers, making a popping sound.

"This was before the storm?"

He nodded. "Captain was still with us."

"And since you were at the helm, he blamed you."

"Couldn'ta blamed the ghost of his dead wife, now, could he?"

"You must have resented Bernard for the flogging."

"Course I did. But that were Bernard. Liked to get in good with the captain, any way he could. Aiming to raise hisself above the rest of us, I'd reckon. If it weren't for Gus, woulda stripped the skin clean off my back. He's a good one, Gus, no matter what folks say."

"And what sorts of things do folks say?"

Douglas shrugged. "Just that he come from money. Got learning. Shoulda been an officer, now, shouldn't he? A real officer, I mean, not second mate. And there's some say he once was first mate, till he got hisself in trouble."

A hollow feeling grew in the pit of Jo's stomach. This was precisely what she'd feared, that Gus was not the man he seemed to be. "If he'd gotten in trouble, why did Captain Watson take him on."

"Knowed each other as boys, those two. Mr. Perkins, he'd been chums with them too."

Chums. At least that explained why Perkins was footing the bill for Gus's hotel room. But it also made her wonder how much Gus resented his friend's authority over him.

"It must have been a shock to Mr. Perkins and Gus when Captain Watson died. It was the fever that took him, wasn't it?" she asked, testing to see if Douglas would agree with Perkins' reasoning on the cause of Watson's death.

Douglas rubbed his jaw. "Weren't the fever that took him."

"His grief over Emma, then?"

He shook his head, then leaned forward. "The curse, that's what it was."

She shifted in her chair. "Ah. The curse. I'm told it started with an old apple peddler, back in Liverpool."

"That's right. After they hauled that old woman off, things went from bad to worse. In my book, the best thing to come outta that storm was the end of the *Iona*."

"Perhaps she can be refloated," Jo said.

"Dismasting. Desertions. Deaths. What's the point in refloating a ship if that's all that will come of it?"

Jo sat up straighter. "Mr. Herrington, I don't mean to be unkind. But I have to say, given the flogging you received at Bernard's hand, you'd have had every reason to kill him."

He held her gaze. "Done my share of sins, Miss. But I ain't no murderer. You want to know who had a beef with Bernard, it's Roger you should talk to."

"What complaint does Roger have?"

He shook his head. "Ask him yourself. I've said enough. You'd best keep your word, Miss. Don't go printing my name in the paper."

"You have my word, Mr. Herrington."

"Good. Now you listen to me." He jabbed his finger in the air. "It's high time you quit asking after the *Iona*. Only brings trouble, and don't I know it."

"I'll take that under advisement," she said. But she had no intention of heeding his advice.

# CHAPTER EIGHTEEN

## Olivia ~ Present Day

The smell of fresh coffee and pastries greets Olivia as she steps into Vi's quilt shop on Saturday morning. Other women from the quilting circle are already there, helping Vi set up for the day's project.

Before coming to Astoria, Olivia had not the least interest in sewing. Under Vi's tutelage, she has learned quite a lot, though within the quilting circle, she's by far the least accomplished. Not that anyone cares. Vi's quilt shop is a no-judgment zone, the atmosphere more about sharing and caring than about proving anything to anyone. Olivia enjoys the sense of community she has found there with women she might not otherwise have met, united around the purpose of creating a quilt to raffle off for a worthy cause.

"Morning, sunshine." Vi is at the coffee pot, filling a mug. "Come try some of Helena's pulla bread. They say there's no one in Astoria who makes it better, and in a town full of Finns, that's saying a lot."

At the cutting table, red-haired Helena blushes. "It's my grandmother's recipe."

Olivia doesn't need to be asked twice. At the refreshment table, she pours herself a mug of coffee. The braided pulla is laid out on a platter, a shiny glaze on top. It smells of sugar and cardamom. "I hate to be the first to dig into it. It looks so pretty."

"Someone's got to be first." Vi sips from her mug. "And I promise, I'll be right on your heels."

With this assurance, Olivia pulls off a hunk of the pulla and pops it in her mouth. It's warm and buttery, with a hint of spicy cardamom.

"Amazing." She licks her fingers, sips some coffee, and indulges in another hunk of pulla, larger this time. "What can I do to help set up?" she asks Vi once she's finished chewing.

"We're pre-cutting squares so we can work on the nine-patch and stars when everyone gets here." Vi nods at the cutting table. "I expect Susie could use some help."

Mug in hand, Olivia goes over to greet Susie, a short, round woman with a ready smile who loves to talk about her grandkids, the sixth generation of Astorians in her family. Today, she's cutting three-inch squares from blue-checked calico.

"Reinforcements have arrived," Susie says. "Good. See those strips of red calico? You can cut them into three-inch squares."

Olivia grabs a pair of shears. "Three inches. That seems small."

"Wait till you see the squares we cut for the nine-patch and the triangles we cut for the stars. Tiny, but pieced together, it'll create a nice effect."

Using tailor's chalk, Olivia marks off three-inch sections. "Vi showed me the piece we're using for the central medallion. Found it in her attic—how cool is that? There must be some story behind it."

"Stories at every turn," Susie says. "You're in the right business with your bookshop."

"I've been reading some about shipwrecks lately. I'd never thought much about how hazardous it used to be, traveling by ship. Especially with the Columbia bar."

"Sure were a lot that went down," Susie says. "I've got a ship's bell in my sunroom from one of those wrecks. It's about the size of that serger." She points to a big machine in the room's corner.

"Wow. Big boats, big bells, I suppose. Is someone in your family a scuba diver?"

"No. My great-great-grandfather hauled it off a ship that went aground near where Fort Stevens is today. Back then, people would turn out to help with a rescue, then stick around to see if there was anything of value they could grab before the ship went to salvage."

"Like vultures circling a kill," Olivia says. This explains the mention of treasure seekers in the Evening Register article. Not people like Jimmy who search underwater, but ordinary folks who grabbed things off a wrecked vessel.

"From what I've heard, it was something of a free-for-all," Susie says. "Lots of the old families around here have salvaged stuff they've passed from one generation to the next. Napkins, silverware, books. Furniture, even."

"How about gold?"

Susie laughs. "Now that would be something, wouldn't it?"

"I don't suppose you know which ship your bell came from."

"I knew at one time, but the name escapes me now." She shakes her head. "Had a fabulous memory when I was young, but these days, it feels like I'm playing hide-and-seek with the facts in my head. Too crowded up there, I guess. We were always told that a couple sailors died in that wreck."

"So tragic," Olivia says.

Susie nods. "But there were happy endings too. Before they shipped out again, some of the sailors from wrecked ships took up with local girls. I can think of a few families whose roots trace back to a sailor who abandoned the sea for the comforts of home. I can imagine one of those wives stitching a quilt like the one we're making, can't you? With a clipper ship medallion in the center."

"A reminder of the sea," Olivia says.

Another woman comes over to help with cutting the squares, and the conversation moves on to other topics. But Olivia is still thinking about that bell. It might not have come from the *Iona*, but it does bring her back to the question of who can keep what from a shipwreck.

Later, after she goes next door to open Tidewater Books for the day, she checks the nautical section. There she finds a used paperback titled simply *Maritime Law*. The copyright is 2002. Recent enough, she hopes, to apply to whatever Jimmy and Jillian are up to.

She skims the section on salvage. As Glen pointed out the other night, there's a basic tenet that sounds a lot like finders-keepers, with salvage rights going to the first person who finds and takes possession of an abandoned ship and its contents. If a salvage claim is disputed, a court will decide who has legal rights to the property.

She runs her finger down a list of factors a court would consider. At the top is location, determining which statutes apply. How much time has passed can make a difference too. The owner's identity may also come into play, along with the identity of whoever salvaged the items. Besides all of that, cultural and historical significance can play a part, as can precedents set by previous courts' decisions.

"All in all, many legal challenges may arise from the recovery of items from a wrecked vessel," the author writes in summary. In other words, the ownership question is as clear as the mud at the bottom of the Columbia River. At this point, no one is likely to dispute Susie's claim to her family's ship's bell. But a stash of gold hauled up from the ocean floor—that would surely raise all sorts of questions.

Maybe that's why the operation Finn's involved in requires so much stealth. If there's gold, and word gets out about it, others might claim they have rights to it.

"There was a court of inquiry after the *Iona* wrecked," she says aloud to Micki, who's sitting nearby, tail swishing. "With a court involved, there must be court records."

The bookshop door swings open, and Naomi comes in. "Talking to the cat again?" Her hair is pulled back in a ponytail, exposing a streak of red in addition to the purple in her hair.

Olivia slides the book back where she found it. "Mark my words. One of these days, Micki will answer. She's just waiting till she has something of value to say."

"More people should follow her example." Naomi swings her big tote bag behind the counter. She flips a switch, and the espresso machine whirs to life.

"It's working," Olivia says.

"Yup. Finn came by yesterday afternoon, right before closing. You were at the post office. Which is just as well. He seems a little peeved with you."

Olivia likes this trait in Naomi. She's kind, but she doesn't mince words. "I was afraid he might be. While I was out yesterday, I stopped by the marina. He was inside a warehouse, building a wall out of crab pots to hide a piece of expensive equipment."

"Some little submarine-thingy, right? He says he doesn't want people asking questions about it."

"Don't you think this whole thing with Jimmy and Jillian is a little too cloak-and-dagger? If it's all on the up and up, I don't see why everything has to be so secretive."

Naomi's brow furrows. "You know, Finn may have a point about you minding your own business."

"It's just that I'm concerned," Olivia says, trying not to sound defensive.

"Look, I don't want to get in the middle of anything," Naomi says. "But Finn's business is Finn's business. He's a big boy, and he can make his own decisions."

"I know, I know. It's just that shipwrecks can, you know, be complicated. There can be conflicting claims. Laws get broken. Sometimes people like Jimmy end up in jail."

"Jimmy has done nothing, Olivia." Naomi's tone is terse. "They're just looking around. So how about you lay off of Finn."

"Fair enough," Olivia says. But it doesn't feel fair at all. This is the closest she and Naomi have ever come to arguing.

As the morning proceeds, they work in silence. Naomi processes boxes of used books. Olivia checks yesterday's receipts and balances the books. A customer comes in and orders a latte. Happily, the machine works its magic without so much as a flicker of the overhead lights.

More customers come in to browse. One of the regulars is Jason Reynolds, an officer with the Astoria Police Department.

"Hey, Jason." Naomi's cheerful demeanor has returned. "I'll bet I know what you're after." She retrieves a book she set aside from the shipment they unpacked a few days ago. "The new Lee Childs, hot off the press."

Jason grins. "That transparent, am I?"

"You've only been asking about it for the past month."

"He can't turn them out fast enough for my liking."

"You should try Michael Connolly," Naomi says. "Right up your alley."

"I've read everything Connolly ever wrote," he says. "Unless there's a new one that has somehow escaped my notice."

"How about Nelson DeMille?" Naomi says. "Lots of action, lots of suspense."

"DeMille, you say? Not sure I've heard of him."

"Follow me." Naomi trots off to the mystery section with Jason following behind. Olivia feels the tension leave her shoulders. Things are back to normal.

Jason leaves happy, the new Lee Child novel and two Nelson DeMille titles tucked under his arm.

"I used to think I was well read," Olivia tells Naomi. "But you're always coming up with authors I haven't noticed, in all sorts of genres."

"When it comes to books, I've always liked a little of everything, I guess." Naomi bends to pet Micki, who is splayed out on a rug in a splash of sunlight. "To me, reading is like travel. Why not explore everything?"

"It's funny that Jason likes to read novels about murder and danger. You'd think he gets enough of that at work."

"In Astoria?" Naomi laughs. "Not much intrigue around here."

"Oh, I wouldn't say that." Olivia reaches for one of the empty cardboard boxes Naomi has unpacked.

"Don't toss that," Naomi says. "I'm saving boxes for building a rocket ship for the next story hour. A little metallic spray paint, a little glue, and we'll be set. A spacesuit for you, and a killer alien get-up for me."

"Nothing too scary, I hope."

"Naw. Think the Star Wars cantina scene."

How Naomi will pull this off is anyone's guess, but Olivia expects she's up to the task. "Make a sketch, and I'll put it in the email notice for the parents."

"Will do." Naomi grabs a pencil and a few sheets of paper from the printer and begins to draw.

With the receipts tallied, Olivia tackles the end cap displays at the front of the store. She's moving books around when Charlotte pops in, ruddy-cheeked and wearing a chic faux suede jacket. It occurs to Olivia that she's never seen Charlotte's car. Maybe she doesn't own one. She seems to walk everywhere, rain or shine.

"Brought you the rest of the Boston cream pie." Charlotte hands over a takeout box. "I've been having a stare down with it in my fridge, and I feared it was going to get the best of me."

"And you thought my waistline needs expanding?"

"Well, there's Naomi."

At the sound of her name, she looks up from her drawing. "Did someone say pie?"

"Utterly amazing pie," Olivia says. "I'll take a sliver, and you can have the rest. Fortification for your project."

"I got us on the schedule for the dive class," Charlotte says. "You and Ethan and me. I know you said you weren't sure, but it was almost full, so I nabbed you a spot."

"You're taking diving lessons?" Naomi says. "I had no idea you were a water rat."

"I'm not," Olivia says.

"I had a friend in town for the shipwreck conference," Charlotte says. "Ethan and I were talking about how cool it would be to learn scuba, and he recommended the class."

"Scuba," Naomi says. "That should help with your space costume."

"Spaceship theme for next story hour," Olivia explains. "I'm the designated astronaut."

"Ask the instructor if you can borrow a helmet. In case NASA doesn't come through," Naomi says.

Olivia's pretty sure she's joking, but with Naomi, you never know. She could have already put a call in to NASA's spacesuit department.

"I'll stick this pie in the fridge," Olivia says. "Charlotte, there's a book in the back room I've been meaning to show you. Do you have a minute?"

"Sure."

Olivia leads the way into the bookshop's back room, where the rare books are shelved. Olivia grabs a volume from the top shelf and hands it to Charlotte. Not a book, exactly, but a bound volume with a cardboard cover and yellowed pages. The stenciled title on the front says *Recollections*.

"A woman from Vi's quilting circle gave this to me on Saturday. She found it when she was cleaning out her basement. She's not sure who it belonged to. Someone from the family who owned the house before her, maybe. I told her I'd pass it along to you."

Charlotte flips through the volume. Some pages are typed, others are handwritten. "Hetta Lindgren," she says, reading the name printed in tidy letters at the front. "1888 - 1889."

"I skimmed through the entries," Olivia says. "I was hoping to find something about a ship that wrecked on New Year's Eve, 1888. I found an entry about a New Year's Eve chafing dish party, whatever that is. One guest was a Point Adams surfman who was called away to aid in a rescue. But no details about the wreck."

"What's with the interest in shipwrecks?" Charlotte says. "You had questions for Glen. And now this."

"It's mainly this one wreck that interests me."

Charlotte puts her hand on her hip. "Why?"

"I'm not at liberty to say," Olivia says, drawing on one of her mother's oft-used real estate lines. "But I was hoping you might help me find a court of inquiry record."

"You mean the judgment from the federal court that rules on maritime matters?"

"I think so."

"I'll need the ship's name, the captain's name, and the date of the wreck."

Olivia hesitates. "I don't want anyone to know I asked."

"Why the stealth?"

"Because someone asked me to keep certain details to myself. I'm worried he's getting into something he shouldn't."

She studies Olivia. "Okay. Mum's the word."

Grabbing a piece of scratch paper, Olivia jots down what she knows. It isn't much. *Iona. Wrecked Dec. 31, 1888, Clatsop Sands. Six survivors. Captain Nicholas Watson, deceased. First mate Howard Perkins in command.*

She hands the paper to Charlotte. "Let me know what you find out."

# Chapter Nineteen

## Olivia ~ Present Day

I t's a mystery to Olivia, how she ended up sitting at the edge of the community swimming pool in a wetsuit, breathing in the smell of chlorine. Not that she hates the water, but she'd rather it involve lounging on a sandy beach, soaking up the sun, instead of donning a bunch of awkward gear and plunging into a pool. Especially if that means relying on a tank of air for the simple act of breathing.

Young and incredibly fit, the pony-tailed instructor squats at the pool's edge, a metal cylinder propped against her leg. "Your tank contains compressed air, filled to a pressure of around 3000 psi." Her no-nonsense manner commands attention. "For deeper dives, you'll breathe a special mix of gases. This valve at the top of the tank controls the flow of air. The pressure gauge tells you how much is left in the tank. It goes without saying that you don't want to run out."

Laughter titters among the students, except for Olivia, who's trying hard to pay attention to every detail.

"Before you go down, you'll want to check the tank for leaks or signs of wear," the instructor says.

"The tank can malfunction?" Olivia says.

"Unlikely, but anything's possible," the instructor says. "Better safe than sorry. Once you're sure the tank's in good shape, you'll want to make sure it's properly attached to your regulator and your BCD."

"BCD?" Olivia wonders why no one else is asking questions.

"Buoyancy control device. It's next on the list." Ethan points to the handout the instructor gave them, listing in order the equipment she's going over. He has that look in his eyes that shows worry, not for himself but for someone else. In this instance, for Olivia, whose nervousness is admittedly getting the best of her.

Holding up what looks like an inflatable vest, the instructor lifts a small rubber hose. "You attach this to the scuba tank, then use the lever to adjust your buoyancy. More air, you float. Less air, you sink."

Why would you want to sink? Olivia wants to say, but she has already asked too many questions.

"You attach the tank here, the regulator here, and the weight belt here." The instructor points to various places on the vest. "When we get in the pool, we'll practice breathing from the regulator before we head underwater. You can practice adjusting your buoyancy too. Just remember that breathing from a regulator isn't like normal breathing. You need to take deep, slow breaths. Be sure to exhale fully, so all the air leaves your lungs."

How deep? How slow? Olivia tries exhaling all the air from her lungs, but she's not sure if she's doing it right.

"Relax," Charlotte whispers. "It's just a pool. Totally safe."

The instructor sets aside the BCD. "In the pool, we'll only be going eight feet deep. But out there," she says, gesturing vaguely toward the door, "you'll go way deeper. You'll wear a weight belt to help you sink. Remember that as you descend, the pressure will affect you. That's why you never want to hold your breath. Holding your breath could cause the air in your lungs to expand, and you might damage them. When you go deep, the pressure may bother your ears. It may even affect the shape of your eyes' lenses. And if you're not able to off-gas nitrogen properly, you can get the bends."

"Decompression sickness." Ethan gives Olivia's shoulder a reassuring nudge. "You won't get it if you pay attention to your depth and dive time. And remember you can control the buoyancy in your vest when you need to go up."

"Slowly," the instructor says. "You go up slowly. That's crucial."

Olivia offers a weak smile, concealing her amazement anyone in their right mind would enjoy something that feels so complicated and unnatural, not to mention dangerous.

"We always dive with a buddy. You watch each other's back and help each other out in case of emergency. So, let's pair up now."

Ethan entwines his fingers with hers. "Buddies?"

"Sure." His touch reassures her.

"You've got to be able to communicate while you're underwater," the instructor says. "So you need to agree on your signals before you go down. To let your buddy know you're good to go, give the thumbs up. If you need to end the dive, signal cut." She makes a slicing motion across her throat with her hand. "You and your buddy should make a plan for your dive and stick to it. Set a maximum depth and dive time."

Five minutes, Olivia thinks. Eight feet. Even that feels like too much.

"If there's an emergency, be ready to respond," the instructor says. "You might need to share your air if your buddy runs out. Or help your buddy get to the surface quickly. Or administer CPR."

She stands abruptly. "That's all for now. Let's get in the water." She tosses each of them a BCD.

Olivia fumbles with the straps, tightening them around her waist and chest, then tugging for a snug fit.

"Looks a little snug," Ethan says. "You don't want to turn blue before we even get in the water."

"Oh," she says. "Right." She loosens her chest strap.

They help each other put their tanks on their backs and attach their regulators. Next come the fins, mask, and snorkels. The instructor comes around, checking the fit. "That mask looks awfully tight," she says when she gets to Olivia.

"I don't want water getting in." Just the thought of this makes Olivia feel panicky.

"Flooded masks happen. We'll practice how to clear them. Okay, folks. Line up at the edge of the deep end and get ready for your first plunge."

Fins flopping, Olivia waddles after Ethan and Charlotte. She feels as if she's mutated into some awkward cross between a turtle and a duck.

"Sit at the edge, then slide in." The instructor demonstrates. "If the buoyancy feels off, adjust it. Bobbing in the water, she points to the valve on her vest.

One after another, the students slide into the pool. Olivia is the last one in.

"Regulators in your mouths," the instructor says. "Inhale. Get the air flowing. Take a few deep breaths and make sure the regulator's working properly."

The rubber feels awkward in Olivia's mouth. Deep inhale. Full exhale. The simple act of breathing has never felt so complicated.

"Now let out some air," the instructor says. "Get those heads under water and check how your masks fit."

Let out air. But Olivia has already expelled all the air she had in her lungs. She looks over at Ethan and sees he's adjusting the valve on his BCD. *Oh, that air.* Slowly, he sinks, like there's a weight attached to his ankles.

She makes a similar adjustment and starts to sink. She fights a feeling of panic. *Breathe, breathe.*

Her head dips below the water's surface, and her mask fills with water. She flails her arms, trying to get her head back above water. The regulator slips from her mouth.

In an instant, Ethan is at her side, adjusting her BCD valve. She bobs to the surface, gasping for air. She yanks the mask from her face, releasing a rush of water.

The instructor swims over. "You've got to stay calm," she says in the tone of a kindergarten teacher addressing a recalcitrant student. "Panic is not your friend. You lose your regulator, you just grab it from behind you and reinsert the mouthpiece. Then take a breath or two to re-establish the air flow."

"But my mask filled up with water."

"That happens," the instructor says. "When it does, push gently on the top of your mask and pull out the bottom to release the water. Exhale hard through your nose to clear any remaining water. Repeat if you need to. Got it?"

Olivia nods. *Top, bottom, exhale.*

"Ready to try again?" Ethan says.

She isn't, but she gives the thumbs up. She puts the regulator back in her mouth, checks it with a few breaths, adjusts her BCD valve, and dips below the surface. Her mask starts to fill again. *Top, bottom, exhale.* Her mask clears. Watching, Ethan gives her a thumbs up.

The other students are milling around in the water, arms and legs moving gracefully. Ethan gestures at her to follow him.

She makes a few tentative kicks with her fins, surprised at how well they propel her. She concentrates on her breathing, the steady inhale, the full exhale. No wonder mermaids entered folklore. If you could do this without all the clumsy equipment, without having to worry about your breathing, the weightless feeling of maneuvering wherever you want in the water would feel amazing.

But they're only in a swimming pool. In the river, in the ocean, there are currents to worry about. The water is murky, so maybe you can't even see your diving buddy. Plus you're sharing the water with creatures that Olivia has only seen behind aquarium glass. For sure fish. Not just little ones either. Finn talks about the big sturgeon he's caught in the Columbia. Out in the ocean, there might be octopus, squid, sharks.

If she's gotten nothing else out of this experience, she at least has new respect for Glen and Jimmy and Jillian and anyone else who ventures into the depths. Glen talked about the thrill of underwater exploration, about how the ocean is the world's biggest museum. But she's more certain than ever that she prefers her museums on solid ground.

The lesson ends without further incident. Back on the pool deck, Olivia strips off her mask and pops the regulator from her mouth.

"No, no, no," the instructor says. "Always shed your tank first, and your weight belt if you're wearing one. In case you lose your footing, you don't want that stuff weighing you down. If you were to fall back in the water, you'd need your regulator to breathe."

Chastened, Olivia slips off her tank, then her fins and her wet suit. She feels light and free and also appreciative of the easy way her legs work on the ground and the ready way her lungs work without her giving them a second thought.

"You seemed a little nervous," Charlotte says as they head for the women's locker room to change out of their swimsuits.

"A lot nervous," Olivia says. "And not much good at hiding it, I guess."

"If you don't want to dive, you shouldn't do it."

"It's not that I don't want to. It's just that…" Her voice trails off. She's not sure how to put it into words.

"Maybe you've got FOMO," Charlotte says. "Fear of missing out."

"Could be. I mean, you and Ethan seem so excited about learning to dive. And I'll get better with time."

"Of course you will. But that doesn't mean you have to keep at it if you're not having fun. We have lots of other things we can enjoy doing together."

"Like eating cream pies?"

Charlotte laughs. "All I'm saying is you wouldn't be missing out on all that much. And no one's going to think any less of you if you don't get scuba certified."

Olivia thinks of the salsa lessons she took because a friend in New York begged her to come along. Of the guitar she tried to learn to play because her mother loved guitar music.

"You know, diving isn't the first thing I've tried without really wanting to," she says. "Mostly because I didn't want to disappoint people whose opinions matter to me."

"Not the best reason to take up a pastime," Charlotte says. "You have nothing to prove. There's lots of stuff you're good at. Lots you enjoy. And it's not as if you never step out of your comfort zone. You've tackled running a bookshop. You're learning to quilt. And you're good at digging into things."

"If I was truly good at looking into things, I'd have taken a deeper dive into, well, diving, before I signed up for these lessons."

"I was thinking more of what you did with Ingrid's missing maid project."

"I never did find what happened to that maid."

"But you haven't stopped thinking about it, have you?"

"Not really."

"And now there's this mystery ship." Charlotte opens the locker room door. Inside, the air is warm and humid. "I did your search, by the way. Checked the archival records for 1889 federal court cases in Oregon. But there's a gap in the holdings. A courthouse fire in Portland, apparently, that destroyed some of the court records, including the ones for the case you're after."

"Maybe that's a sign I should leave well enough alone."

"Not much of a sign, considering the era. Fires destroyed quite a lot of records back then, especially in the West. Too many wood buildings, and the firefighting efforts were valiant but crude. And there was little redundancy built into record keeping like there is today."

"You'd think they'd have stored important records in a vault."

"Generally, they did. But as it turned out, some of the vaults back then weren't all that fireproof. And records that were awaiting processing weren't necessarily in the vault."

"Well, thanks for checking. It was mostly just curiosity on my part. Always been a weakness of mine, I'm afraid."

Charlotte stops short. "And where in the world would we be without curious people?"

"Curiosity has gotten me in trouble more times than I can count. As my mother likes to say, sometimes the less you know, the better."

"Maybe. But I still maintain it would be a sorry world if we didn't have people like you who go the extra mile to figure things out."

Charlotte is a true friend, Olivia thinks as she strips out of her swimsuit and dons her clothes. She doesn't just accept Olivia as she is. She helps her see herself in a whole new light.

Her canvas tote swung over her shoulder, Olivia leaves the pool building hand in hand with Ethan. Like her, he smells faintly of chlorine. She reaches up to touch his hair. She loves how the ends curl when it's damp.

Her hair is damp, too, the locker room dryers working so slowly there was no way she could finish before the pool closed for the night. But she doesn't mind. The night air is calm and only moderately cool, tingling her skin. Overhead, a gibbous moon casts long shadows over the sidewalk.

Reaching the entrance to Ethan's duplex, they stop. Olivia looks up at him. "We can still be buddies even if we're not diving buddies, right?"

"Buddies with benefits." He draws her into a kiss. "Want to come in for a nightcap?"

"I'd love to," she says. "But I was in such a hurry to get to the lesson on time that I left without feeding Micki. I'll be getting the evil eye as it is. Rain check?"

"Absolutely." He touches her cheek. "You sure you don't want me to walk you home?"

"No, you should get inside and dry your hair. Can't have you catching your death, as my grandmother used to say."

He rakes his fingers through his hair. "As you wish. But for the record, I believe that theory about cold and illness has been disproven."

"Probably so." She watches as he unlocks the door and waves goodnight. Then she continues down the sidewalk. Micki can certainly get in the way of a good thing. But she's been a steady companion for Olivia from the start, spurring reluctant admiration for a species she previously had little use for. The bookshop wouldn't be the same without her.

The streets are deserted, the storefronts locked and dark. Such a change from New York, the city that never sleeps. You can't get a pizza at 2 am here, but there's something incredibly soothing about strolling along Astoria's streets in the moonlight, soaking up the silence. She feels safe in a way that she has nowhere else.

Some of that has to do with the people she's met here, and the way they've welcomed her into their community, stranger or no. Some has to do with immersing herself in a place steeped in history. Not all that history has been kind, especially to the indigenous people who were here first. Still, it gives her a sense of belonging that she feels deep in her bones.

She turns toward the building she and Finn own. Her concerns about him linger. She could try to put them aside, stay out of his business. But as Charlotte pointed out, she's good at looking into things. She shouldn't have to apologize for that. She shouldn't let her concern about disappointing people keep her from learning the truth.

She stops in front of the bookshop door and digs her key from her pocket.

"Look who's out and about." From the shadows comes a man's voice "Been snooping around the docks again, have you?"

She whirls around and comes face to face with Jimmy Stone. "Good lord," she says. "You frightened me."

"Nothing to be scared of." He edges toward her. She holds her ground. She's not going to let him back her into a corner. "Your hair's wet. Been for a swim?"

She straightens, holding his gaze. "What if I have?"

"What? You don't like me checking up on what you're doing?" He laughs as if this is some big joke. Then his face turns serious. "You know, Olivia, where I come from, people give each other some space. They don't go poking their noses where they don't belong."

"And where do you come from, Jimmy?" She shifts her bag, her wet swimsuit having soaked through the canvas. "I don't believe you've ever said."

"Why would I? It's not as if we're pals. As I believe Finn has made clear to you, Jillian and I are here for a specific purpose. When we've fulfilled that purpose, we'll move on. In the meantime, we'd appreciate you not going around asking questions. This is important work we're doing, and it needs to be handled with discretion."

"In other words, secretly."

The glint of his eyes makes her wary. "Your choice of words, not mine."

"I care about Finn," she says. "I don't like the idea of you drawing him into something that may not be entirely above board."

"Ah yes. Permits. You wanted to make sure Finn knew we needed them." He thrusts his hand in his jeans pocket and withdraws a folded square of paper. "Jillian and I are not novices, Olivia. We know what we're doing."

"I never said you didn't. But this is all new to Finn."

"Who is a grown man, I might point out. A man capable of making whatever business arrangements suit him without intervention from you or anyone else."

"I'll take that under consideration," she says cooly. "Now if you'll excuse me—"

He thrusts the folded paper at her. "Have a look."

She plucks the paper from his hand. Unfolding it, she sees the state seal of Oregon printed at the top of the page. *Archaeological Permit* reads the heading. She scans the details. *Shipwreck Iona* is the project name. Under Excavation Summary, the location given is *Pacific Ocean* followed by a set of GPS coordinates. The applicant is Jillian Woodhull, and her institutional affiliation is the Seaworthy Institute, which has a UK address.

She barely has time to take in this information before he snatches back the paper and thrusts it back in his pocket. "As you can see, all is in order. Should you have further questions, I suggest you bring them directly to me."

Before she can respond, he turns heel and walks away, his boots clomping briskly on the pavement.

Her fingers shaking, Olivia finds her key and unlocks the door. She can't get inside fast enough.

# Chapter Twenty

## Josephine ~ 1889

Josephine's chat with Douglas amplified her concerns about Gus Leighton. She understood Douglas's gratitude for Gus's sparing him an all-out flogging. Still, what sort of sailor defied his captain? Especially since, according to Douglas, Watson and Gus had been friends.

She also didn't understand why a man with Gus's upbringing and education would sail as a second mate instead of assuming command of a ship, or why he'd have to rely on charity to get by in Astoria.

She hoped she could convince Amity to back away from Gus. More than with the other men she'd rejected, she would have every reason. If Jo couldn't talk sense into her, maybe Noah could. Though he was Amity's younger brother, she respected his opinion.

And to Jo's delight, Noah and her father would be returning from California by steamer this afternoon. In the meantime, she had a newspaper to put out. Having sent Amity to retrieve the daily police sale report, she sat down at the typewriter. But she found herself typing in fits and starts.

"Done with page two," Nan called over from the bench. "Ready for that page one article."

Jo pulled another failed attempt from the typewriter roller, balled it up, and tossed it in the wastebasket. "I wanted to print something more about the *Iona*. But at every turn, the facts get more confusing."

"Why not just wait for the court of inquiry and report on what they decide? We can put another wire on page one."

Jo shook her head. "I want to keep the *Iona* fresh in people's minds till the court convenes. Another article might prompt someone to come forward with more information."

Nan raised an eyebrow. "About the murder, you mean?"

"Yes. I've been thinking maybe there would be some clues about what happened among the stuff people took from the ship. Something broken or missing, maybe. But our notice has had little effect. No one's bringing anything in."

"What about the crew? You've talked with all of them?"

"Yes. But they give different accounts. And it all seems to circle back to that blasted curse."

"Then write about the curse," Nan said. "People love a good curse."

Jo laughed. "I've never heard anyone call a curse *good*."

"Curses get people talking. That's what you want, isn't it?"

"Yes. But—"

"And you want to see what people took from the ship. If they think what they've taken is cursed, they'll be lined up outside the police station wanting to get rid of it all."

"A story about the curse," Jo said. "You know, that just might work."

She rolled a clean sheet of paper into the typewriter and began pounding away at the keys. When she finished typing, she pulled the paper from the roller and read her story out loud.

*Wrecked Ship Cursed, Sailors Say*

*Surviving seamen from the* Iona*, the vessel that wrecked on Clatsop Sands on New Year's Day, maintain the storm she suffered was one in a series of mishaps they attribute to a curse.*

*The trouble started in Liverpool, one man said. An old woman peddling apples had come aboard shortly before the* Iona *was due to set sail. As she was escorted from the vessel, she shouted a curse over the vessel and crew.*

*Waiting in Astoria for the court of inquiry to convene, the survivors speak of the bad luck their ship encountered. Early on, they were forced to contend with foul weather, a dismasting, and a grounding on the Heads near Liverpool.*

*As the misfortunes mounted, two of her sailors deserted. Then another two left. Yet another seaman from the* Iona *slipped on a San Francisco dock and drowned.*

*En route from California to Portland, the captain's wife, who was sailing with her husband, succumbed to a fever she contracted during the voyage. Shortly after her death, the captain died too.*

*They suggest the curse culminated with the wrecking of the* Iona *during this week's storm. Adding to their woes, a sailor's body was found on a Clatsop beach. With a stab wound to the chest, the man appears to have been murdered.*

*No wonder a curse is feared. Only one small dog seems unconvinced. Said to have been a pet of the captain's wife, the canine was rescued from the ship yesterday morning.*

"That should get folks talking," Nan said.

"Maybe I should add a reminder that items taken from the ship must be returned to the police," Jo said.

"I wouldn't," Nan said. "You don't want the article to come off as a ploy. Even if it is."

"That makes sense," Jo said. "Especially since we're running the notice."

Hoping for results, Jo offered to go to the police station the next morning to pick up the police sale report. Having spent the entire evening with Gus, Amity was happy to let her go. It would spare her having to fend off the interests of Officer Melbourne, who was nothing if not persistent.

At the police station, Melbourne made little attempt to hide his disappointment. "I hope Miss Elliot is well," he said as he handed over the daily police sale report.

"She's fine," Jo said. "Just finishing up a few things back at the office."

"Be sure to give her my regards. The day isn't as bright without her."

Why couldn't Amity go for someone like him instead of the mysterious Gus Leighton, Jo wondered. Melbourne hadn't traveled the world, and his looks weren't as striking. But he'd been born and raised here. She'd know what she was getting into.

"I'll tell Amity you asked after her," Jo said. "While I'm here, I'm wondering if you've seen any results from our notice."

His brow furrowed. "Notice?"

"About items taken from the shipwreck. Have any been returned?"

"Oh, that notice. Slow at first, but earlier this morning, we had folks lined up down the block."

"What a pleasant surprise. Folks do pay attention to the paper after all. Could I have a look at what they brought in? We might want to run a follow-up."

"Good idea. Follow me." He motioned her around the end of the counter, then led her down a hallway to a closed door. Using a key from his ring, he unlocked the door and swung it open.

The closet was jam-packed with items large and small. Her gaze darted about the closet. A parasol. Several ladies' dresses. A dulcimer. An open trunk filled with shirts and trousers. Three framed oil paintings. A silver tea service.

"This must be at least half of what was aboard the *Iona*," Jo said. "And some valuable items too. Mr. Perkins must be overjoyed."

"I'm sure he will be once he comes by and has a look."

"And what's this?" Her heart quickened as she reached for a leather satchel propped beside a stack of books. It was surprisingly heavy.

"Why, this must be the bag the boy has been asking about," she said. "Though it's hard to know for certain with the language barrier."

"Take it to him if you like," Melbourne said. "If it's not his, you can just bring it back. How's the lad faring?"

"Quite well. Effie dotes on him. He doesn't seem to mind."

Bob laughed. "A welcome change from having to hide himself from a bunch of sailors, I'll bet."

Carrying the satchel, Jo left the station, eager to get away before Perkins showed up. She was glad, too, that Chief Bailey had been out. He would have no doubt remembered Perkins going on about his satchel. It wasn't as if Jo was stealing it. She only wanted a look inside.

On her way home, she nearly collided with Roger Conrad. Head lowered, hands in his pockets, the tall sailor was striding briskly toward the police station.

"Sorry," he mumbled. "Didn't notice you."

She swung the satchel, concealing it behind her skirt. "Good day, Roger. I've just come from the police station. Quite a few of the items taken from the *Iona* were turned in to the police this morning."

"That's where I'm headed, to the station."

"I hope you find some of your belongings." She noted he seemed a good deal politer than when she'd caught him studying her house. "Do your shipmates know to come too?"

"Arthur and Doug, they're on their way. Mr. Perkins and Gus, they're out at the wreck."

"At the wreck. I wonder why."

He shrugged. "Underwriter's agent didn't take inventory of what was left. Ship was too unsteady, he said."

"I hope they're careful. I was out that way yesterday. I doubt that ladder will take much weight." She paused. "I ran into Arthur out at Point Adams. I wondered why he was there, but he wasn't exactly forthcoming."

A look of concern crossed Roger's face. "I advise you to keep your distance from Arthur, Miss."

"Why is that?" A dead weight at the end of her arm, the satchel was growing heavy.

"He's done time for murder."

She drew back, "Murder," she repeated, recalling the way Arthur had eyed her in the cannery warehouse. Her and Clara both.

"It's only 'cause of Gus that Captain took him on."

"But why would Gus want to bring a murderer aboard the *Iona*?"

Roger straightened. "You'd have to ask him, Miss."

Yes, she would, once she found a way to bring it up. "I talked with Douglas yesterday. He said Gus stepped in on his behalf while Bernard Ainsworth was carrying out the captain's orders. Something about a flogging. After that, I presume Gus and Bernard were at odds with one another."

"Might be that they were. Bernard could rub folks the wrong way. A little too eager to get on the captain's good side, folks thought."

"And are you one of those folks?"

He shrugged. "Bernard and I had our differences. But when it came right down to it, we were pals." Anguish showed in his eyes, more noticeable now than when he'd been among his fellow sailors at the breakfast table the other day.

"But didn't he catch you trying to desert?"

"He did."

"Why did you try to leave?"

"I ain't generally one to truck in superstition, Miss. But I never seen such a run of bad luck as that ship had. When folks started dying, I figured I'd best cut out or I could be next. Bernard caught me getting ready to sneak off, and he set me straight. Said I'd no right to leave them shorthanded, 'specially after the others left. And he promised that if I'd stay, he wouldn't tell the captain."

"So, this was before Captain Watson died."

"Right. But Victor, he was dead. Had that fall in San Francisco, which weren't no accident if you ask me. Then the missus, she passed a few days later, at sea."

"You mean Emma Watson."

"Emma Craig."

"I thought she and the captain were married."

He shuffled his feet, shifting side to side. "Depends who you ask."

Curious. But then so much about this wreck was.

"So you had no complaint against Bernard, even though he kept you on the ship when you wanted to leave?"

"Couldn't let my fear get the better of me, could I? Not when we were already down five men, and the crew small to start with."

Down five men. Victor, plus the two who'd deserted in Brazil, plus the two who'd jumped ship in Mexico.

"It seems Mr. Ainsworth was right. Even when the ship wrecked, you came away with your life."

"Don't mean she ain't cursed, Miss."

"I suppose not. You've given me much to think about, Mr. Conrad."

They went their separate ways. As Jo approached her house, she felt the satchel weighing on her in more ways than one. So many accusations swirled around the *Iona*, and none of them seemed to align. There must be a way to sort them out.

She found Effie in the kitchen with Pablo, who was cutting out biscuits under the maid's watchful eye. "Well done," she said at the sharp circle he held up for her review. "You've a nice firm hand."

"Thank you," he said, his pronunciation precise. Effie had been working with him on his English, and he was making considerable progress.

"The soup smells delightful." Jo slid the satchel onto the table, glad to be free of its weight. "And fresh biscuits too."

Pablo's eyes darted to the leather bag. He stepped back, holding his hands up in a gesture of surrender. "No está ladrón."

"English, please," Effie said, the faintest edge of sharpness in her voice.

"I am..." Pablo began. "Am not..."

Effie gave an encouraging nod. His eyes flitted from one corner of the room to the other, as if the word he was after might suddenly appear.

"A thief?" Jo guessed.

He nodded. "I am...not...not a thief."

Effie wrapped her arm around his shoulders. "Of course you're not a thief. Why would anyone think you were?"

"You did sneak aboard the *Iona,* Pablo." Jo leveled her gaze at the boy. "You rode without paying."

"No hay dinero," he protested.

Effie set her hands on her hip. "English, Pablo."

"You had no money," Jo said. "Is that it?"

He nodded. "No money."

"But you wouldn't take what isn't yours?"

He shook his head, his gaze fixed on the satchel.

"But this bag means something to you."

"No...no good."

"That's enough, Miss Jo," Effie said firmly. "You're scaring the child. Pablo, run down to the cellar and fetch a jar of preserves from the shelf I showed you."

He dashed from the kitchen, looking relieved to be out of the spotlight.

Effie set her other hand on her hip, giving Jo the stern look she remembered all too well from her childhood, when the maid caught her doing something wrong. "And why is it you insist on terrorizing that poor child?"

"As you'll recall, that poor child came off a ship where someone was murdered. The ship's first officer, Mr. Perkins, showed a keen interest in this satchel being returned."

"So why bring it here?"

"The boy tried not to be seen. But that doesn't mean he didn't see things himself."

"True. But this old thing?" Effie nudged the satchel. It didn't budge.

"Heavy, isn't it?" Jo lifted the latch and opened the satchel. She peered inside. "Lead weights."

"Like my father used, fishing. Why would anyone care about finding those?"

"Puzzling," Jo said. "You said you found quite a lot in Pablo's pockets when you emptied them to wash his clothes. What happened to those items?"

Effie straightened. "I told him we aren't pack rats here, and as long as he's staying in this house, he was to keep his belongings in his dresser drawer. Not many clothes in there. I intend for him to have a new shirt and trousers at least."

"So that's why you've been staying up nights. You're sewing for him."

She jutted her chin. "And who else, pray tell, does the child have to look out for him?"

It was a hard point to argue.

# Chapter Twenty-One

## Josephine ~ 1889

On her way to return the satchel to the police station, Jo stopped at the newspaper office to see how the evening edition was coming together.

"Just in time." At her desk, Amity was perusing the wire stories. "I've got room for either *Chicago Anarchists Active* or *Eleven Seamen Drowned*. Which should we run?"

"Seamen drowned." Jo dropped the satchel on the floor beside her desk. "More local relevance."

"But the ship went down in the Irish Channel. That's halfway around the world. And I thought that a story about eleven men drowning might feel too unsettling after the *Iona*'s wreck."

"Good point. Let's use the anarchists then. People have a strange fascination with anarchists."

"What's in your bag?" Amity said.

"It's not my bag. It came from the *Iona*. Someone returned it to the police station."

Nan looked up from her work. "The curse story worked."

"It did. After we ran that front-page item on the cursed ship in last night's paper, Bob Melbourne says people were lined up outside the station this morning, wanting to return things they'd taken from the ship. By the way, Amity, Bob sends his regards."

Amity rolled her eyes.

"He's a nice man," Jo said. "With a good, steady job. And he worships the ground you walk on."

"None of that explains how you ended up with this satchel," Amity said, ignoring her remark.

"I took it home to see if Pablo knew anything about it."

"And did he?"

"I think he knew more than he let on. He wanted me to know he wasn't a thief."

"Does that mean there's something valuable in there?"

"Not really." Jo unfastened the latch.

Amity leaned over, peering into the satchel "Lead weights?"

"Had to have been something else in it, don't you think? Something valuable, and whoever took it replaced it with these."

"Gus said the captain's wife came from money. Maybe she stashed her jewels in here."

"Or her money."

Nan looked up again from her compositor's stick. "Now we've got lost treasure?"

"Could be," Jo said.

The door swung open, and Gus Leighton came in. "Good morning, ladies." He glanced at the clock ticking on Jo's desk. "Or good afternoon, it seems. I've brought you some news. I trust I'm not too late."

"Not at all." Smiling, Amity tipped her chin. "We'll make room on page one."

"If the news is consequential," Jo said.

"It is to me." Gus ran his hand through his hair. "The *Iona* is gone. Last night's tide came in higher than we expected. Must have floated her loose."

"A ghost ship," Amity said. "Adrift with no crew."

"Mr. Perkins must be fit to be tied," Jo said.

"To put it mildly," Gus said. "He's trying to get a tug to go out and search for her. But broken up like she was, my guess is she has already sunk."

"Sounds like front page news to me," Amity said.

"Me too," Jo said. "Let's set the anarchists aside. Amity, can you type something up? You know the spot it needs to fill."

"Of course." Amity rolled a sheet of paper into the typewriter and plunked on the keys.

"Mr. Leighton, do you have a moment?" Jo said. "I have a few questions."

Amity stopped typing. "Something to add to the article?"

"No. Just looking to satisfy my curiosity on a few points." Jo sat at her desk. "Have a seat, Mr. Leighton."

"Your curiosity." Amity frowned as Gus sat in a chair beside Jo's desk. She started typing again, though more slowly now, as if she was hoping to hear what they said.

Jo took up her pen. "I understand you've some medical training, Mr. Leighton."

"Two years of study in London. That training has proven useful at sea. Even on a cargo ship, it's useful to have someone aboard who knows a bit about medicine."

"With your training, I'm curious what you think about some of those who died about your ship. I understand the ship's steward slipped on a San Francisco dock and drowned. Some of the crew seem to think his death wasn't an accident. Did you have an opportunity to assess the situation? From a medical perspective, I mean."

"I didn't witness Victor's fall. To my knowledge, no one did. We'd tied up just after dark, and Perkins refused to let anyone disembark."

"And Perkins was in charge at that point? Because Captain Watson had died?"

"That's right. Emma died three days out of Manzanillo. Nick died two days later."

"She died of yellow fever, I'm told. Some seem to think Pablo brought it aboard the ship."

"Hiding in the anchor compartment, he wouldn't have survived if he had the fever. Emma probably caught the fever in Panama. She and Nick spent a good deal of time ashore. There's some talk that mosquitoes spread it."

"Did Emma linger long?"

"Not at all. She came around asking for something for a headache, which I gave her. She said she felt sick to her stomach too. The next day, Nick summoned me to their cabin to see if I could do anything else for her. By then, her skin had turned yellow, and she was hemorrhaging from one ear. Classic signs of yellow fever. I did what I could to ease her discomfort, but at that point, there was little hope."

"And Captain Watson died soon after?"

"A few days later." Gus rubbed his chin. "He and Emma were quite close. Naturally, he was despondent when she died. Holed up in his cabin. Went through a jug of rum a day, Perkins said." He paused. "You won't print that in the paper, will you? Folks might get the wrong idea about Nick."

"She won't." Amity paused her typing. "I'll make sure of it."

Jo shot her a look. "I'm only trying to piece together what happened," Jo said. "No need to disparage your captain."

"He was also my friend. Never saw anyone so despondent. He couldn't bring himself to attend the little service we held for her."

"A burial at sea?" Jo asked.

"Yes. Hard on all of us, that. Emma was a fine lady."

"Some say Captain Watson died of a broken heart," Jo said. "Is that your opinion too?"

"That's what Perkins told us. It happens, you know, with people so in love that when one dies, the other follows shortly after. And if those two weren't in love, I don't know who is. Only..." His voice trailed off.

"Only what?" Jo said.

"Like I said, Nick and I were chums. Chums from way back, actually. So I gave him some time to grieve, and then I went and checked on him, even though Perkins warned us to leave him be. Nick could scarcely get out of bed. His chambers reeked of vomit."

"He drank too much rum?"

"It was more than that. I tried getting him to drink some water, but it came right back up. His skin was pale and clammy. I feared he was on the brink of losing consciousness, I begged him to allow me to get my bag and attempt some cure, but he ordered me away. I did as he said." He shook his head. "I wish I hadn't. The next morning, he was dead."

"If it wasn't yellow fever, and it wasn't a broken heart, what do you think killed him?"

He hesitated. "You're sure this won't end up in the paper?"

"Tragic as these deaths were, they aren't exactly news. There would seem no need for me to publish your remarks."

"Or to attribute them to me?"

"Correct."

"Well, then," he said. "My best guess? It was poison."

"You think he took his own life?"

"I suppose that's possible. But Nick had seen enough of the world to know the ways one could die. I don't see him choosing an agonizing death by poison over a clean shot from his pistol."

Amity looked up, her fingers frozen on the typewriter's keys.

"Sorry," Gus said. "I'm being too blunt."

"Not at all," Jo said. "You're being forthright. I appreciate that."

"It's my nature. Likewise, you strike me as a woman who doesn't mince words, Miss Felch. You seem to have quite a strong interest in these unfortunate incidents, yet you haven't truly said why."

"I like getting at the truth of things." She felt the weight of Amity's gaze. "So you suspect the captain suffered the effects of poison. If this was not at his own hand, then who was at fault?"

"I'd rather not speculate," Gus said.

"But you must have some opinion."

"None that I care to share."

"Jo," Amity said. "You're pushing."

"Back to your steward. You say he disobeyed orders, going ashore after dark. What pressing business would have led him to hurry off the ship under cover of night? A penchant for whiskey, perhaps? Or women?"

"Jo!" Amity said.

Her frankness seemed not to ruffle Gus. "Victor was as strait-laced a man as you'd ever meet. Held himself to high standards, and the rest of us too."

"And yet he was careless about his footing. And disinclined to swim when his life depended on it."

"I had a look at his body the next morning. Big lump on his head. Must have hit on a rock going in. Got knocked unconscious and drowned."

"Unless someone knocked him unconscious, and that's why he fell in. Might someone from your crew have had a grudge against him?"

Gus laughed. "Someone? Try everyone. Victor wasn't the easiest man to get along with."

"And what about Bernard Ainsworth? You sailed north, ran into weather, and as the ship was foundering, someone apparently killed him.

Douglas showed me the stripes where Bernard flogged him. If a man hurt me like that, I might be tempted to strike back."

"Douglas isn't the sort to carry a grudge."

Amity quit typing. "And anyhow, Gus put a stop to the flogging."

"Even though the captain ordered it," Jo said.

"It was the day after Emma died," Gus said. "Nick wasn't in his right mind. I tried telling him it wasn't Douglas's fault, that the chronometer was off. But as I said, Nick had been in the rum. When Douglas went on and on about having seen Emma's ghost, it was too much for him. He ordered Douglas flogged. I refused to do it. A man shouldn't be punished for what wasn't his fault. Bernard was always ready to do whatever the captain wanted done, so he grabbed the nine-tails and laid into Douglas. Got in a few stripes before I stopped him."

"And Mr. Perkins agreed you were in the right?"

"I wouldn't say that. He and I exchanged words, but in the end, Perkins let it go. Couldn't afford to have the crew turn against him, shorthanded as we were."

Amity pulled the paper from the typewriter and walked it over to Jo. "I should think you've taken up enough of Gus's time for one day."

Jo took the paper and skimmed the story. All the facts were there—a recap of the wreck, Perkins and Gus returning to the wreck, the vessel's disappearance, Gus's theory about how she'd been jarred loose from shore.

"Looks good." She returned the paper to Amity. "Ready for Nan."

Gus stood. "I'd best get going." He nodded at Amity. "See you tonight."

"Looking forward to it." Amity's gaze followed him as he went out the door. Then she turned to Jo. "You've had your word with Gus. Now I want a word with you."

She handed her article to Nan, then marched toward the back door. Jo followed her out the back and into the alley. The wind had died back a bit, but the air was chilly. Jo hugged her arms to her chest.

"Do you know how you sounded in there?" Amity's eyes flashed. "Like one of those Grand Inquisitors from the history books."

"If you haven't noticed, we're in the news business," Jo said. "That requires asking questions. Hard questions."

"What is it with you and Gus? You sounded as if you were trying to get him to admit to some crime."

"That sailor didn't stab himself," Jo said. "And from the sounds of it, that steward may have met with foul play too. Not to mention the captain possibly being poisoned."

"Which you only know because Gus told you." Amity fisted her hand on her hip. "I understand your curiosity, Jo. I understand your wanting justice to be served. But it's not all up to you. You can't just make it happen."

"A fact I know all too well," Jo said. "Birdie Magness is still missing. Cecil is still dead."

"None of that is your fault. You've got to quit taking on every unsolved case, Jo. It's not your fault that man got away. And it certainly doesn't give you the right to go around insinuating that Gus Leighton is somehow to blame for every bad thing that happened aboard the *Iona*."

"But he could be involved somehow. Can't you see that? He comes from money. He's well educated. He should be the captain of some ship, not a second officer. For that matter, why would he go to sea at all? Why would he not stay back and oversee his family's estate, or whatever it is the wealthy British do to occupy their time."

"Gus's situation is complicated."

"But of course he has explained everything to you. His version, anyhow."

"That's the only version any of us can tell, Jo. The one that makes sense to us."

"Fair enough. But the fact is, one of those men from the *Iona* is a murderer. I should think you'd want the truth to come out, if only to remove suspicion from your precious Gus."

"You needn't say that with such derision. He's my friend. I care about what happens to him."

"And I care about you."

"Then back off on Gus."

Jo hesitated. Overhead, a gull screeched as a big crow winged its direction. "I just want to get to the bottom of what happened," she said. "I don't like the idea of a murderer getting off scot-free."

# CHAPTER TWENTY-TWO

## Josephine ~ 1889

Heading back to the police station, Jo shifted the satchel from one arm to the other. She wondered how far the *Iona* had drifted. Despite the damage from the storm, she seemed a tough little vessel.

It wouldn't be the first time a ghost ship had drifted away. When Jo was a child, her father had pointed from the cannery dock to a ship bobbing in the distant waves.

"That's the *Mindora*," he'd told her. "Struck Sand Island. Her crew rowed to Astoria in lifeboats. But when the pilot schooner went back there, the *Mindora* was gone. Now she's sailing all on her own. We call that a ghost ship."

For a six-year-old, the word *ghost* rose above all the other details. Watching the schooner swing about in the waves, Jo envisioned misty apparitions working the rigging.

Transfixed by this memory, she nearly collided headlong into Howard Perkins. There was a hard set to his mouth and a grimness to his gaze.

She swung the satchel behind her skirt, hoping to hide it. "I'm sorry to hear that the *Iona* has broken loose from shore. That must be disheartening."

"If the underwriter's agent had acted with more haste, we wouldn't be in this predicament," he grumbled.

"The tug will go after her now, I presume."

"For what good it will do."

"She may yet turn up on some other beach," Jo said. The *Mindora*, she recalled, had eventually come to rest north of Shoalwater Bay on the Washington side, near where Amity and Noah's parents now lived.

"Wherever she lands, I'm sure those worthless beachcombers will rush in to strip her of whatever's left."

"At least quite a lot of what was taken earlier has been returned." Jo held fast to the satchel, her arm straining under its weight. "I suspect all that talk of a curse has got folks rattled."

"As well it should."

"Mr. Leighton seems unconvinced there's a curse," she said.

Perkins laughed sharply. "He won't admit to it because he's the one that brought it on. Bad luck follows men who defy their captains."

"Why would Mr. Leighton defy the captain? I thought you and he and Captain Watson were friends."

"We were," Perkins said. "Not even Gus Leighton would stoop so low as to challenge Nick. But aboard another ship, he led a mutiny."

"He turned the crew against the captain?"

Perkins nodded. "Him and that worthless murderer Arthur Trill. Nick had no business bringing Trill onto the *Iona*."

*Or for that matter, bringing on Gus.* "It does seem a lapse in judgment. I wonder why Mr. Leighton would take up the cause of a murderer."

"The way he tells it, you'd think Arthur was entirely innocent. The court begged to differ, though if you ask me, their judgment was far too lenient. Five years for killing your captain? Trill should've hung."

She shook her head. "I know little of the laws of the sea, but I shouldn't think any captain would have taken either Art or Gus after a mutiny."

"Nick was too softhearted for his own good. And Gus has a way of persuading people over to his way of seeing things. Your pretty friend would do well to take that into account."

"Amity has a good head on her shoulders." *At least she used to.*

Perkins leaned to one side, peering around Jo. "What's that you've got, Miss Felch?"

"I was here at the station earlier today, picking up the daily police sale report." She swung the satchel around to the front as if she had not the slightest reason to hide it. "An officer allowed me a look at the items brought in from the *Iona*, and I spotted this satchel. I took it, thinking it might belong to the boy. But after I got it home, it occurred to me that you were the one I heard asking about a satchel. So, I'm bringing it back." Hoisting the satchel in both arms, she offered it to him.

Taking it from her, his expression relaxed. "Our little stowaway must be progressing rapidly in his mastery of English, to be conversing with you about a satchel."

Jo straightened, holding his gaze. "Our maid has taken a liking to him. She helps with words he doesn't know."

"She'd best not get too attached. I don't trust that lad farther than I can throw him."

"I'm glad the bag has found its rightful owner," Jo said. "I hope it's some consolation amid the losses you've suffered."

"You have no idea." He tipped his hat. "Good day, Miss Felch."

Turning from the station, Jo tried to calm her thumping heart. It was only a small lie she'd told Perkins, knowing full well he was the one who'd asked about the satchel. But unlike some men who were only too willing to believe a lady incapable of holding a thought in her head, she feared the first mate might have seen right through her ruse.

The matter of the satchel was behind her now. But as she circled back past the newspaper office on her way home, the words she'd spoken in the alley came back to her. Birdie Magness, the maid she'd set out to find months ago, was still missing. Cecil Wisener, the newspaper's original publisher, was still dead. Nor had she secured the release of Cecil's wife, Stella, who was being held against her will at the state mental asylum.

Overall, not a litany of successes. But Jo's mother had always praised her persistence—her stubbornness, some might call it—and Jo clung to that now. It wasn't just her natural curiosity that made her want to know the truth about the *Iona*. If Gus Leighton had had any part in those untimely deaths, she wanted Amity to know it. They'd been friends since childhood. Lately, they'd grown closer than ever, teaming up at the Register—until Gus showed up.

As Jo turned toward her house, the steeple bell chimed four o'clock. She had time to stop by home before meeting Noah and her father at the steamer.

The smells wafting from the kitchen told her Effie was making good on her promise to prepare a dinner that would rival any Lewis Felch had enjoyed in California. Making as little noise as possible, Jo ascended the stairs. At the top, she went to the door of what had once been a playroom and now, with the addition of a cot, was where Pablo slept.

She turned the knob and cracked the door. The bright wallpaper her mother had picked out, the chest brimming with toys - little had changed since Jo's childhood. Had her mother lived, she'd likely have turned this into a sewing room or perhaps an office where she could sort through the papers her husband brought home from the cannery. But without her, the room remained as it was.

Pablo's cot was neatly made up, though whether by him or Effie, Jo wasn't sure. The boy himself wasn't there. Effie had probably put him to work peeling potatoes or cutting up apples for pie. Either that, or he was in the backyard throwing a ball for Queenie to fetch.

Jo went quickly to the dresser. Pulling open the top drawer, she found the items Effie had pulled from Pablo's pockets, all the earthly belongings the stowaway had squirreled away in his pockets. A seashell. A rosary. A tiny book written in Spanish, with an illustration of the Virgin Mary behind the title page. A bottle cap. A polished stone.

But the items that most interested Jo were a single gold coin and a round cardboard container the size of her fist. The coin's lettering was in English, so she didn't think Pablo had brought it from home. More likely, he'd found it—or taken it—while aboard the *Iona*.

But it was the container that set her heart thumping. *Rough on Rats* read the bold lettering on the lid. And above that, *POISON!* Beneath, in smaller print, was what amounted to a guarantee. *With 90% arsenic, your rat troubles are over.*

If Gus's description of the symptoms was accurate, Captain Nicholas Watson hadn't died of fever. Nor had he died of a broken heart. He'd ingested poison. With the love of his life sent to a watery grave, that could have been at his own hand. But if that were the case, why would Pablo be carrying around an empty poison container?

She slipped the container into her skirt pocket and went down to the kitchen. Effie was bent over the open oven, prodding a fork into a hunk of roast beef. Looking up at Jo, she closed the oven door. "All ready for your father's homecoming. And Noah's," she added with a wink.

"I'll admit, I missed them both," Jo said.

Effie stirred a pot of Swiss white soup, a favorite of Jo's. "I suppose you're on your way to the docks. Be a dear, won't you, and fetch some parsnips from the cellar before you head out. Pablo's gone out back to run some energy off that little dog. I declare, I've never seen any creature so rambunctious for its size."

"I'll get the parsnips. But first, I'm wondering what Pablo has to say about this." Jo pulled the Rough on Rats container from her pocket.

"Why should he say anything? Rats are thick on ships. There's bound to be rat poison. And that container is just the right size to fit into a boy's pocket."

"The ship's captain died during the voyage, Effie. Gus Leighton says he showed signs of having been poisoned."

"Amity's Gus?"

Jo didn't like referring to him that way. "The ship's second mate. He has some medical training, apparently."

Effie lifted her spoon from the soup. "That's a horrible thing, for a man to be poisoned. But surely you can't be thinking the boy had any part in it."

"It's possible. Maybe the captain discovered he'd stowed away. Maybe he was going to have him punished."

"And maybe the moon's made of green cheese."

"I'm not being fantastical, Effie. The captain isn't the only one who died while sailing on that ship. And in truth, what do we know about Pablo? He may not be as innocent as he appears."

"We know Pablo is a long way from home." Effie touched the spoon to her lips, tasting the soup. "With not a soul to look after him besides us." She added a pinch of salt to the pot. "I'll not have you go around making unfounded accusations against him. Jedediah Bailey has done enough of that already."

"I'm not generally one to agree with Chief Bailey, but in this case, his suspicions may be warranted." Jo slipped the container back into her pocket. "I'd never forgive myself if I've brought a murderer into this house. And the fact is, Pablo's a stranger. We have no reason to trust him. Or any of these men, for that matter."

Effie set down her spoon. She wiped her hands on her apron. "I came to this country like Pablo did. Didn't speak the language. Didn't know a soul outside my family. Easiest thing in the world it was, being fearful, not trusting a soul. But it's no way to live, Miss Jo. At some point, you've got to give folks the benefit of the doubt. And trust yourself too. Now fetch me those parsnips." She made a shooing motion with her hands. "I haven't got all day."

# CHAPTER TWENTY-THREE

## Josephine ~ 1889

Jo's father, Lewis Felch, pushed his chair back from the table. "Not a finer meal to be had in the entire state of Oregon, Effie." He patted his rotund belly.

"Or California," Noah said.

Effie beamed. "That's kind of you to say. Although the chicken croquettes were a bit dry for my liking."

"The chicken croquettes were outstanding," Jo said. At her feet, Queenie thumped her tail.

"It seems you've got a friend, Jo," her father said.

"It's only the morsels I shared with her that make her appreciative. And I'll warn you, she makes the rounds. From what we've sneaked to her beneath the table, it's a wonder she hasn't doubled in size."

"Spoiled rotten." Effie added an empty platter to the stack on her arm.

"Is that the dog you mean?" Noah asked. "Or a certain guest?"

"The boy's earning his keep," Effie said. "Aren't you, Pablo?"

Pablo looked up from the dish of tapioca custard he was devouring at record speed. "I have helped in the kitchen," he said in slow, careful English. "With the..." He looked at Effie.

"Parsnips," she said.

"Parsnips," he repeated.

"And the potatoes," Effie said. "And the scalloped cheese."

"Before you know it, he'll be demanding wages," Jo's father said.

Pablo looked at him quizzically. "Wages?"

"Money," Effie said. "Coins. Like I showed you."

*Like the coin you kept in your pocket,* Jo thought, but this wasn't the time to bring that up.

"I want no money," the boy said. "Your..." He paused, seemed to search for a word. "...kindness is like...like gold."

"A fine sentiment." With his napkin, Jo's father dabbed at his mustache. "On that note, I believe I'll retire. I must admit, traveling tires a man."

"Miss Effie?" Pablo set his empty dish to one side. "May I be....?"

"Excused," Effie said. "Yes, you may. But no staying up late with your nose in a book."

Jo's eyes widened. "You can read, Pablo?"

"Un poco," he said. "I mean, a little."

"He knew his letters already. I've been showing him how they come together to make words." With this, Effie pushed through the swinging doors and into the kitchen.

Pablo pushed his chair back and left the table, following Jo's father from the dining room. From the hallway, Jo heard the two of them conversing. She couldn't make out what they were saying, but she heard her father laugh as their footsteps retreated.

"Father seems to be walking better," Jo said. "Do you think the hot springs waters eased his gout?"

"It seemed so," Noah said. "But not enough to keep him away from here. I suggested extending our stay, but he couldn't wait to get home."

"I'm glad you're back." Jo set down her cup and took his hand, his grip warm and sure. "Though I must confess I've had little time to pine away in your absence."

"I've never thought you one to pine away over anyone. But if you were, I should like it to be me."

"And so it would be." She hesitated, not wanting to spoil their reunion but feeling as if she must speak. "Noah, I'm concerned about Amity. I didn't want to say anything with Father here, but—"

Effie swung back through the doors to the kitchen, carrying the tea tray. "I thought you two would have retired to the library already."

"We're headed that way," Jo said.

Hand in hand, she and Noah headed for their library. Effie came along behind them and set out the tea.

"There you are. I expect you have a good deal to catch up on." With a wink at Jo, the maid left, shutting the door behind her.

"If she had her way, we'd be saying our vows tomorrow," Jo said.

"I can think of worse ways to spend the day." Noah pulled her into his arms, and they shared a kiss, long overdue.

"I like how you take your time, Noah Elliot," she said softly. "Especially with me." Months ago, she'd broken off her engagement with attorney Warren Hatch. Though her affection for Noah felt different, she didn't entirely trust her feelings yet.

They sat side by side on the settee, and Jo poured their tea.

"Now tell me about this gentleman friend of my sister's," Noah said. "The one important enough to cause her to miss my homecoming meal."

"From what I told at dinner tonight, you know the circumstances of their first meeting."

"Quite dramatic. I hadn't pegged you and Amity as the life-saving types."

"I wonder now if the drama of it all predisposed Amity to befriending him so quickly. On the surface, he seems a nice enough fellow. Well-educated, well-traveled. Good-looking, though not as handsome as you."

Noah laughed. "I have a feeling my sister would beg to differ. But handsome men have tried to court Amity before, and she's always spurned them. There must be something special about Gus Leighton."

"Supposedly he comes from money." Jo sipped her tea.

"That's never much mattered to Amity."

"Just as well since he seems not to have any now. He's relying on the charity of folks around here to get by. Now he's planning to find some sort of work so he can pay them all back."

"Seems honorable enough."

"I suppose. But if he comes from money, why has he been working at all? Why go to sea?"

"Adventure, maybe," Noah said. "Although didn't you say he was second mate? Seems like a man of stature would have aspired to a higher rank."

"On a previous voyage, he sailed as first mate. But then he led a mutiny, and the captain was killed."

Noah drew back. "He led a mutiny and took a man's life?"

"It wasn't Gus who killed the captain. It was a man named Arthur Trill. After his release from prison, Gus convinced the *Iona*'s captain to hire him on. Now Arthur is here in Astoria, waiting for the court of inquiry to rule."

"A murderer here in Astoria," Noah said. "That doesn't sound good. I wonder why any captain would permit such a man on his crew, even if the second mate encouraged it."

"The captain and Gus were childhood chums, apparently."

"And you said the captain died at sea?"

"Yes. One of a series of unfortunate incidents leading the crew to believe the ship was cursed. If I were less inclined to the facts, I might begin to believe that myself."

Noah glanced away, then returned his gaze with an intensity that felt as if it wrapped around her. "I understand your concerns about Gus Leighton. And I appreciate your looking out for Amity's best interests. But I have to wonder how much of this is you being cautious with strangers, Jo. You've every reason to be."

She held his gaze. "I'm trying to be objective. Sorting through the facts. Whatever happened on the *Iona* before she wrecked on our beach, it ended with a seaman's body washing up on shore. Someone stabbed him. In all the fuss over salvage rights, this poor man's murder seems all but forgotten. And I'm starting to wonder if the wreck and the murder are connected."

He tipped his head, looking puzzled. "How's that?"

"The morning after the *Iona* wrecked, locals from down the beach went aboard and grabbed whatever they thought was of value. The first officer, Howard Perkins, ran them off. But quite a lot had already been taken, including the sailors' belongings. That morning, Perkins was shouting about a missing satchel. Later, he mentioned it to Chief Bailey. It turned up the other day after we printed a story about the ship's curse."

"No one wanted to keep items that might be cursed. Is that it?"

"Exactly. Nan suggested the story. It had the desired effect."

"Well, then. The first officer must have been pleased to get his satchel back."

"He was. But I expect he feels differently now. I looked inside. It contains only lead weights, the type used for fishing."

He looked puzzled. "What were you doing with his satchel?"

"I recalled how eager he was to get hold of it. While I was at the police station this morning, I saw it had been returned. So, I asked Bob Melbourne if I might borrow it to see if it belonged to Pablo."

"I'm confused. Why would the first officer care about Pablo's satchel?"

"To be honest, I never thought it belonged to Pablo. Then again, Pablo is a mystery. There's much I don't know about him."

"And yet you've allowed him to stay in your house."

"I couldn't bear to see him languish in jail, and Bailey resting back on his laurels as if he'd solved the murder of the century by arresting a child. Once I brought Pablo home and Effie took him under her wing, any second thoughts I had were immaterial. Anyone who wants to get at Pablo will have to get past Effie first."

He gave a lopsided grin. "And Effie is a force to contend with. Did you confirm the satchel doesn't belong to Pablo?"

"Yes. When I showed it to him, he stepped back with his hands in the air and said he wasn't a thief."

"Curious. You think someone took whatever was inside and replaced the contents with lead weights?"

"Maybe. But if that's the case, why return it at all? You're either worried about a curse or you're not. It makes no sense to keep part of the loot and return the rest."

"Greed might override superstition if what they found was truly of value."

"But if someone here changed out the satchel's contents, how does one explain—"

The library door opened, causing Jo to fall silent.

"My missing brother." Amity stood inside the doorway, arms outstretched.

"My missing sister." Noah got up and hugged her. "Where are you hiding this man who's stolen your affections?"

"I wanted him to come meet you." Amity sat in the chair next to the settee. "But he's changing hotels and wants to get settled into his new room."

"I thought Howard Perkins was footing Gus's bill at the Occidental," Jo said.

"Some sort of problem arose, I guess. Gus says he'll be better off at the Grand. The superintendent at the mill arranged a line of credit for Gus there, till he gets his first paycheck."

"Millwork," Noah said. "I trust he knows what he's in for."

Amity threw back her shoulders. "Gus isn't afraid of hard work."

"I've been filling Noah in on what happened with the *Iona*," Jo said.

"Thank heavens that court of inquiry is finally set to convene," Amity said. "Gus has been on pins and needles."

"I don't see why he'd care how they rule on the salvage question," Jo said. "He has no financial interest in the *Iona*, does he?"

"He just wants it over with. Put that part of his life behind him and move on. Maybe then people will forget about that blasted curse."

"I didn't think Gus believed in the curse," Jo said.

"He doesn't. But everyone else seems to. It's the talk of the town. Anything goes the least bit wrong, folks are blaming the curse. Horse throws a rider. Fox nabs a chicken. A man trips, mounting the stairs. People think that's all from the curse."

"That must be hard on Gus," Noah said. "I expect some folks eye him with suspicion."

"Him and the rest of the crew," Amity said.

Noah stood. "Well, ladies, I should get going. Lewis will be well-rested by morning, and he'll be wanting to go over the notes I took while we were in San Francisco."

"Is he planning another expansion of the cannery?" Amity said.

"Possibly. He definitely wants to upgrade some of the machinery."

Jo shook her head. "Last summer, all he talked about was how the fish runs were declining. Now he's keen to invest more in the business?"

"Just some efficiencies to improve the bottom line." Noah pecked his sister's cheek, then Jo's. "Good night." His eyes lingered a moment on Jo. Then he left.

Amity leaned back in her chair. "I expect you gave him an earful about Gus."

"He was curious. Especially since you chose dining with Gus over Effie's grand welcome-home meal."

"I didn't intend any slight. But all this consternation over the *Iona* is taking a toll on Gus. I'm the bright spot in his days, he says. I hate to deny him that."

"You could have brought him here for dinner. Effie cooked enough to feed an army."

"And have you grill him with questions that make him look like a criminal?"

"He led a mutiny on a previous ship," Jo said, trying not to sound defensive. "To many, that would make him a criminal."

Amity's eyes narrowed. "Who told you about the mutiny?"

"Howard Perkins. He said Gus and Arthur were aboard a ship when the crew turned on the captain. To hear Perkins tell it, Gus was the ringleader. He says Arthur served time for killing the captain. It seems an unsavory affair all around."

"If you think to shock me with these facts, you should know Gus has already told me all about what happened. He and Art were aboard a schooner carrying supplies around Australia. The captain was a hard man. On the slightest provocation, he'd lock a man in irons, Gus said."

"Provocation may be a matter of interpretation."

"Even so, a man in irons is helpless. And yet this captain ordered these men left on the deck, exposed to the elements. He threatened anyone who brought food or water to the men in chains."

"If Gus found this behavior so egregious, he should've taken it up with the authorities at the next port. A court of inquiry can rule on misconduct aboard a ship."

"True, but this captain disregarded the course the helmsman put before him. He pointed them due south, toward Antarctica. Gus feared the man was losing his mind. They were running short on provisions. Someone had to act, or the entire crew would have ended up dead."

"So Arthur took it upon himself to kill the captain. And Gus stood by him. Maybe even encouraged it."

"That's not how it happened," Amity said. "The crew came to a unanimous decision. They took command of the ship."

"You mean Gus took command."

"Because he was first mate. It was his duty to lead in the captain's absence. And Gus is a man who takes his duties seriously."

"And was it not his duty to punish Arthur Trill for murder?"

"Art didn't kill the captain. The crew put him in irons—belowdecks and out of the elements, mind you. They fed him and made sure he had fresh water, given the rations they'd imposed after going off-course.

The crew took turns keeping watch over him. During Arthur's watch one evening, Gus heard a shot fired from below. He ran to see what had happened. There was Art, pistol in hand, and the smell of gunpowder in the air. The captain lay dead, shot through the chest."

"And yet Gus claims Art didn't kill him?"

"It was an accident. Art was setting down the tray with the evening meal, and the captain lunged for his revolver. Art lost control of the gun, and it went off. Gus thinks the captain must have fired on himself, perhaps intentionally, perhaps not. Either way, Art swears he didn't pull the trigger."

"Then why did he go to jail?"

"The captain had been especially hard on Art, Gus says. Some among the crew figured Art had gotten his revenge. Their testimony swayed the tribunal. Even if he was guilty—and Gus is confident he wasn't—he'd served his sentence and been released when Gus reconnected with him and suggested he join the *Iona*'s crew. He's an accomplished seaman, Gus says. Able with the rigging. Hard worker. Tough. And Gus believes in second chances. So did Nick Watson, apparently. The world could use more like the two of them."

"Look, Amity. All you know about Gus is what he tells you. What if he's deceiving you about all of this?"

"Like you were deceived, you mean?"

Jo was silent a moment. "I should have been more wary. And I think you should be too."

"These circumstances are different. All I'm asking is for you to trust my judgment."

"But you've never fallen like this for any man."

"Maybe that's because I've never been in love like this. Don't you want me to be happy?"

"Of course, I want you to be happy. It's just that—"

"Then please, back off with your suspicions about Gus. Don't make me choose between him and our friendship."

Jo drew a sharp breath. "All right. I'll give Gus the benefit of the doubt. As long as you agree to admit to the facts wherever they lead."

# CHAPTER TWENTY-FOUR

## Olivia ~ Present Day

Sitting on the front rug, Micki greets Olivia with a yowl of hunger. Clearly, the diving lesson is no excuse for a delayed meal.

"I know, I know." Closing the door behind her, Olivia flips the deadbolt. "Unacceptable."

After her encounter with Jimmy, the smells inside the bookshop send waves of comfort through her veins. Wood polish, the result of Naomi's obsessive cleaning. Coffee beans, ground at the espresso bar. And most of all, the smell of books, a magical potion of paper and glue and stories waiting to be explored.

She goes upstairs and opens a can of souffle of salmon, which Micki gobbles up. Between her diving panic and confrontation out front, Olivia is coming off a rush of adrenalin that leaves her feeling dog-tired. She changes into her PJs, but instead of going straight to bed, she curls up on her couch with her phone.

*Jimmy Stone,* she types into her browser's search bar. Dozens of listings pop up, including a Kentucky barbeque champion and a felon arrested for supplying alcohol to minors. But none of the men have anything to do with oceans or diving. She switches to an image search, but none of the photos even remotely resemble the man who confronted her on the sidewalk tonight.

She goes back to standard search mode and tries *Stone treasure*. No Jimmy, only a Stone Brewing Company in Palo Alto featuring a Treasure Island Lager and a shopping website featuring "treasure stone" jewelry, whatever that is.

For all the adventures Jimmy Stone claims to have been involved in, there's no internet trail to show for it. She suspects that's what he wants.

She has more luck searching for Jillian. There's a Facebook page for Jillian Woodhull, and the profile photo is a match, depicting a slightly younger Jillian aboard a boat, the wind in her hair, the sun on her face, and the ocean in the background. Her cover photo is a beach-front sunset. Not being her Facebook friend, that's all Olivia can see. Jillian's privacy settings are tight. Olivia can't hold that against her. At least she exists online in a way that Jimmy seems not to.

Olivia does a new search, this time for *Jillian Woodhull Seaworthy Institute*. A basic webpage for the Seaworthy Institute comes up, in a style that suggests it's overdue for an update. The home page shows an old stone building that looks like it used to be some sort of cottage. Maybe it still is. Next to the red front door is a plaque that reads *Seaworthy Institute, Est. 1962*.

The text on the page says only that the institute is devoted to archeological expeditions at sea. At the bottom of the page is an address in Hastings, UK. There's also a phone number.

Besides the home page, there are only two tabbed pages on the site. Olivia clicks on the one labeled *Current Projects*. But nothing is current here, the most recent project on the list dating from four years ago. The page contains three links, but every one of them registers a *404 page not found* error. Whatever the Seaworthy Institute is up to these days, website maintenance isn't among its priorities.

The other tab links to an "About Us" page. There Olivia finds a staff photo showing five people involved with the institute. In the center of the picture stands a tall woman with closely cropped white hair. Standing to one side of her is a younger-looking version of Jillian, smiling broadly. Then there is a youngish man with wire-rimmed glasses, handsome in a studious sort of way. His arm is flung around Jillian. On the other side of the white-haired woman are a bearded man and a red-haired woman, both grinning.

Beneath the photo is a staff list. The Institute's director is named as Marianne Woodhull. Jillian shows up as assistant to the director. There's an Andrew Woodhull, too, listed as operations manager. He must be the young man with his arm around her, Olivia thinks.

She searches for *Andrew Woodhull UK Seaworthy Institute*. All that comes up is an old LinkedIn listing that hasn't been updated in years. An image search brings up the Institute's About page photo and also a head shot of the same man, looking slightly older. The head shot comes from the staff webpage of a London arts institute.

Jillian and Andrew could be brother and sister, but Olivia suspects they are married. Or, more likely, they used to be married, since Jimmy and Jillian are a couple now. That would make Andrew Marianne's son or grandson, with Jillian related by marriage.

Either way, the Institute named in the permit Jimmy flashed in her face does exist, and Jillian is associated with it. Olivia wishes she'd had a chance to study the applicant's signature on the permit more closely. But it was one of those hasty-looking signatures that's hard to make out, especially in the dim light.

She closes out of her browser. There are state officials who look into applications for permits. Everything must have checked out, or they wouldn't have issued one. If what Jimmy and Jillian are doing is legal, why should she care if Finn wastes away his time and his gas searching for treasure at the bottom of the ocean?

But she does care, enough that she reopens her browser and pulls up the Institute's website again. She punches London into her phone's world clock. Eight hours ahead of Astoria puts it at a little past six a.m. Her call will go to voice mail. So much the better. She doesn't want to have to explain why she's phoning from halfway around the world.

She dials the number listed on the website. After one ring, she gets a message saying that the number she's attempting to reach is no longer in service. Not so surprising, considering how outdated the site is. Maybe the Institute has changed locations, and with that, changed phone numbers.

She scrolls through the search results. Farther down, she finds a couple of news items about archeological finds from shipwrecks off England's southern coast. Both include quotes from Marianne Woodhull. But the news items are dated 2011 and 2013. Olivia finds nothing more recent.

"Enough," she says to Micki. Having filled her belly with Souffle of Salmon, the cat is curled up beside Olivia on the couch. "Time for bed."

For Olivia, a good night's sleep often brings clarity. But when she wakes up the next morning, questions about Jimmy and Jillian are still on her mind. Most of all, she wonders why Jimmy felt compelled to track her down and dangle their permit in front of her. She wishes she'd confronted him about that. If he thinks she has some sort of sway over Finn, he's mistaken. And what would it matter if she did? For better or worse, Finn is all in on this venture.

And it is for the worse, as Olivia discovers when Naomi comes in. Without her usual eyeliner and shadow, she looks shaken and bleary-eyed.

"You feeling okay?" Olivia asks.

"I'd feel better if I'd slept more than three hours last night." Naomi stashes her purse in the drawer beneath the register. "And if Finn hadn't gone and almost drowned himself."

Olivia's heart skips a beat. "What happened?"

"He showed up on my doorstep at 2 a.m. He was soaking wet, and his teeth were chattering. And the look on his face...Olivia, I've never seen fear in him before. I tried to get out of him what had happened, but he was pretty incoherent. He kept mumbling about Finn's something, and I kept saying 'Finn's what?' Once I got him toweled off and warmed up, I finally figured out he wasn't talking about himself. He meant flipper fins. You know, the kind divers use."

"Something went wrong with Finn wearing fins?" Olivia says, remembering her own duck-like waddle to the pool's edge last night.

"Not Finn. Jillian. It took a while, but eventually, I put together what happened. Finn took Jimmy and Jillian out last night like usual. Apparently that submarine thingy found something they wanted to explore, so Jimmy and Jillian decided they'd dive down and investigate."

"In the middle of the night." After Olivia's brief experience with diving, this seems even more unfathomable than it did before.

"They have headlamps on their diving helmets, apparently. Everything was going fine, Finn said, but then the current picked up earlier than they were expecting, so they worked their way up the line to the surface. As they got close, Finn said he could see how the current was pulling them away."

Just hearing this, Olivia feels her diving lesson panic all over again. With dread building in the pit of her stomach, she can scarcely form words. "They got...swept out to sea?"

"No, not that."

Relief floods over her. Whatever is going on with Jimmy and Jillian, she wouldn't wish that sort of disaster on anyone. "Then what was it?"

Naomi runs her hand through the purple swath of her hair. "Finn helped them onto the boat. They were worn out. Jillian pulled off her mask and spit out her regulator. Then she reached down to pull off her fins, and she lost her balance and fell back into the water."

Last night's instructions are fresh in Olivia's mind. "What about her tank? And her weight belt?"

"Still wearing them. She dropped straight to the bottom. Her regulator swung behind her head, and she was having a hard time reaching it. Jimmy knew she was in trouble. He dove in after her. But the current took him, and he was having a hard time swimming against it. Finn tossed him a rope and pulled him in."

"But Jillian..." Olivia's voice trails off. This is her worst nightmare, for Jillian and also for the men, who are helpless to save her.

"They heard a thump at the bottom of the boat. She came up for a few seconds. They reached for her, but she went down again. Jimmy wanted to jump in again, but Finn yelled for him to stay put. He tied off to the boat just as she bobbed back up, sputtering and gasping for breath. She'd finally gotten her weight belt off and activated her buoyancy compensator. Finn swam to her. At the end of his rope, in more ways than one, he said."

Olivia lets out a breath she hadn't realized she was holding. "She's okay?"

"Yup. Mad at herself for putting them all in danger."

"How terrifying," Olivia says.

"Tell me about it." Naomi swipes away the tears that are welling in her eyes. "I get shook up just thinking about how it might have turned out. Not just for her but for all of them."

Olivia puts her arm around Naomi's shoulder and gives her a squeeze. "Hopefully they've all learned a lesson. No amount of gold is worth losing your life over."

"That's what I told Finn. And there might not even be any gold. Isn't that what you've been trying to tell him?"

"Right. But I don't feel like he's heard me. Maybe he'll be more apt to listen now."

"I hope so. But when he got up this morning, it was like what happened last night was just part of some grand adventure. He's ready to go back out with Jimmy and Jillian again tonight. Olivia, I know I asked you to quit pestering him about this project. But if you can knock some sense into his thick skull, by all means do it."

"I've tried. But he doesn't like me interfering. Neither does Jimmy. He came by here last night before they went out. I was just getting home from my first diving lesson."

"So that's how you know about weight belts and regulators."

"Right. And how I found out I'm not cut out for scuba."

"What did Jimmy want?"

"He was angry that I'd mentioned permits to Finn. He flashed one in my face and basically told me to lay off. The light wasn't great, but the permit looked authentic. It was issued to a Seaworthy Institute in the UK."

"Where Jillian's from."

"Right. I found the institute online. Looks like a small operation. She shows up as being on the staff with a couple of other Woodhulls. An older woman named Marianne Woodhull is in charge, according to the website. Jillian's listed as her assistant. But the site hasn't been kept up. And in the past few years, it doesn't look like the Institute has been involved in any explorations at all."

"So why this one?" Naomi says.

"I wonder that too. There are thousands of shipwrecks around the world they could be exploring. And according to Charlotte's friend Glen, marine archeologists tend to focus on sites where they know they'll get paid. Government entities and private corporations hire them to satisfy historic preservation mandates that waterfront sites be free of historical artifacts before development proceeds."

"Which can be done during daylight."

"Right. All above board. It's treasure hunters like Jimmy who operate on the fringes. But even if they find treasure, there's no guarantee they'll get to keep it. Depending on the circumstances, insurance companies who paid out claims back when the ship wrecked may get to keep anything of value."

For the first time this morning, Naomi cracks a smile. "You've been researching this, haven't you?"

Olivia smiles back. "Maybe a little. Finn let slip the name of the ship. I found a reference to it in this book Jimmy asked me to hold for him." She retrieves the book from the Holds shelf, flips to the photo, and holds it out for Naomi to see.

*"The schooner* Iona," Naomi reads from the caption. *"Captain Nicholas Watson, from Manzanillo, Mexico, for the Columbia in ballast, was wrecked in January 1889, off Clatsop Sands. All but one of the crew got off safely, and they made their way to Astoria.* Nice looking ship."

"But it was carrying ballast, not gold."

"Right." She closes the book and hands it back to Olivia. "Weird that Jimmy put this on hold but hasn't come back to pick it up."

"He did the same thing at the library. Put three books on hold, each with some sort of reference to the *Iona*. Last time I was there, he still hadn't claimed them. I think he's trying to make sure no one else can find out about the wreck."

"He doesn't know how persistent you can be when you want to know something."

"Nosy, some people call it. But once I get going on something like this, I want to know everything there is to know. Especially when it affects people I care about. Anyhow, Margaret over at the library let me have a look at the books Jimmy put on hold. Plus I found a newspaper account of the wreck. Turns out the *Iona*'s captain died at sea."

"So he's the person who didn't survive the wreck?"

"No, he died earlier. One of the sailors died during the storm. His body washed up on shore the next day. He'd been stabbed."

"A ship without a captain. A murder. And now Jillian almost drowns trying to get at the wreck." Naomi shakes her head. "It's like that ship's cursed."

"I don't know about that. But the whole thing raised enough questions that I asked Charlotte if she could find the records of the court of inquiry proceedings. That's where questions of salvage rights would have been adjudicated. I thought if I could show Finn that someone else, like an insurer, had claims to the wreck, he'd see the light. But Charlotte says the records were destroyed in a courthouse fire."

"So now what?"

Olivia drums her fingers on the register counter. "There's something else Jimmy Stone doesn't know about me. Push me too hard to quit something, and I tend to double down. The fact that he doesn't show up anywhere online makes me suspicious. I'm going to do some asking around."

"I won't try to stop you," Naomi says. "But I don't like how this is all adding up. Be careful."

"I will be. In the meantime, I think it's best if neither one of us pushes too hard on Finn. If that near disaster last night hasn't discouraged him, nothing we say will. At least not till we have rock-solid proof that this whole business isn't on the up and up."

"I'll do my best to keep my mouth shut. For a few days, anyhow."

Customers start coming in. Olivia and Naomi turn their attention to helping them find the books they've come looking for. Like Officer Jason, some have specific genres or authors or titles in mind. Others come in with a vaguer sense of what they want. A young mother who wants to spend her toddler's nap time escaping into a story. A recent widower who needs a distraction from his grief. A construction worker looking for a title he and his bookish girlfriend will both enjoy.

Between customers, Olivia ponders her next steps with Finn's situation. She could be projecting her own fears of plunging beneath the waves, but it feels like danger is lurking all around this foolish venture, and next time, the outcome could well be more tragic. Not to mention that Jimmy seems to be hiding something. Why else would he bother to confront her? Jillian's involvement with the semi-defunct Seaworthy Institute seems suspect too.

Around lunchtime, Olivia's phone pings with a text message. It's from Finn. *Need you to meet me at First National. 3 pm?*

"Finn wants me to meet him at the bank this afternoon," she says. "Do you know anything about that?"

"Didn't say a word to me," Naomi says. "Although with what I know of his overall finances, I doubt he's planning on giving you money."

"One way to find out." Olivia types her response. *3 pm. See you there.*

Leaving Naomi in charge, Olivia takes off early. On her way to the bank, she stops at the Colonial Inn. The night at the sushi restaurant when Finn introduced her and Ethan to Jillian and Jimmy, Ethan asked where they were staying, and they said the Colonial. Not for the first time, she appreciates Ethan's gift for small talk, which has a way of yielding up helpful information.

She sees nothing colonial about the Colonial Inn. Painted orange with a low-sloping roof, the motel is a throwback to the sixties when car travel was at its peak and every little town along any self-respecting highway had at least one motel with identical rooms looking over its parking lot.

The young guy at the registration desk looks up from reading a book when Olivia enters. She's pretty sure she has also seen him waiting tables at a local brewery.

"I heard a friend of mine from out of town might be staying here," she says. "Out of the country, actually. She's British. I was hoping to catch up with her, but I've lost track of her phone number. I'm pretty sure she said she was going to stay here. Can you check? Her name's Jillian Woodhull."

"Sorry. We're not allowed to give out information about guests."

"Oh, right. That makes sense. Privacy. Well, maybe you could tell me when would be a good time for me to catch her. Assuming she's staying here, that is. Then I could come around and maybe surprise her here in the lobby."

He sets his book down. It's a spy novel, John LeCarre. "If by chance there was a British woman named Jillian staying here, I'd look for her right before dusk or right after dawn." He shakes his head. "People keep some strange hours."

"That's Jillian. Love her to death, but she's got some odd habits. I tease her about being an old lady vampire."

"I'm with you on the vampire part. Not sure about the old lady."

"Her aversion to credit cards," Olivia says, testing her theory. "I expect you've noticed."

"Oh yeah. Her and that guy she's with, they pay only in cash. Pain in the rear. Our system's set up for credit." He shakes his head. "And those prepaid phones. Geez. Can't believe there's still a market for those."

*Only among criminals,* Olivia thinks. But what she says aloud is, "I expect Jillian's found some loophole that makes them worthwhile. International calls, maybe. While she's abroad."

He shrugs. "Maybe." He picks up his book.

"I'll come back around later this week. If it's a choice between dusk or dawn, I'm all in on dusk. Never have been much of a morning person."

"Me neither." He's trying to be polite, but she can tell he's itching to get back to his book.

"Don't say anything to Jillian, please. I want to surprise her."

"Never saw you before in my life," he says.

Leaving him to his book, she heads for the bank. Paying in cash. Using burner phones. Not long ago, in the mystery section of her bookshop, she came across a used paperback called *How to Be Invisible.* The handwritten inscription inside the front cover read, *Here's how D.B. Cooper fooled you. Merry Christmas from Joe and Nan.*

Puzzled, she showed the book and the inscription to Naomi. She laughed and said it's a story that's been circulating around Astoria since before she was born. Back in the 1970s, a guy calling himself D.B. Cooper hijacked a flight from Portland to Seattle, extorted $200,000 cash at the Seattle airport, and demanded to be flown to Mexico. Once they were airborne, he parachuted from the plane with the cash. Aside from some bills that landed in the wilderness, no trace of him was ever found.

According to Naomi, some locals swore the police sketch of Cooper looked a lot like a guy who'd hung around Astoria before the hijacking. During that time, he swindled people who befriended him out of an undetermined amount of money. "I'll bet that book was a gag gift for someone he duped," Naomi said. "I wonder how that went over."

Flipping through the book, Olivia saw it didn't belong in the fiction section. It was an actual manual of sorts for people who wanted to disappear. She recalls some of the advice: Avoid buying or renting a vehicle. Find temporary housing under an assumed name. Don't stay too long in any one place. Pay in cash. Use burner phones.

Jillian isn't operating under the radar, but it sure seems as if Jimmy is. Why? The obvious answer would be that he has gotten into some sort of trouble and is on the run. That would explain the burner phone, the cash payments, the temporary housing, the lack of a vehicle. It would also explain him being so forceful about making sure she saw the permit, lending the appearance of compliance with the law.

His name isn't actually Jimmy Stone. She'd put money on that. But without knowing his real name, she feels as if she has hit a roadblock. All the evidence she has so far is circumstantial.

Rounding the corner to the bank, she spots Finn outside. Jimmy and Jillian are with him. None of them look shaken in the least by Jillian's near-drowning last night.

"Hey, Olivia!" Jillian waves as if she's the long-lost friend Olivia made her out to be when talking with the motel clerk. "Long time, no see."

Jimmy stares as Olivia approaches, as if he's daring her to confront him.

"I heard the three of you had quite the adventure last night," Olivia says, coming up to them.

Finn tugs at the brim of his cap. "You could say that."

"My own stupidity," Jillian says. "You'd have thought it was my first time out. Good thing these two knights in shining armor were at the ready."

"Naomi was pretty shook up, just hearing about it," Olivia says. "Considering what could've happened."

"Just a little dip in the ocean," Jimmy says.

Olivia locks eyes with him. "More than a little dip, I'd say."

"Ah, but we had the proper permit for it," Jimmy says. "That's all that matters, isn't it?"

Ignoring the jab, Olivia turns her attention to Finn. "What's up that you need me at the bank?"

"Come in, and I'll explain."

She looks to see if Jimmy and Jillian intend to follow, but they've turned and are heading away from the bank.

"Ciao, Olivia." Jillian turns and waves. "I'll stop by and see you at the bookshop one of these days. Jimmy tells me you've got an amazing inventory for a small store."

"Sounds good," Olivia says. "And Jimmy, don't forget you've got a book to pick up."

He answers with a backhanded wave, acknowledging he heard but nothing more.

Finn ushers her inside. A familiar musty smell greets her. Judging from its drab exterior, she guesses the bank building dates from the 1950s or 1960s. Inside, too, it's decidedly lacking in charm. But this is where Olivia's great-aunt Ingrid had always kept the bookstore's accounts, and since Ingrid's passing, the staff has been nothing but friendly and helpful to Olivia.

She follows Finn into a corner office. At the desk is a man Olivia has seen before but never had occasion to speak with. His suit is nearly the same shade of gray as his hair. His necktie is gray, too, dotted with maroon fleur de lis.

He stands as they enter and extends his hand to Olivia. "Daryl Robbins," he says. According to the plaque on the desk, he's a senior vice president. "And you must be Olivia Crawford. Finn has told me what an exceptional job you're doing with the bookstore."

"It's a work in progress," she says.

After shaking hands all around, they sit. "Finn asked if I'd explain a request he's making of the bank," Daryl says, getting down to business.

"I figured he'd do a better job of it than me," Finn says. "Being a financial guy and all."

"Explain away." Olivia leans back in the leather chair, striking what she hopes is a casual pose, but her alarms are up. "I'm all ears."

"I've looked over the arrangement the two of you have worked out for Ingrid's building." Daryl taps a paper on his desk. "Joint ownership on a three-year trial basis, with you leasing back the bookshop and Finn handling the maintenance in exchange for a share of the income from the rental units. Seems fair."

"Tom Jensen drew up the agreement," Olivia says. "He said it was unusual but not without precedent."

"Tom knows what he's doing. As joint owners, you both have certain rights to the property under common law, even if they're not explicitly stated in the agreement." Daryl clears his throat. "One of those rights is encumbrance."

Encumbrance. Olivia's inner alarms crank up higher. She turns to Finn. "You want to take out a loan and use the building as collateral?"

"Money's tight," he says. "Gas, maintenance. Everything's going up."

"Finn has agreed to a thirty-month payback period." Daryl swivels the loan application so she can see it. "That aligns with the terms of your joint tenancy agreement. But his portion of the income from the building falls short of our loan requirements. He needs a co-signer."

Olivia looks over the numbers. "One hundred thousand dollars," she says. "That's a lot of gas money."

"The boat needs some upgrades. It's my livelihood, you know. Like the bookstore is for you."

"Which is why I can't put the building at risk by allowing a lien."

Finn glares at her. Compared to when they first met, with Finn angry over Olivia's inheriting what had been his favorite uncle's property, they've come a long way, built trust and camaraderie. She's come to think of Finn as the brother she never had. Annoying at times, but well-intentioned. Hard-working. Considerate.

In the awkward silence, Daryl stands. "I've got some business to tend to out front. I'll leave the two of you to discuss things."

Three strides, and he's out of the room, shutting the door behind him.

"This is about the gold, isn't it?" Olivia says. "That's why you think you can make these huge payments."

"Have you checked the price of gold lately? With my share of what's down there, I can pay this off in full with plenty of money to spare. We'll be able to afford some of those renovations you've been talking about."

"You don't even know there's gold down there."

"Jillian's certain it's there. And Jimmy says we're this close to bringing it up." Illustrating, he displays his thumb and forefinger, inches apart. "Once we get a magnetometer and side sonar on the site, we'll be all over it."

"That's what this money is really for, isn't it? As far as I'm concerned, if Jimmy and Jillian need equipment, they should buy it themselves. Or is their cash supply running out?"

Finn ignores her remark. "It's an investment, Olivia. You have to spend money to make money. Think of what I can do with equipment like that on my boat. You know how many shipwrecks are out there? I'll be the go-to guy whenever anyone wants to go looking for them."

"Lots of those ships went down with little or nothing of value. And even with those carrying cargo that was worth something, who knows what's become of it, or who has rights to it. Even if Jimmy and Jillian find this gold, others might have claims to it."

"This isn't their first rodeo, Olivia. They're professionals."

An assistant posing as an archeologist and a treasure hunter using an assumed name and a burner phone, she's tempted to say. But then he'll know she's been going around asking questions.

"Professionals who nearly got you killed," she says.

He shakes his head. "Don't you get it? None of that would've happened last night if we'd had the right equipment."

"I'd think professionals would have the right equipment from the start. And they'd have investors backing them."

"I'm their investor. Like I said, they can't go around telling everyone about this wreck, or someone else will get to it first. They trust me, and that's why they've offered me this opportunity."

Opportunity. Isn't that what every scam claims to be?

"I'm sorry, Finn. I just can't put the building at risk."

He stands. "I should've known you wouldn't help me out. Never mind. I've got others who will."

"Do what you have to do, Finn. I just wish you'd open your eyes to the risks you're taking."

# CHAPTER TWENTY-FIVE

## Olivia ~ Present Day

That evening, Olivia calls her mother.

"Darling, it's so good to hear from you," Steph Crawford says. "It's been simply ages."

"It's been a week, Mom. And the phone works both ways, you know."

"Of course. But I can't tell you how busy I've been. Just when the summer rush is finally slowing down, I get these buyers who insist on seeing simply everything in their price range, which is substantial, let me tell you. I swear I've put a thousand miles on my car in the past two days. And of course, they're wildly indecisive. First, they insist on a pool. Then it's a hot tub. Then it's a garden tub in the master bath."

"I'm sure that's been frustrating, Mom. But, hey—"

"Frustrating doesn't begin to describe it. I'm worn to a frazzle. I've got half a notion to leave town and dump them on Judy. She owes me big time after the last buyers she pawned off on me. I've been thinking I should get out your way and see what you've done with the bookshop. We could drive down to Napa and do some winetasting."

"I'd love to see you. But honestly, it's a little too soon." If her mother comes out, it will take her no more than an hour to come up with a list of improvements Olivia simply must make to the property, none of which will be remotely within her budget. And as for the wine, Olivia already has concerns that her mother's drinking too much. She doesn't want to encourage it.

"Too soon." Her mother sighs. "Really, Olivia, you could at least come up with a more original excuse. I'm beginning to think you're hiding some outrageous development from me."

"I'm not hiding anything. But I do have a question. A real estate question."

In the background, a car's horn honks. "The way people drive around here," her mother says. "I swear it gets worse every day. Now, what's this about real estate? Have you come to your senses and decided to sell that building and start a real career?"

"I'm not even close to wanting to sell. I want to know about joint tenancy. Can one owner take out a loan and use the property as collateral without the other owner agreeing?"

"This is exactly what I've been worried about, Olivia. You're in over your head with an old building that's nothing but a money pit, and now you're going to go into debt. Ruin your credit score, and you'll never be able to buy a house."

"I don't need a house. I have Ingrid's apartment. And I love this historic building. You know me. I'm careful with my money."

"I thought I knew you, Olivia. I really did. But then you disappear without telling anyone, and next thing I know, you're entrenched in some little town on the other side of the continent."

And her mother wonders why Olivia doesn't call more often. "You've made clear that you disapprove of my life choices, Mom. But they're my choices, and I'm happy with them. If you don't want to answer my question, that's fine. I'll do an internet search."

"And get a head full of wrong ideas. To your question, yes, one joint tenant might encumber the property without the other's approval. But lenders typically prefer that both come on board. And you can be sure they'll take a close look at the substitution language in the joint tenancy agreement. In case of foreclosure, the bank needs to be able to step in and assume the interests of the owner who defaulted."

"That makes sense." Steph Crawford knows her real estate. "I knew you'd have the answer I was looking for."

"I wish you'd consulted me before you entered into a joint tenancy arrangement with that man. You owed him nothing. Ingrid left you that building, free and clear."

"I'm happy with my decision. It was the right thing to do under the circumstances."

"Water under the bridge at this point, I suppose." There's some jostling at the other end of the line. Olivia envisions her mother gathering her belongings up from her Porsche, which she refers to as her mobile office.

"Sounds like you're home. I'll let you go, Mom. Thanks for the information."

They hang up. Olivia strokes Micki, who's curled on her lap. It's hard now to imagine how she lived so many years in New York without a pet. She's tried to get her mother to get a cat or a dog like they had when Olivia was young. Half the reason her mother gets so wrapped up in her work, Olivia thinks, is that she's got nothing to come home to.

"You'd have done the same thing about that loan, wouldn't you, Micki?" She circles her fingertips over the soft fur behind the cat's ears. "Only now I've got to worry about what Finn's going to do next."

She soon finds out. The next day, Naomi fills her in on Finn's new plan. "He's going to see his uncle in Portland. Something about a loan."

"I thought Finn wasn't close with his family," Olivia says.

"He isn't," Naomi says. "He's mentioned this uncle before, but not with what you'd call affection. Apparently, he has a reputation for getting himself involved in shady deals."

"Ugh. That's the last thing Finn needs."

"I'm worried about him, Olivia. He's obsessed. Jimmy's putting all sorts of ideas in his head."

"About the gold, you mean."

"Not just that. After you wouldn't co-sign that loan, Jimmy told Finn you've got no business sense. He said I should quit working here. I told Finn it would be a cold day in hell before I'd do that. I love this job. And I love Finn too." Naomi's voice quivers. "Or at least I think I do. I don't like how Jimmy's trying to drive a wedge between us."

"You know, I'm liking that guy less with each passing day," Olivia says. "There's something off about him. And it feels like he's trying to isolate Finn from the people who care about him."

"Except for when he needs money. I guarantee Jimmy is behind this push to see the uncle in Portland."

"This whole thing has gone on long enough. There's too much at stake. People's livelihoods."

"And lives," Naomi says grimly. "I just can't figure out how to get Finn to see it."

"I hear you on that. Without hard evidence, there's no convincing him that Jimmy and Jillian aren't on the up and up. So, we'll just have to come up with that evidence. Somehow."

"My grandma used to say where there's a will, there's a way. I hope that applies in this situation."

"I've been accused of being strong-willed," Olivia says. "Though I prefer to think of it as being persistent. And I'm pretty sure there are more stones I can turn over to find the truth about Jimmy Stone. I just need to figure out what they are."

The day gets busy after that, with customers coming and going. Vi stops by mid-afternoon with a plate of leftover pulla bread she stashed in the freezer after last week's quilting circle. Together, they indulge in a mid-afternoon coffee break.

"You never told me there were snacks like this at the quilting circle." Naomi licks pulla crumbs from her fingers. "Maybe I can get up by eight on Saturday mornings after all."

Vi laughs. "We start at eight, so you'd have to roll out of bed before then. But we'd love to have you join us, even if you're in your PJs. Need more young folks to keep things lively. And you've got a flair for art." She nods at Naomi's tattooed forearm. "You might be surprised at how fun it is. Olivia can tell you."

"I give her a full report every Saturday," Olivia says. "Including the Astoria gossip."

"You should see how she doles it out," Naomi says. "Like puppy treats. Drops little hints here and there till I'm begging for the whole scoop."

"Join us, and you'll hear it all firsthand." Vi's eyes sparkle. "You can even toss in a few juicy bits of your own."

Naomi straightens in mock seriousness. "I am the model of discretion, I assure you."

"And what about that man of yours? People are talking about him hanging around with a couple of strangers. Friends of the family, he says, but no one's buying that."

Olivia jumps in so Naomi doesn't have to. "Finn's tight-lipped with everyone. Even Naomi."

"Business and pleasure," Naomi says. "I've got these books, Finn's got his boat."

"Speaking of boats, you should see the quilt we're making now," Olivia says, turning the conversation away from Finn. "Vi found this cool old fabric in her attic with a ship printed on it. We're using the ship as the focal point for our quilt."

"Another benefit raffle?" Naomi says.

"For the Maritime Archeological Society. A friend of Charlotte's is involved. They had a conference here recently."

"I expect we'll finish our masterpiece tomorrow," Vi says. "Olivia, can you get word to Charlotte's friend? Maybe send him a photo when we're done so he can promote the raffle with the group's members?"

"Will do. And of course we'll hang the quilt here and sell tickets like we've done before."

Naomi eyes the space above the register. "Guess that means there's a ladder in my future."

"I don't do heights," Olivia explains. "Not if I can help it. One of many reasons I value Naomi."

"Who may explode if she eats any more of this stuff." Naomi nudges the pulla plate toward Olivia.

Vi returns to her shop, and Naomi helps a customer who comes in looking for books to give her granddaughter for her birthday. Olivia takes the pulla upstairs and stashes it in a container. She's tempted to have one more piece, but she and Ethan are checking out a new waterfront restaurant tonight, and she doesn't want to spoil her appetite.

When evening comes around, she's glad she held out. The restaurant is charming, with killer views of the river, and the food is amazing. Olivia and Ethan split plates of cannelloni and eggplant parmesan in a marinara sauce that rivals any she ever tried in New York, which is saying something.

As is always the case with Ethan, the pace of the meal is leisurely. It's one of many things Olivia loves about him—he gives the impressions he has all the time in the world for her. No matter what they're discussing, he listens intently, seeming genuinely interested in her perspective.

Tonight, she tells him about the new books that arrived at the shop this week, including a long-anticipated sequel to a book by one of her favorite authors. That gets them sharing more about their favorite authors and why they like them.

But when Olivia asks about how the next diving lesson went, Ethan has little to say. Instead, he pivots back to her quilting with Vi's Saturday circle. She updates him on the quilt to benefit Glen's group, a ready segue back to the diving lessons.

"You all went out in the lagoon this week, didn't you? That must have been exciting."

He gazes at her with a familiar look, one that touches her deep in her soul, encompassing care but not worry. "I didn't want to say too much. You made the right choice for you, and you should have no regrets."

"I don't," she says. "But I still want to know what it was like for you. That way, I can experience it vicariously. Like things we're fascinated to read about in books but don't want to experience ourselves."

His face relaxes. "Being out there was like nothing I've experienced before. I'm not sure I have words to describe it. There's this whole world beneath the surface. Fish, pilings that had fallen in the river, little critters crawling over the sand. Nothing outlandish, and yet I felt awestruck. I came across a hunk of timber, all covered in barnacles. Who knows where it came from or how long it has been there. I thought of how hidden it was. How well-preserved. Like it had settled into its final resting place and became part of the landscape. Or waterscape, I guess. Is that a word?"

"If it's not, it should be." All this undersea talk makes her want more than ever to tell him about what's going on with Finn, but she holds back, wants to wait till they're out of the restaurant and can speak more privately.

They finish their meal, topping it off with a slice of mascarpone cheesecake and a glass of port. Leaving the restaurant, Ethan proposes they stroll the river walk, soaking up the scenery while burning off a few of the calories they've consumed.

Olivia readily agrees. They head west, following the river in its never-ending journey toward the sea. Beyond the bridge, the sunset streaks the sky in brilliant hues of orange and red.

The evening is cool, the sky clear. She hugs her sweater to her waist, wishing she'd thought to wear her jacket. Ethan slings his arm around her shoulder. He draws her close, and she finds herself warming inside and out.

She hates to break the spell of good feelings. But she values Ethan's opinion, and she needs to get out the thoughts that have been swirling in her mind since her talk with Naomi.

There's no sense tiptoeing around the subject. Ethan is quick to pick up on that sort of thing. "Finn tried to get me to co-sign a loan," she says. "Using the bookshop building as collateral."

He slows his pace. In his gaze, she sees his concern. "Why does he need a loan?"

"It's those people he's gotten involved with. The ones we met at the sushi place. He's been taking them out in his boat every night. They've got him convinced there's..." She catches herself. She promised Finn she wouldn't mention the gold to anyone, and even with the trust between them eroding, she wants to keep her word as long as she can. "There's something valuable that they're after. Treasure of some sort."

"Like that guy told the kids at the bookshop—what's his name again?"

"Jimmy. Jimmy Stone. At least that's what he says his name is."

Even in the dim light, she sees the furrows in Ethan's brow. "You think he's using an alias?"

"Something's off with him. The other night, after the diving lesson, he confronted me outside the bookshop. Finn must have told him I'd mentioned them needing archeological permits for what they're doing, and Jimmy came marching over to show me they had one. It looked legitimate, but it also raised more questions."

"That he confronted you at all raises questions with me. The way he did it sounds threatening."

"You could say that. He clearly wants me to quit asking questions. Which of course only makes me want to ask more. I did an internet search for the institute named on the permit. There's a website, but it doesn't look like there's been much of anything happening there for the past few years. Jillian is affiliated with it, but only as an assistant."

"So, she's not actually an archeologist."

"Not that I could see. And I couldn't locate any Jimmy Stone or Jim Stone or James Stone online whose vitals and image match up with the guy she's involved with."

"You think he's hiding something."

"I think he's running from something in his past. Something he wants no one to know about. Not so different from what I did when I left New York and didn't want anyone to find out I'd lost my job."

He pulls her into a sideways hug. "I knew I should have done an internet search before I got involved with you. Next you'll be telling me that your real name is Hazel Crumpet."

She laughs. "Not a chance. I never felt the need to reinvent myself that completely. But Jimmy clearly has. I went to the motel where he and Jillian are staying. They're paying in cash, same as they pay Finn. And Jimmy's using a burner phone."

"Those seem like red flags to me."

"But not to Finn. I don't know what it will take to get him to see reason. The other night, the three of them almost got themselves killed out in the ocean. And yet Finn is still all-in."

"Wow," Ethan says. "I understand your concern."

"Of course, I told him I wouldn't cosign the loan. Now he's going to hit up some rich uncle of his. Naomi's a wreck, worrying about him. I'm not far behind. Especially if he encumbers our building. I've got to find out what's really going on with Jimmy and Jillian and that shipwreck."

"If anyone can sort this out, it's you." Slowing his pace, Ethan wraps his arms around her. "But promise me you'll be careful. People who have something to hide can be dangerous."

She looks up at him. "I'll be careful. But I'm not going to stop till I get to the truth."

# CHAPTER TWENTY-SIX

## Olivia ~ Present Day

Saturday morning, Olivia wakes up with ideas about where she can get at least some of the information she's after. But first, she's got Vi's quilting circle to attend. The design they're doing for the Maritime Archeological Society is intricate, and Vi says it's all hands on deck—pun intended—to finish it this week.

Fortified by a cream cheese Danish, Olivia pairs up with Susie again. They're tasked with creating a border of alternating dark and light triangles to go around the ship medallion that occupies the quilt's center. It's painstaking work, but Olivia finds the rhythm of it conducive to helping sort out the thoughts that have been floating in and out of her head.

She snips a thread. "I wonder if whoever made this medallion had a particular ship in mind."

"I'll bet they did," Susie says. "Back then, anyone who lived near any sort of waterway or ocean would have spent plenty of time watching ships come and go. Our big old cargo ships these days don't look nearly so romantic as those big schooners with their sails unfurled."

"True enough. Those cargo ships are functional, but I doubt we'll ever see one featured in a quilt."

"That's for sure." Susie sizes up a finished border strip next to the medallion. "One more triangle." She hands the strip of fabric back to

Olivia. "Say, remember how we were talking last week about heirlooms salvaged from shipwrecks?"

"Like your bell." Using her template and a piece of chalk, Olivia outlines another dark triangle.

"Right. You asked about gold. I totally forgot about the Kivinens."

"Sorry?"

"Longtime family here. Hanna Kivinen is my neighbor. Her grandfather—or maybe it was her great-grandfather - worked at a cannery out by Hammond. I remember her telling me one time that he'd found gold on a ship that wrecked on the jetty when it was under construction."

Olivia looks up from her work. "When was that?"

"Oh, boy. Let me think. They built our jetty first, then the north one. About the time the railroad came through, I think. 1880s? 1890s? Something like that."

"Did Hanna ever mention the name of the ship?"

"She might have. I don't recall. Why?"

"Oh, I was doing some reading. There was this beautiful schooner that wrecked on the jetty. New Year's Eve, 1888. I've heard rumors there was gold on board. Local salvors had a field day toting items off the ship, apparently, but there's no mention of what happened to the gold. I wonder if Hanna could shed some light on that."

"Maybe. She's a treasure trove of family stories, and she loves a captive audience. Want me to see if you can come by for a chat?"

"Sure. After work today?"

Susie gives her an odd look. "You really are interested in that wreck, aren't you?"

"Like a dog with a bone, my mom always says. Once I get onto something, I don't let go. I've lost sleep over lesser matters than a shipwreck."

"Oh, I hear you on that. I swear I lay awake for an hour last night trying to remember what I needed to add to my shopping list. Finally, it came to me. Avocadoes. Tell you what. I'll stop by Hanna's on my way home and let you know what she says."

"Perfect. I can already feel a good night's sleep coming on."

By the time Olivia leaves to open up the bookshop, the piecing is done, with only the backing and quilting left to finish. With the artful arrangement of patterns and colors drawing the eye to the ship at the center, the quilt is shaping up to be one of the nicest they've made since

Olivia started taking part in these projects. She snaps a photo to send to Glen, and Vi says she'll be by later this week with raffle tickets and the finished prize for Olivia to display.

Back at the bookshop, Olivia shows the photo to Naomi. "Ooh, I want to win that one," Naomi says. "I'd give it to Finn for his birthday."

"How'd it go with his uncle in Portland?"

"Not good," Naomi says. "Or good, depending on how you look at it. The uncle said that unless Finn could produce some proof that they've found the right wreck and there's gold on it, he doesn't see it as a viable investment. Or a reason to co-sign a loan. On the one hand, I'm glad. But Finn's feeling really defeated. Seeing his uncle stirred up a lot of old family issues that he's been trying to put behind him."

"That's too bad. If only..." Olivia's voice trails off. She's learned the hard way that there's little point in lamenting a situation unless you intend to do something about it. "I'm about ready to try talking to Finn again. With just a bit more evidence, maybe I can get him to give up this whole enterprise."

"I hope so. He wants to do the right thing. Problem is, Jimmy and Jillian have convinced him he's doing it. Finn's the kindest, most generous guy I know. But when he gets his mind set on something, it's like talking to a brick wall."

There's a big demand for Saturday morning books and coffee. Naomi keeps the espresso machine humming while Olivia handles the retail end. Finally, the rush tapers off. Olivia slips into the back room and texts Glen using the number Charlotte gave her. *Quilt is ready,* she writes, attaching the photo. *Raffle starts next week.*

*Amazing!* he texts back. *Our members will be clamoring for tickets, myself included. Huge thanks to your Astoria crew for making this happen.*

*It's been a fun project,* she replies. *Hey, do you have a minute for a call? Sure,* he says.

She dials his number. "Glad you could talk," she says when he picks up. "Charlotte says your conference went well?"

"Swimmingly," he says. "Sorry. Bad marine pun. How are the diving lessons going? She told me the three of you signed up."

"To be honest, I got scared off after the first lesson. But from what I hear, Ethan and Charlotte are having a blast."

"Don't feel bad," he says. "Diving's not for everyone. Life's too short to waste time on things you don't enjoy. There's plenty else in the world to explore."

"Good point. I wanted to ask you about some folks who are in town exploring a shipwreck. I thought maybe you've heard of them. Jimmy Stone and Jillian Woodhull."

"Stone doesn't ring a bell. But I don't know everyone in the field, not by a long shot. Woodhull..." He pauses. "Is she with the Seaworthy Institute? In the UK?"

"That's the one."

"I haven't heard of Jillian Woodhull. But she must be some relation to Marianne Woodhull. She founded Seaworthy back when few women were in the field. She and her crew made some impressive discoveries. But Marianne was diagnosed with dementia a few years back. She must be well into her eighties now, so I suppose it's not a big surprise. Still, it's disheartening to lose a great mind like hers. And as is often the case when there's a capable, charismatic founder at the helm, the Institute has rather fallen apart without her involvement."

"So you wouldn't expect them to have a permit to explore around here?"

"Not unless someone new has taken charge. This Jillian Woodhull, she's a marine archeologist?"

"She says she is. But on the Institute's website, she's listed as Marianne's assistant. And the man she's here with, Jimmy Stone, he says he's after treasure. From what you told us, I'm wondering how often an archeologist teams up with someone like him."

"Pretty much never. Not with their goals and methods so far apart. Archeologists aim to honor and preserve remnants of the past. Treasure hunters are looking to pillage and profit."

"When we spoke that night in Astoria, you mentioned a treasure hunter who was on the run from the law."

"Tommy Thompson," he says. "He found the *Central America* wreck decades ago. Took his investors' money and ran. Stayed under the radar for years till the authorities finally caught up with him. Wish I could say that was unusual, but I could name several others who've gotten sideways with the law."

"I suppose pillage and profit are incentive enough to run the risk," Olivia says.

"Sadly, that seems to be true. Do you have any idea what these folks are after out there?" Glen asks.

"A ship that wrecked on the jetty in 1888," she says.

"They made you swear not to tell anyone the name of the vessel, did they?"

"More or less. Through a friend they've pulled into their scheme."

"Warn your friend to be careful. If this venture is sketchy, he could be charged as an accessory."

"I've tried to warn him," she says. "I'll try again."

She thanks Glen for his time and hangs up. She goes back out front, ready to fill Naomi in on what Glen told her, when Jillian comes into the shop.

"Hey, there, you two." Jillian says brightly. "How's your Saturday going?" From her tote bag, she takes out five books, all mysteries, and stacks them on the counter. "Thought you might want to add these to your inventory."

"Let's have a look." Pulling the stack toward her, Naomi sorts through the titles. Till Olivia gets the shop's database up and running, they rely on Naomi's memory for inventory decisions.

"We've got three of these Graftons already," she says, setting one book aside. "But we're short on Tana French and Kate Atkinson, so we can buy those. You get a better deal with in-store credit, though."

Jillian waves her hand in the air as if swatting away a fly. "Oh, you can just have them. Lightens my load."

"That's kind of you." Olivia tosses the Grafton in the Goodwill box and moves the other four books to the bin for used books waiting to be shelved. "But we're happy to pay you."

"How about a cappuccino for the road?" Jillian says.

"You got it." Naomi fires up the machine.

Olivia reaches beneath the register and pulls out the book Jimmy selected. It seems like ages ago. "Did you want to pick this up for Jimmy?" she says, speaking loudly to be heard over the machine. "He asked me to hold it for him."

"Oh, that man." As the machine shuts off, Jillian's voice drops to normal volume. "His eyes are always bigger than his stomach."

Olivia's not sure this cliché applies to books, but she gets Jillian's drift. "Okay. I'll re-shelve it." She adds it to the bin with Jillian's books. "Guess you can always pick up a fresh supply when you get back to the Seaworthy Institute."

A look of puzzlement flashes across Jillian's face, as if she's trying to recall having told Olivia the institute's name.

"Supply of books, I mean," Olivia says, as if this is what needs clarification. "Although I expect you have a lot more than that to deal with when you get back to home port. Sorting and cataloguing your finds, that sort of thing."

"Oh, right." The crack in Jillian's composure mends itself. "There's always a ton of stuff to take care of."

"It must be especially hard with Marianne's dementia. From what I hear, she was quite a powerhouse in her day."

"She was." This time, Jillian makes no attempt to hide her puzzlement. "But how do you know Marianne?"

"There was a shipwreck conference here recently. A friend helped organize it. I was hoping to connect you with him, but I guess you were out of town that weekend. Anyhow, I learned about the Institute from Jimmy, and when I told my friend about it, he mentioned Marianne. She's your mother?"

"Grandmother," Jillian says. "In law, actually."

"Good of you to keep things going for her during this difficult time," Olivia says.

"Since you're an archeologist yourself and all." Naomi hands her the cappuccino.

"Well, to be honest, I'm more of an assistant," Jillian says. "Marianne's the one who signs off on everything. Well, hey, I'd better get going." Jillian starts for the door, then turns. "I don't suppose you've thought any more about co-signing the loan? We could really use that equipment."

"You mean Finn could really use it," Naomi says.

"Right. Finn," Jillian says.

"As a matter of fact, I have been giving it some thought," Olivia says. "I feel bad for Finn, with his uncle turning him down. And if there's actually gold down there, it could be a good investment. The only thing is, I'm a little fuzzy on why you all are so sure about the gold. And why you're the only ones who seem to know about it."

Jillian hesitates a moment. "We've got firsthand information. Well, as close as you can get to firsthand for something that happened so long ago. My great-great-grandfather was the *Iona*'s first mate. He took command after the captain died at sea."

"So he's the one who wrecked the ship," Naomi says. "Bummer."

Jillian shoots her a look. "It wasn't his fault. There was an awful storm. They ran into the jetty, and they had to abandon the ship."

"And its cargo of gold?" Olivia says.

"The cargo wasn't gold. The gold belonged to the captain's wife. She came from money. In fact, she owned the ship, and she traveled on it. Sadly, she died, and the *Iona* wrecked. Before my great-great-grandfather Howard could get to the gold, the ship floated out to sea and sank. And there it's sitting to this day, at the bottom of the ocean."

"That's quite the story." Naomi looks skeptical.

"It's all true, I swear." Jillian makes a cross-your-heart gesture. "We've got new images from the ROV suggesting that we've zeroed in on the location. With a side sonar and a magnetometer, we'll be able to pinpoint the gold."

"I'm starting to see why Finn's a believer," Olivia says.

"So, you'll consider the loan after all?" Jillian says.

"Maybe." Olivia ignores the look Naomi shoots her. "How about we meet up for drinks at the Dockside before you all go out tonight, and we can discuss it further? Nine o'clock, say. You, me, Jimmy, and Finn."

"I don't think Finn should be drinking before we go out," Jillian says.

"The Dockside offers free coffee for the designated driver," Olivia says. "I'd say Finn qualifies."

Jillian smiles. "Then it's a date. I'll let the guys know." She saunters out, shutting the door behind her.

"Have you lost your mind?" Naomi says. "You're supposed to be stopping Finn from this foolishness, not encouraging it."

"Don't worry. You okay looking after the shop for a while? I've got a few things to take care of before our little outing."

"You have a plan, I hope," Naomi says.

"Part of one, anyhow. Depending on how things go. Does Jason pull weekend shifts at the station?"

"He was complaining about it last time he was in, wishing one of the older guys would retire so he could move up a notch and let the newbies take weekends."

"Good deal." She grabs her jacket. "I'll be back in a while."

"I hope you know what you're doing," Naomi calls after her as she heads out the door.

# Chapter Twenty-Seven

## Josephine ~ 1889

T he notice submitted to the *Evening Register* was brief.

Court of Inquiry
regarding the wreck of the *Iona*,
registered in Liverpool and
sailed under the command of
the late Captain Nicholas T. Watson
Convenes tomorrow
9 am, County Courthouse

"Page one, next to the police sale notice." Jo handed the paper to Nan. "Set it large, so folks will see it."

"Maybe this will finally put an end to the nonsense about a curse," Amity said. "A dull ruling on the disposition of property."

"That article on the curse might not have been such a good idea after all," Nan said. "From the talk around town, you'd think the sea was going to come and swallow us up, all on account of some ship and its curse."

"Even so, I don't regret running that story," Jo said. "It got people to return what they'd taken."

"Except for whatever went down with the ship," Amity said.

"We don't know that the *Iona* sank. She might still be drifting."

"I wired Father, just as you asked." Amity's father was the sheriff across the river in Pacific County. "He's heard no reports of sightings. Maybe we should print that as an update. Might put folks at ease."

"Let's hold off till tomorrow. I've been thinking…" Jo glanced over at Nan, who was plucking letters to set the notice. She leaned close to Amity, speaking in a low voice. "The court of inquiry. What if they rule on more than just the disposition of property?"

"Like a certain sailor's getting stabbed to death amid a raging storm?" Amity said.

"And the captain dying at sea. And the steward who drowned where he shouldn't have."

"But who's going to bring any of that up? Other than arresting Pablo, Bailey hasn't lifted a finger concerning Bernard's death. Although for Pablo's sake, I'm rather glad for his complacence."

"You're right," Jo said. "None of the crew will want to bring up those deaths. Because of the flogging, Douglas had every reason to want Bernard dead. Roger might have wanted him dead, too, after Bernard kept him from deserting."

"And then there's Arthur," Amity said. "Convicted for murder, even if he didn't deserve it."

"What about Gus?" Jo said. "Would he bring up the deaths?"

Amity shook her head. "He just wants this all to be over with so he can get on with his life. After the hearing tomorrow, he'll start work at the mill. He's over there right now, having a look around." She glanced at the clock. "I'm to meet him at five o'clock for dinner. If you've got everything under control here, I'd like to head home and freshen up a bit."

"Go on ahead," Jo said. "Just don't stay out too late. We've got a big day tomorrow."

"You sound like my mother again." Amity reached for her wrap.

"I'll take that as a compliment, knowing your mother as I do."

Amity left. Finished with her typesetting, Nan followed shortly after.

Idly, Jo filed papers from the stack on her desk. She wished Amity's mother lived closer. She'd spied for the Union in the War Between the States, and while she refused to say much about that experience, she had good instincts when it came to reading people. Jo would love to know what Hattie Elliott thought of Gus.

Gus wouldn't speak up about the deaths, and neither would the men who'd served under him. Neither, Jo suspected, would the ship's mercurial first mate, Howard Perkins. And maybe there was no reason to bring them up. Maybe it was just a string of bad luck.

But Bernard hadn't stabbed himself. Someone had killed him. And if the court of inquiry didn't open an investigation into potential wrong-doing aboard the *Iona,* chances were no one ever would. Whoever had killed Bernard would get off scot-free. And would anyone care? He was just another sailor. Expendable, at least in the eyes of some.

Antero came in and started up the press. If a year ago, someone had told Jo that she'd come to love the smells of machine oil, newsprint, and ink, she'd have flatly denied it. But here she was, lingering at her desk, breathing them in. She suspected Cecil, the former publisher, had relished those scents too.

Cecil had never been one to let a matter drop. He had a way of looking where others didn't, of noting what was concealed behind the obvious. In the end, that had been his undoing.

What was most obvious about the *Iona*? The fact that she'd wrecked. The idea that she was cursed. These were what folks would be talking about long after all else about the ship was forgotten. In their minds, the two would be connected. A curse on the ship, so she wrecked. That's what the crew seemed to think. For that matter, so did Perkins. Only Gus had flat out denied the curse.

What power that old apple woman had exerted. She'd likely never know how the seed she'd planted in anger had grown, nurtured along by each unfortunate incident that befell the ship and her crew. Even with the *Iona* drifting out to sea, people were still talking about the curse.

People shared a propensity for superstition. Still, someone might benefit from promoting the idea of a curse. Someone who needed people to believe no human played a part in the *Iona*'s tragic fate.

As the press clicked and clacked, Jo slipped on her cloak. From her desk, she took the box of sponge drops she'd brought from home that morning. Effie had packed the treats for Jo's father to take to the cannery this morning. But he'd forgotten them, and so Jo had offered to drop them off. She'd intended to get there earlier, but she'd gotten busy and nearly forgotten the errand.

Maybe she could convince Noah to take off work early. In the off-season, he kept a more leisurely schedule. With the court of inquiry looming, she'd love for the two of them to slip off for a quiet dinner alone, like Amity and Gus so often did. Or maybe the four of them could even dine together. That would show Amity that Jo was sincere about giving Gus the benefit of the doubt, even if that wasn't entirely the case. Maybe, through their conversation, Jo could pick up more pieces to the puzzle the *Iona* had put before her.

Funny, she thought, how folks spoke of a ship as a person, and a woman at that. Yet in recent days, Jo had to admit she'd felt a sort of intimacy growing between herself and the vessel. She felt bad for the ship in the same way she'd feel bad for a friend who'd suffered a run of bad luck. She hated to think of her sinking to the bottom of the ocean, to be covered up by mud and sand, an inglorious end to what had by all accounts been a stately vessel.

Under the big Felch's Canning and Packing sign, Jo turned toward the office building, perched closer to the road than the warehouses and packing plant. As she reached for the door, Howard Perkins approached.

"Miss Felch. What a pleasant surprise. But then this is your father's enterprise, isn't it?" He glanced up at the sign. "Seems he's done quite well for himself. But I understand how easily one might overextend in a business like this. The fish runs are declining, I hear. No wonder he's strapped for cash."

She straightened, holding his gaze. "My father's business is none of your concern."

"I assure you, I have only his best interests in mind."

"And what might those interests be?"

"I understand Mr. Leighton has found employment. That he intends to remain in Astoria. I fear some of your townspeople are too trusting for their own good."

"Perhaps. But that has nothing to do with my father."

"We are our brother's keepers, are we not, Miss Felch? I've yet to make your father's acquaintance, but even as a stranger, I'd hate to see him get mixed up with the likes of Gus Leighton. The other business owners I've spoken with today have been grateful for the warning."

"My father hasn't hired Mr. Leighton. I believe he's found work at the mill." She folded her arms across her chest. "But I'm confused, Mr.

Perkins. Why should Mr. Leighton's employment prospects concern you?"

His gaze intensified. "Because of the company he keeps. I spent the better part of this morning at the police station, attempting to convince Chief Bailey that I've been robbed. Unfortunately, he sees things differently. So, I've been forced to take matters into my own hands. You had my satchel in your possession, did you not, Miss Felch?"

"And I returned it. As I found it. Filled with lead weights."

"You seem to take me for a fool. A fool who carries worthless dead weight around in his satchel."

"What you keep in your satchel is none of my concern, Mr. Perkins. It's possible, of course, that whoever took the satchel from the *Iona* in the first place used the weights to replace something of greater value. If that's the case, I'd be happy to place a notice for you in the paper. Free of charge since you've found the police chief less than cooperative. I like to see justice served. I'll simply need a description of what's missing."

"I believe you know what's missing."

"I assure you, I don't."

"If you and your pretty friend have colluded with Mr. Leighton to rob me, I assure you that won't end well. I've ample evidence to prove Leighton has more money than he claims to have. Those fancy meals he's been buying your friend can't be cheap. This business of him finding work is all a ruse to add to the illusion that he's some poor schmuck who's down on his luck."

"I've colluded with Mr. Leighton on nothing. If anything, I share your suspicions of him. If you'll tell me what was taken, perhaps I can help you find it."

He eyed her sharply. "I think not, Miss Felch. I'm not convinced where your loyalties lie. In any case, I intend to clear this all up with Mr. Leighton before the court of inquiry tomorrow."

"You plan to confront him?"

"I do. It's the best course, don't you agree? Get things out in the open before a court charged with investigating misdeeds on the high seas. Mr. Leighton seems to be averse to that possibility. He has checked out of the Occidental Hotel. No one seems to have hired him as he claims." He stepped closer. "Perhaps your friend knows where he's gone. Perhaps she has told you. If the two of you are protecting him, for a share of the..." He stopped short.

"A share of what, Mr. Perkins?"

His eyes flashed. "Damn it, girl. Don't play games with me."

"I assure you, I'm not being coy. As a reporter, I'm simply trying to get the facts straight in my head."

"And how will it be for your future as a reporter if I bring charges of robbery and collusion? You certainly seem to be protecting Mr. Leighton."

"I expect you'll find him at the court of inquiry tomorrow." She pulled open the door to her father's cannery, gripping the handle hard to conceal the shaking of her fingers. "Good day, Mr. Perkins."

# CHAPTER TWENTY-EIGHT

## Josephine ~ 1889

"I promised Effie I'd deliver these sponge drops." Steadying her voice, Jo set the box on Noah's desk. "Father forgot them this morning."

"His mind is on cogs and wheels," Noah said. "He's been out in the plant all afternoon, supervising the installation of the machines he brought back from California. Shall I walk you out to see him?"

"No thanks. I know how he gets when he's in pursuit of some goal. He won't appreciate the interruption."

"Like father, like daughter." He looked her up and down. "If I'm not mistaken, you've got something on your mind as well."

"A few somethings."

"Anything you care to share?"

"Not just yet." Though her nerves had settled, her thoughts were whirring.

"Perhaps I can stop by tonight with whatever is left of these sponge drops. You'll likely have it all sorted out by then, and you can enlighten me."

She forced a smile, her encounter with Howard Perkins having erased her idea of a quiet dinner with Noah. "I do love Effie's sponge drops. Just don't let on that I waited till afternoon to bring them by."

He reached into the box and withdrew a cookie sandwiched with jam. "I'll see that the supply's depleted just enough."

Jo kissed him goodbye. Leaving the cannery, she tried to sort through her thoughts about Perkins. She should have found herself allied with him. He'd all but confirmed what she'd been trying to tell Amity, that Gus Leighton wasn't entirely what he claimed to be. But she didn't like the broad net Perkins was casting, accusing her and Amity of conspiring to steal from him.

Whatever was once in that satchel, Howard Perkins seemed desperate to get it back. He also seemed determined to pin the theft on Gus.

Jo knew what Amity would say, that Gus was among the least likely to have stolen from the first mate. They'd been friends, after all—Gus and Howard and Nick Watson. And it was Arthur, not Gus, who'd gone out to Point Adams to nose around the pilfered goods, though of course Gus could have put Art up to it.

She should leave Gus and Perkins to sort out their differences. But she worried what Perkins might do. If any harm came to Gus, Amity would be devastated. Wishing he'd quit seeing Amity was one thing. Allowing harm to come to him was another.

Jo turned toward the Grand Hotel, three blocks up the street. Conflicted as she felt over Gus, she was glad she hadn't told Perkins which hotel he'd moved to. She could stop by and warn him of Perkins' agitated state. If Amity was to meet him at five o'clock, he must be back from the mill by now.

She ascended the hill. Entering the hotel, she approached the front desk. "I'm here to see Mr. Leighton."

Looking up from his ledger, the clerk glanced sideways at the key cubbies. "He's not in his room. Left around noon, as I recall. Is there a message for him?"

She glanced at the clock. Five minutes till Amity was to meet Gus. "You're sure he's not here?"

"Positive." The clerk nudged his glasses higher on his nose.

"And no one has been here looking for him?"

"No. Is he in some sort of trouble? I hear that ship was cursed."

"That ship's likely at the bottom of the ocean now. I'd say we're all safe, wouldn't you?"

Color rising in his face, the clerk returned his attention to his ledger.

Feeling troubled, she left the hotel. To the east, the mill whistle blew, loud and shrill. Quitting time. She pictured workers streaming from the mill, Swedes and Norwegians headed for Uppertown, Finns headed the opposite direction.

Shielding her eyes from the afternoon sun's glare, she looked both directions, thinking she might spot Gus Leighton. He wasn't supposed to have been working today, just getting his bearings. Where was he? And where was Amity?

She regretted having mentioned the mill to Perkins. She should have left well enough alone. Whatever the conflicts among the *Iona*'s crew, they were the ones who'd have to live with them.

As for her concerns about Gus, maybe Amity was right. Rather than any flaw of his, maybe her worries stemmed from having been duped before. And her failure to keep Stella Wisener out of the asylum, coupled with her failure to learn for certain what had become of the missing maid Birdie Magness, made her even more determined to get this one right.

And yet something was going on with the men who'd sailed aboard the *Iona*. A death that looked like poisoning. An empty poison container stashed in a stowaway's pocket. An unlikely accident involving the ship's steward. A sailor stabbed in the chest as a storm raged. A coveted satchel containing only lead weights.

As she started for home, her thoughts returned to the curse. Even after the *Iona* drifted out to sea, someone was keeping the curse front and center in people's minds. Someone who would benefit from turning attention away from his own misdeeds.

Douglas Herrington had a lot to say about the curse. But his trepidation struck Jo as genuine. Nor could she see what Roger or Arthur would gain from promoting the idea of the curse. When she'd talked with them, neither man had brought it up without prompting.

That left Gus and Perkins. Gus had rejected the notion of the curse outright. Perkins, on the other hand, had brought it up over and over. With the crew. With the police. With her.

Thanks to the article she'd published, the curse had gotten his satchel returned, albeit without its original contents, whatever that might have been. But the curse could be useful in other ways too.

On the front lawn of her house, Pablo was tossing a ball to Queenie. For as small as she was, she had amazing stamina, dashing from one end of the yard to the other to retrieve the ball, then trotting back to Pablo so he could throw it again.

Jo stepped through the gate. Queenie dropped the ball at her feet, then looked up at her, panting and wagging her tail. "All right, all right," Jo told the dog. She tossed the ball toward the front steps, and Queenie scampered after it.

Pablo straightened his shoulders. "Good afternoon, Miss Jo. Fine weather we're having." His precise enunciation reminded her of their Chinese gardener Lee Quong, who along with Effie had been helping the boy improve his English.

"Indeed it is, for January." She glanced toward the house. Having reached the stairs, Queenie was swiping with her paw at the ball, which was lodged under the bottom step. "Have you seen Miss Amity?"

"Miss Amity was home. But she left."

"Did you see which way she went?"

He shrugged.

"How long ago did she leave?"

He shrugged. "I don't know."

Jo shook her head. Hadn't her mother always said she had an over-active imagination? Amity was fine. She'd met Gus at the mill. The two of them were likely already at the restaurant, ordering their dinner.

She went to the steps and retrieved Queenie's ball. She tossed it, and Queenie took off after it.

"Quite the bundle of energy, that one."

Pablo cocked his head. "Sorry, Miss Jo. I do not understand."

"The dog. She is active. Lots of running. Lots of fetching."

His face brightened. "Ah, yes. Run. Fetch."

Jo started inside. At the sound of her name, she turned. Gus was coming up the walkway. He seemed out of breath.

"Have you seen Amity? She was supposed to meet me at the mill. I was detained a few minutes inside. I thought she'd be waiting when I came out. But she wasn't. It's not like her to be late."

Jo bristled inwardly at this familiarity. He'd only known Amity for a few days. But she couldn't argue his point. Amity prided herself on being prompt. "Last time I saw her, she was leaving work. She told me she was going to freshen up, then meet you for dinner."

"Maybe she got confused and went to the hotel," Gus said.

"I don't think so. I just came from the Grand. She wasn't there."

"What were you doing at the Grand?"

She swallowed hard. "Looking for you. I ran into Howard Perkins, and he was eager to find you."

His face clouded. "I hope you didn't tell him where I'm staying."

"No. But he's got some notion in his head about you and Amity and me conspiring to steal from him."

Gus ran his hand through his hair. "The last thing I wanted was for you and Amity to get dragged into this."

"Into what?"

He sighed. "Like I said, Howard and Nick and I were friends when we were lads. We attended the same boys' school. But the older I got, the more I saw how little Howard and I had in common."

"You had a falling out?"

"Not exactly. We just drifted apart."

Jo understood. It had been the same with her and Dorinda Hamilton—they'd been friends until they got older, and Jo realized how differently they viewed the world. "Why did you sign on with the *Iona* if you knew you'd have to answer to Howard?"

"I hadn't many options," he said grimly. "Amity says you know about the mutiny. Once you defy a captain, it's hell trying to get another one to take you on."

"Why would you go back to sea at all? Amity tells me you come from money. I'd think you had other prospects."

"There were complications. Not to mention my own stubbornness. And pride. Plus there's something about the life at sail that gets in your bones." He shook his head. "I'm over that now."

She held his gaze. "Mr. Perkins is quite concerned about whatever he had in that satchel. Do you know what it was?"

"I swear, I haven't a clue."

"Satchel." Pablo came toward them. Jo had all but forgotten he was there. "It is the...object one carries?"

"That's right," Gus said. "Mr. Perkins has a satchel. Do you know what he had in it?"

"Miss Emma. She had...money." Pablo thrust his hand in his pocket and pulled out the gold coin Jo had seen in his dresser drawer. "Many, many money. Like this one."

"How do you know about her money?" Jo asked.

"I come out at night," Pablo said. "Mr. Gus knows."

Jo turned to Gus. "You knew he was stowing away?"

Gus nodded. "Found him hiding in the anchor locker when we were not long out of Manzanillo. I told him if he made no trouble, I'd keep his secret. He was doing no harm."

"You came out at night," Jo said, turning her attention back to Pablo. "And you saw lots of gold coins. Where?"

"A window." He pointed toward the house. "Like that one. Small. Looking down."

"Emma had a skylight put in," Gus said, explaining. "To brighten the captain's quarters. Who did you see with the money, Pablo? Miss Emma?"

"One time, Miss Emma." The boy held up his finger. "Next time, Mr. Perkins. With his.... satchel."

"He was putting Emma's gold coins in the satchel?" Jo said.

"Yes. Many, many gold," Pablo said.

"I heard talk about Emma bringing a fortune aboard with her. Never looked into it one way or the other. None of my concern."

"That would explain Perkins' interest in the satchel." She looked over at Pablo, who was toeing the dirt with his boot. "Pablo, do you know what happened to the gold?"

He looked up, eyes wide. "I am no thief, Miss Jo. I did not take the money. Only..." His voice trailed off.

"Only what?" Gus said.

"Only this one." Pablo pressed the gold coin into Gus's hand.

"You're a good boy, Pablo, to want to return it. But it doesn't belong to me. Besides, I think Miss Emma would have wanted you to have it." He folded Pablo's fingers over the coin. "I expect you have more need of it than anyone else from the ship."

Jo eyed him. "Perkins would ask how you can afford to be so generous."

"If you're suggesting I took the gold from his satchel, I wish it were true. I'd have seen it returned to Emma's next of kin. Her ship is gone, and with it, her gold, assuming what Pablo says is true."

"I don't doubt the boy," Jo said. But she'd doubted Gus. Why? Because Amity had fallen head over heels for him.

From the river, a ship's horn blew, announcing its arrival. A pair of gulls careened overhead, catching updrafts of wind. Eying the Felch mansion, Gus shoved his hands in his pockets. "I need to find Amity."

Jo wanted to get at the truth. So, it seemed, did Howard Perkins, but only so he could lay claim to Emma's gold. And yet as a friend of Nick Watson's, he should have had only Emma's best interests in mind. And yet in a person's mind, Jo knew, perceptions could easily become reality.

"The mill." She felt gut-punched. "I told Perkins you'd be working there. He must have gone looking for you and found Amity waiting for you."

# CHAPTER TWENTY-NINE

## Present Day ~ Olivia

Jason is on the phone when Olivia arrives at the police station. An officer asks if she can be of help, but Olivia says she'll wait for Jason. The call is protracted, something involving a feud between neighbors over a fallen tree branch and a barking dog, from what Olivia surmises.

Finally, he extricates himself from the call and comes over to greet Olivia. "Sorry to keep you waiting. Had to diffuse World War III over on Franklin Avenue."

"Thanks for your efforts. We'll all sleep easier tonight." She eyes the officer at the other desk. "Is there somewhere we can talk in private?"

"Conference room. Follow me."

He leads her down the hallway to a room with a long table and eight chairs. Mounted on one wall are photographs of Astoria's police chiefs dating back to 1876. Jason pulls two chairs from the table, and they sit. "What can I do for you?" he asks.

"You might be thinking I've read too many of those mysteries you like so well. But I believe there's a man hanging around who might be trouble."

He frowns. "Is someone bothering you at the bookshop?"

"Not exactly. This guy has gotten in tight with Finn Parsons, and I've got a feeling he's running from the law. Pays for everything in cash, uses a burner phone. Now he's trying to get Finn to take out a loan so he can buy some expensive equipment. He's convinced Finn that they're going to get rich finding some treasure lost at sea."

"Mountain of a Thousand Holes," Jason mutters.

"Come again?"

"Neahkanie Mountain, down by Manzanita. A Spanish galleon wrecked there back in the 1600s. Ever since, there have been stories about the treasure the survivors supposedly buried there. So many folks have gone digging around there that people started calling it the Mountain of a Thousand Holes. Finally, the state figured out how to weed out the treasure hunters and let the archeologists have a go at it."

"What did they find?"

"No treasure, unless you count the hunks of beeswax that have been washing up on the beach ever since the wreck. Which were valuable back in the day, as I understand it. But back to your stranger. Those behaviors you mentioned do raise suspicions. But none of it's illegal."

"I figured as much. But I thought maybe if I could get fingerprints or something, you could run them to make sure he's not wanted for some sort of crime."

Jason leans back in his chair. "I can run prints, but I'd need something more to go on. Something that would pass for probable cause."

"This guy confronted me outside the bookshop the other night."

"Did you feel threatened?"

"Definitely. I'm pretty sure that was his goal."

He sits forward. "Good enough for me. I don't like the idea of strangers accosting local residents, especially in the dark. Can you get this guy to handle something, then bring it in so I can lift the prints? Nothing wooded or made of stone."

"I can do that. I'm going to meet up with him and some other people tonight."

"I'll get you an evidence bag. Make sure you don't contaminate the prints. And bring it straight to the station when you're done. I'll be here till midnight. I can enter the prints in the database before my shift ends. If there's a match, it should come back the next day or two. No match, and your guy's not a criminal. Or he hasn't gotten caught yet."

He takes a plastic evidence bag from a cabinet. She folds it in half and slips it into her tote. Leaving the station, she checks the address Susie texted her. *Hanna's excited to meet you,* the message says. *Come by my place first, and I'll take you over and introduce you.*

Olivia walks up the hill. Her calves strain at the incline. But it feels good to be outside. And at last, she might just be making progress. Maybe Jimmy has done nothing nefarious. But if he has, she'll have the evidence she needs to convince Finn.

She wonders what Hanna will say about the gold. It could be nothing more than family legend, amplified and distorted over the years. For that matter, Jillian's claims about her great-great-grandfather could be family legend too. But the name Howard rings a bell, maybe from one of the newspaper articles she has read.

She turns up the walk to Susie's house, a meticulously maintained Craftsman home with big rhododendron bushes on either side of the front walk. Wearing an apron, Susie greets her at the door.

"Decorating a cake for my granddaughter's birthday." She shows her fingertips, tinged with purple and pink food coloring. "With all those baking shows on TV, the expectations get higher every year. I'll run you over and introduce you. Then I'd best get back to the cake."

Hanna's house is across the street and kitty-corner from Susie's place. It looks smaller by half than Susie's Craftsman but equally well-kept. The woman who comes to the door looks as if central casting sent her over to play someone's great-grandmother in a Hallmark movie. She stands a head shorter than Olivia, who is by no means tall herself, and she's thin enough that Astoria's brisk winter winds might be enough to bowl her over. Like Susie, she's wearing an apron, though hers is faded and worn.

Her eyes light up at the sight of them. "Here's the lady I told you about," Susie says. "Ingrid's niece. Grandniece, rather. She runs the bookshop now."

"Ingrid was a lovely woman," Hanna says. "Did a lot of good around town."

"She did," Olivia says. "I miss her still."

"I'll leave the two of you to chat." Susie sniffs the air. "If my nose doesn't deceive, you're in for a treat, Olivia. Hanna makes the best munkki in town."

Munkki, Olivia discovers when she's seated at Hanna's kitchen table, is a delightful Finnish deep-fried treat, coated in sugar.

"You must eat munkki with a fresh cup of coffee," Hanna says, setting a cup and plate in front of Olivia. "Decaf." She wags her finger. "Otherwise, we'd be up all night."

Olivia samples the munkki. "Delicious." She licks sugar from her fingers. "Like a donut hole, only better."

"My grandmother's recipe. She taught me to make it, the same as her grandmother taught her. My grandmother's mother came straight from Finland. Took up with a fisherman here, and that was that."

"Susie tells me your family lived out by Point Adams."

"That's right. The men, they fished for the cannery out that way. Some of the women, they worked the line. Hard work, but back then, folks didn't complain." She chuckles. "Leastways, that's what they told us when we were kids."

"Lots of weather out Point Adams way." Olivia sips from her coffee, rich and dark, percolated the old way.

"Storms like you wouldn't believe. My grandmother stayed living out there even after the cannery shut down. I'd go out to visit, and when those storms would blow in, she'd tell stories about the Point Adams men going out in the thick of it to rescue ships in trouble. Saved many a sailor, she said."

"Did she ever see a shipwreck herself?"

"Oh, my yes. Mostly when she was a girl. Lots more gadgets and gizmos keeping ships safe these days. You won't see them big cargo ships run aground. Back then, it was all schooners and steamers. Had their troubles, they did. You've seen them ship bones out at Fort Stevens?"

"The Peter Iredale," Olivia says. It's the only wreck she's seen up close and personal, the eerie-looking skeleton of what must have once been a proud ship.

Hanna nods. "Grandmother told me all about that wreck. Her cousin was on the lifesaving crew back then. 1906, I think it was. Or maybe 1905." She taps the side of her head. "When you get to be my age, the details get jumbled. Anyhow, this cousin of hers helped bring the captain in from one of the surfboats. Said he was aiming for a fast run up the coast, trying to cut five days off the usual time. Just like folks that go speeding up the highway today. No good comes of it."

"True enough." Olivia shifts in her seat. She wants to get around to the *Iona* and her gold. "Going too fast, you can lose control."

"That's what happened with the Iredale. Captain said he picked up the Tillamook light in the middle of the night, so he had the hands set the sails, thinking they'd get a pilot off the bar after daybreak. But he misjudged the ship's course. That plus a big wind and strong current, and before they knew it, they were in the breakers and onto the sand. When she hit, her masts snapped like twigs, Grandmother said."

"What happened to the crew?" Olivia asks.

"Captain gave the call to abandon ship. Every one of 'em got rescued."

Olivia spots her opening. "I've heard local folks would go in for the salvage after a ship was abandoned."

"Indeed they did. But the Iredale wasn't one of the better wrecks for that, Grandmother said. Big gale and heavy seas kept folks away at first. Got half-buried in sand. But her father got plenty off other wrecks. A sextant. Pair of candlesticks. Men's shirts."

"And your family hung onto all that?"

"Well, now. When Grandmother passed, some of it went to the museum. But I still have the candlesticks in my china cabinet. Polish them once a month. Real silver, they are. People don't go in for that much anymore. But Susie says it's the gold you've come to hear about."

"I've heard something about a ship that wrecked with some gold."

Hanna leans forward. "Don't want folks talking about that. But Susie says I can trust you to keep quiet."

"Your story is safe with me."

She nods, then reaches into her apron pocket and sets three gold coins on the table. "Got a little nest egg we pass from one generation to the next. Not that there's much left now, mind you. Folks have a need, they dip into the stash."

"May I?" Olivia asks.

Hanna nods.

Olivia takes a coin in her hand, the metal cool against her skin. It's surprisingly heavy. She sets it back on the table in front of Hanna. "Your grandfather salvaged these coins from a wreck?"

"These and a whole lot more."

"Do you know which ship it was?"

Hanna leans back in her chair. "Don't rightly recall. It was a strange name. I remember that much."

"Could it have been the *Iona*?"

"Maybe. Can't say for sure. But I remember the shoes."

"Shoes?"

"Fancy ladies' shoes. Grandmother said her father found them in the captain's quarters. Looked about her mother's size, so he grabbed a pair. Heavier than he expected, but he was in a hurry, so he didn't stop to see why. The first mate was after him and his friends to get off the wreck. Later, he found gold coins stuffed in the toes of those shoes. Imagine that." She chuckles. "Stashing gold in your slippers."

"How strange," Olivia says. "I wonder why anyone would do that."

"A bunch of other Finnish men, they took shoes too. They found that gold, they all got together and made a plan. None of them had been in America that long, and they all looked out for each other. Canneries dropped the price they were paying for fish, and the Finns organized a strike. Why, they even had their own Finnish newspaper, right here in Astoria."

"What sort of plan?" Olivia asks.

"Well, they called a meeting of everyone who'd gone on that ship, out in somebody's barn. Decided it wasn't right that some had found gold and some hadn't. So, they put it all together and divided it up between them. Then they made a pact not to go around showing it off, less somebody try to take it from them."

"And no one ever tried to take it from them?"

Hanna shakes her head. "They kept quiet. Plus that wreck didn't stay put. The sea took it, and so far as anyone knew, it took the gold with it."

"How clever of them," Olivia says. But she has to wonder—did they get all the gold?

# CHAPTER THIRTY

## Olivia ~ Present Day

It's nearly closing time when Olivia gets to the library. Margaret looks up from helping a patron as Olivia proceeds to her usual spot at the microfiche reader. She pulls up the 1899 reel for the Astoria Evening Register, where she found the detailed New Year's Day report on the wreck of the *Iona*, including mention of the local salvors. Some made quite a haul, she knows now.

She spools up the reel and scrolls into history, scanning the headlines. *Feather Workers Win This Fight. Suicide on an Ocean Steamer. The Prohibition Campaign.* Then she finds it—another article on the *Iona. Wrecked Ship Cursed, Sailors Say,* the headline reads.

Cursed. Like what Naomi said after Finn and his friends nearly drowned. Scanning the article, Olivia reads of an old woman peddling apples who cursed the vessel on its launch from Liverpool. At least that's what some of the wreck's survivors said.

And in fact, the *Iona* went on to endure multiple storms, a dismasting, and a grounding. Several from her crew deserted. One man, the ship's steward, slipped on a dock and drowned. The captain and his wife died at sea. Lots of bad karma, for sure. And Olivia recalls reading in a different article that a sailor was stabbed too.

As if to counter these weighty matters, this article closes with mention of a little dog that was rescued days after the crew abandoned the ship. But there's no mention of gold coins. Or shoes.

Olivia scrolls on. She stops at a front-page headline. Iona *cast into the waves*. Beneath this, in smaller print: *Now a Ghost Ship*. The article is written with less finesse than the previous pieces, but the facts are all there. Convinced the wreck was not as dangerous to enter as previously believed, the *Iona*'s first and second mate returned to see what they could salvage. But after an unusually high tide accompanied by a stiff wind, they found the ship had drifted out to sea. Sightings of the ghost ship would no doubt follow, the article concluded.

This confirmed what Hanna told her, that the *Iona* drifted away not long after her great-grandfather and his friends made their haul. Again, there's no mention of gold. But then the ship's officers likely wouldn't want people knowing about that.

She scrolls on and hits pay dirt. *Court of Inquiry Rules in Matter of the Wrecked Ship Iona*.

She glances at the clock. Five minutes till closing. Margaret is over at the computer island, shutting things down.

Olivia skims the article. After reviewing the facts, the judge declared the *Iona* abandoned. But then additional evidence was entered. And that evidence was...Olivia goes over the sentence twice to make sure she hasn't misread...a dog that remained aboard the vessel after the call to abandon. A dog named Queenie, to be exact.

The judge cited precedent regarding a cat found aboard a wrecked ship. The court ruled that since the cat was aboard, the ship hadn't been abandoned after all.

With that, the judge amended his ruling: The *Iona* was not abandoned. "Should the *Iona* be recovered at sea, the insured retains a claim to her value," the judge said.

Finn needs to see this. Even if Jimmy and Jillian find gold in the wreck of the *Iona*—and after what Hanna has told her, Olivia doesn't think they'd find much—the vessel's insurers will lay claim to it.

With minutes to spare, she frames the article on the screen and hits the print button. She's ready to shut off the machine when she notices another headline below the fold: *First Mate Held on Charges of Kidnapping, Murder.*

Olivia reads through the story. At the court of inquiry, the judge also heard testimony concerning the first mate of the *Iona*, accused him of three murders and a kidnapping. His name? Howard Perkins. The source of Jillian's family story about gold. The source, it seems, of Olivia's recent troubles with Finn.

She's dying to show Finn. But first she needs to know whether Jimmy Stone is in trouble with the law. If she plays her cards too soon, he might get away. She needs to tread carefully, follow through with her plan.

It's convenient, in a way, that Ethan is out of town this weekend, helping a friend in Portland navigate some roadblocks on a historical preservation project there. He won't have to worry over any risks she must take.

At home, she heats up leftovers for herself and dishes up the usual salmon soufflé for Micki. The cat gobbles up her dinner, then curls next to her favorite pillow and waits for Olivia to join her on the couch, book in hand, their usual evening ritual.

"Sorry, girl," Olivia says, washing up her plate and fork. "I've got another commitment."

She changes into a shirt that's more suitable for evening. Nothing too fancy, but she's noticed that Jillian is on top of such things, and this is no time for her to feel bested. She grabs her tote bag and, with another apology to Micki, sets out on foot.

Clouds roll lazily over the darkened sky. Stars pop out and then disappear, as if they're playing hide and seek. The air is moist and cool, the autumn rains just around the corner. Listening to the clack-clack of her boots on the pavement, she thinks again of Ethan, wishing he were at her side. No, she reminds herself. It's better this way.

The Dockside is part of a complex of shops and eateries built over the river on pilings. Olivia makes a mental note to ask Ethan about the building's history. From the outside, it looks like it might have started out as a warehouse.

She goes inside. There's a fanciful vibe to the Dockside, with its rotating faux-crystal chandeliers and portholes built into the walls.

As she hoped, she has arrived ahead of the others. The tables overlooking the water are full, but the rest of the place is nearly empty. She grabs a round table tucked in a dark corner where they should be able to talk freely. She's studying the drink menu when Finn, Jimmy, and Jillian come in.

"What a unique spot," Jillian says, looking around the bar.

"Local favorite." Finn scoots in his chair. He looks worn out. Or maybe it's just the light. "How's it going, Olivia?"

"Great," she says brightly. "Lots of sales at the shop today."

"Good," Finn says. "Good." He can't seem to settle his eyes on anything.

Perusing the menu, Jimmy doesn't say a word. He looks sullen, like a kid who's been forced to come along to some function he abhors.

The server takes their order, wine for the women, coffee for the men. Finding his voice, Jimmy orders a basket of fries. He avoids Olivia's gaze. This throws her off. But she's made her plan, and she's going to stick to it.

"I expect Jillian told you two that I'm reconsidering," Olivia says once the server is gone. "About the loan. She explained about her family connection to the...um...project. That puts it in a different light."

Jimmy leans forward. "So that's all it takes. A different light."

"I'll admit I was skeptical," she says. "So, I did some research of my own. And what Jillian told me checks out. Especially about her great-grandfather's involvement."

Jillian smiles. "Of course, it did. I wouldn't make up something like that."

"Still, I'm curious," Olivia says. "About how the two of you got together on this project. Since you come from rather different backgrounds, professionally speaking."

"Professionally, maybe. But we've been friends since we were kids," Jillian says. "Jimmy's folks lived in England for a time. His dad was an engineer at the UK-division of some American outfit. Electrical something or other, wasn't it, Jimmy?"

"Uh-huh," Jimmy says.

The server delivers their drinks and the fries. Jimmy nudges the basket so it's between him and Finn, and the two of them dig in.

"You were saying," Olivia says, "about being friends when you were young."

"Right." Jillian sips her wine. "Jimmy's family moved away after a few years. But after we were grown, we reconnected, the way people do these days, and found out we share an interest in shipwrecks. Jimmy had done lots dives, and he remembered me telling him our family story. So naturally he was keen on checking out that wreck. With my connections at the Institute, we were able to make it happen, though not quite with the financial backing we need. Especially since, as you know, Marianne can't raise funds as she used to."

Dabbing a fry in a pool of ketchup, Jimmy glances sideways at Olivia. "Dementia does that to people."

But it's not the dementia that bothers him, Olivia thinks. It's that Olivia found out about it and told Jillian, who told him. Which raises the question of what else she's learned.

"That all makes perfect sense, now that you explain it," Olivia says.

"All you had to do was ask," Finn says. "Instead of snooping around on your own."

"You know, Finn, when I was younger, I'd have taken that criticism to heart. But I don't feel as if I need to apologize for checking into things. We might all be better off if people did more of that." She sips her wine. "At any rate, things are checking out. With the proper clauses in the contract, I'll reconsider signing for that loan."

Finn flashes a winsome smile. "I told these guys you'd come around eventually. You won't be sorry."

"Let's meet at the bank on Monday." Two days from now. She hopes that's enough time.

"Great news," Jillian says. "Isn't it, Jimmy?"

"Sure." He sounds less than enthused.

This affects her purpose not in the least, Olivia reminds herself. Setting aside the matter of the loan, she gets Jillian talking about differences between the UK and here. Finn joins in, noting words he has misunderstood when talking with Jillian. Chips, biscuits, knackered. They have a laugh over Finn's refusal to allow that *pants* could refer to what a person wears underneath his clothes. Even Jimmy cracks a smile.

By the time they get up to leave, things feel less tense. They're nearly at the door when Olivia says, "Oh no. My bag." She glances back at the table, where her tote bag is slung across the back of her chair. "You all go on ahead. Finn, give Daryl a call first thing Monday, and let me know what time he can see us."

"Will do," Finn says.

They say their goodnights. Olivia hurries back to the table. The busser is headed that way. Fortunately, he stops at another table to fill some water glasses.

Olivia reaches for her tote. Withdrawing the evidence bag, she slides over to Jimmy's seat. She grabs his coffee mug by the rim, taking care to avoid touching the handle.

The busser approaches. Holding the evidence bag and the tote, she ducks her head beneath the table as if she has lost something.

"Something I can help with?" the busser asks.

"My wallet. I must have dropped it." Speaking from under the table, she drops the mug in the bag, seals it, and tucks the bag in her tote.

"I'll get a flashlight," the busser says.

She pops her head back above the tabletop. "False alarm." She pats the side of her tote. "It was here all along."

"Happens all the time," the busser says.

She leaves the Dockside. Stepping into the night air, she nearly runs smack into Jimmy.

"Oh," she says. "You startled me. Where's Finn? And Jillian?"

"Hit the can," Jimmy said. "Me, I've got a bladder of steel. Have to, in my line of work."

She's not sure what to say to this. "I suppose so."

"Nice you finally came around about that loan," he says. "But it's too little, too late. We're leaving town."

"Leaving town? When? Why?"

"In a few days. Haven't said anything about it to Finn. Or to Jillian. You're the first to know. Appropriate, seeing as how you're the one that ruined it all."

This wasn't at all what she had in mind. "But I said I'd do the loan. You'll have your equipment."

"All the equipment in the world won't matter now. Now that you're flapping your jaw about what we're up to, the whole thing's ruined. Hope you're happy."

"I haven't told anyone the ship's name. I haven't said anything about..." She looks around to see if anyone's listening. "The gold."

In the moonlight, his eyes look steely. "Here's what you might not know about treasure. Something you might not have picked up from reading your books." He says *books* like it's some sort of disease. "When you're hunting for treasure, you don't forget the people who get in your way. Ask any pirate. They get their revenge."

With that, he turns heel and walks back toward the Dockside. Finn and Jillian are coming out the door, the two of them laughing.

Too rattled to speak, Olivia scurries off, pretending she hasn't seen them.

# CHAPTER THIRTY-ONE

## Josephine ~ 1889

The smell of fresh-cut timber enveloped Jo as she neared the mill. Wisps of smoke trailed from the smokestacks, faint remnants of the black clouds that belched from them during the workday. In the millpond floated hundreds of logs hewn from forests on both sides of the Columbia. Passing by here, she sometimes felt a twinge of sadness, thinking of the majestic trees that had been felled. And yet Astoria was built on lumber as much as it was on salmon, with the town's mills providing a livelihood for many a working man.

Today, she had no time for such thoughts. Gus strode beside her, his boots clomping on the boardwalk. She'd tried to dissuade him from coming along, but he wouldn't hear of it.

She slowed her steps in front of the sprawling complex of pitched-roof buildings. "We can't allow Perkins the advantage of spotting us first. You toured the mill this afternoon. If he's got Amity and he's hiding, where might he be?"

"I was getting my bearings," Gus said. "Not looking for where a man might hold an innocent woman hostage."

She understood his agitation. But under the circumstances, they needed to be more clear-headed than emotional. "They secure the buildings when the workers go home for the night, I presume."

"Right. A watchman was going around locking doors while I was searching for Amity."

"Where were you supposed to meet?"

"The west entrance." He pointed.

She studied the mill's layout. "Perkins must have lured Amity away from there, maybe with some story about you being detained in a different part of the mill. And he'd have to have given her some reason for his being there, or she'd have been suspicious."

"I suppose he could've said he knew the foreman. Howard likes to impress folks with how well-connected he is. Maybe he told her the foreman and I were at the office."

"Which is where?"

"Over there." He indicated a two-story red building at the far end of the complex.

Jo frowned. "I don't see an easy path from the west entrance to there. He'd have had to have led her around the front of the pond while the workers were heading out for the day."

"Hard to pull off an abduction with that many men looking on," he said grimly.

"What about that big building over there?" She pointed at a large building directly north of the west entrance, raised on pilings set partly over the river and partly on shore. "Those piles of sawdust block the view. He could have forced her under the building."

"And it's not a place the watchman is likely to look," Gus said.

"Let's head over there," Jo said. "If we cross in front of the mill on the boardwalk, he shouldn't be able to see us coming, if in fact he's there. Then we can double back around the pond. That should put us right behind the piles of sawdust."

She started for the boardwalk. He grabbed her arm. "If he's got Amity, it's because he's trying to get to me. I can't let you put yourself in danger. I'll go alone."

She shook free of his grip. "I'm going too. It's my fault he found her here in the first place. I should have kept my mouth shut about the mill."

"And I should have confronted him about how agitated he's been these past few days instead of just trying to get away from him."

She looked up at him. After all she'd questioned, this was the closest she'd come to trusting him. "Then we are two people with less than perfect judgment," she said.

"And a strong desire to get it right this time."

Side by side, they proceeded down the boardwalk, stepping lightly. Neither spoke, both lost in their concerns for Amity, Jo supposed. Whatever Gus might or might not be, whatever he might be hiding about his past, he truly seemed to care for her.

As they passed in front of the mill, a ship's bell clanged. They turned toward the water, waves lapping at the shoreline, then made their way around the east end of the complex. Jo hoped her logic was sound. Perkins would be expecting Gus to approach from the west end, where he and Amity had agreed to meet.

She squinted at the area underneath the building. Only the first rows of pilings were visible. Darkness swallowed the rest. No movement that she could see. No sound other than the river's water beating against its banks.

Reaching the mounds of sawdust, they crouched, concealing themselves. Jo's elbow brushed against the wood-scented pile, stirring up sawdust and tickling her nose. She stifled a sneeze as she peered around the edge of the pile. From here, she could see more of the pilings that held up the building, stretching from land to water. She looked methodically from one to the next.

"There he is," she whispered. "Perkins. And he's got Amity."

Gus hovered over her, searching. "Where?"

"Under the building, this side of the entrance. Tide's coming in. They can't venture too far from there."

"I'm going after her."

"No." She grabbed his arm, holding on with all her might. "Look closely. He's got a gun. If he's worked up, he won't hesitate to shoot you."

"Better me than her."

"Do you not understand how she feels about you? I've lost count of how many men have tried to court her. And yet you're the only one she cares about. And you're the only one Perkins cares about too." She searched his eyes. "I need you to trust me, Gus. It's the only way."

Without waiting for an answer, she strode from behind the sawdust toward the building. "Queenie!" she called out as she neared the pilings.

Mud sucked at her feet. "Queenie! Now you've done it, you little rascal. Ruined my best shoes."

Out of the corner of her eye, she saw movement. On the pilings, the building was raised high enough that she didn't have to duck to get underneath.

"Who goes there?" Perkins' voice was unmistakable.

She swung around, feigning surprise. "Why, Mr. Perkins." He stood with his right hand behind his back, concealing his gun, she thought. "We seem to meet in the most unexpected places. I don't suppose you've seen that little dog. I was taking her for a walk, and..." Her voice trailed off. "Is that you, Amity? It's hard to tell in this light."

"It's me." Amity was feigning cheerfulness, but Jo heard the strain in her voice. "Mr. Perkins seems to have some sort of..." She grimaced, and Jo realized Perkins was twisting her arm behind her back.

"I've no complaint with you, Miss Elliot. It's Gus Leighton I'm after. You need only bring me to him, so I can persuade him to coming around to my way of seeing things."

Amity wrenched, trying to twist from his grasp. "When I see him, I'll advise him to stay as far away as he can."

"And now we've got your friend to contend with." Perkins swung the pistol around, pointing it at Jo. "Perhaps she has some insight into Mr. Leighton's whereabouts."

Jo straightened. "Have I not made myself clear, Mr. Perkins? I mistrust Mr. Leighton as much as you do."

"Mistrust isn't the half of it. The man's a liar and a thief."

Jo turned to her friend. "Now do you believe me, Amity?"

As Amity opened her mouth to speak, Jo caught her eye. A look passed between them, a look they'd exchanged whenever Dorinda Hamilton got carried away with her gossip. A look that said Amity would follow Jo's lead.

"You would do a great service, Mr. Perkins, if you'd put down that pistol and lay out the facts for my friend," Jo continued. "Mr. Leighton's charms have overridden her reason. He took your gold, did he not? The gold that by rights should have gone to Captain Watson when his wife died."

Perkins laughed bitterly. "Watson had no right to Emma's gold. He wasn't good enough for her. She never loved him, not truly. But she'd bought him that ship, so she couldn't very well break things off, could she?"

"How hard it must have been for you, knowing you should have been the one to be with Emma instead of Nick Watson," Jo said, testing out a theory she'd been rolling over in her mind. "You had all the responsibility, he had all the fun."

Perkins sneered. "You have no idea. Every port we stopped in, the two of them would dress in their finest and gallivant about town. It's a wonder Emma had any gold left. In Mexico, I begged her not to go ashore. Too much fever." He shook his head, his eyes filled with sorrow. "If not for Nick, she'd have listened to me. She'd have understood that I was the only one on that ship who truly cared about her."

"You must have been devastated when she died," Jo said gently.

"A senseless tragedy," he muttered. "Just when she was starting to see the light."

"Starting to see that you and she were meant to be together, you mean," Amity said.

"No wonder you had to punish Nick Watson," Jo said. "Using rat poison. Only the steward found out."

Perkins jutted his chin. "I gave strict orders when we docked in San Francisco. No one gets off the boat without my permission. But that pompous little do-gooder apparently didn't think my rules applied to him."

"You caught him leaving the ship," Jo said. "And you figured he was going to the police with his suspicions."

"No figuring about it. The man told me as much."

"Then Emma's gold went missing," Jo said. "And you knew there was another on your crew who couldn't be trusted."

"Gus Leighton," Amity said hollowly.

"Not Gus," Jo said. "Bernard Ainsworth. He saw you taking the gold, didn't he, Mr. Perkins? To keep quiet, he demanded a share of it. But you weren't going to let him get the best of you. When the storm blew in, you seized the opportunity and stabbed him in the heart."

"Dirty business, blackmail," Perkins said.

"No matter what the perceived slight, Howard has always fancied himself judge and jury," Gus said, stepping from the shadows.

"Ah, there you are at last." Perkins yanked Amity in front of his chest and pointed the pistol at her head. "I was starting to doubt your affections for the girl."

Gus stepped closer. "Let her go. This is between you and me."

"No need for her to rush off just yet." Perkins' mouth twisted in a half-grin. "Not till our business is settled."

"And what business would that be?"

"The gold. What have you done with it?"

"Nothing. Until recently, I didn't even know it existed."

Perkins' eyes narrowed. "Then who, pray tell, enlightened you?"

Gus's face fell. Jo knew he hadn't meant to implicate Pablo.

"Bernard Ainsworth," she said. "As the storm came up, he told you. That's what you told me, isn't it, Mr. Leighton?"

He nodded slowly. "Yes. Bernard."

Jo shifted her gaze to Perkins. "The last thing you need, Mr. Perkins, is someone making accusations about you and that gold. Especially with the court of inquiry convening. Besides, it must surely be at the bottom of the ocean now."

"No!" Perkins' voice shook. "It can't be. Gus took it."

"Having no great admiration for Mr. Leighton, I'd be inclined to agree," Jo said. "But I must say, I've never met a man who could refrain from flaunting his wealth, no matter the circumstances. And Amity has told me how frugal Mr. Leighton has been as he courts her. Why, she's had to pay for their meals on more than one occasion, haven't you, Amity? It's one of the many reasons I've tried to convince her to stop seeing him."

Amity glanced at Gus. Jo saw the apology in her eyes, but from where he stood, Perkins couldn't. "Jo's right. I've been a fool not to listen to her. Gus is penniless. And, from what you say, Mr. Perkins, he's a scoundrel as well."

"There you have it, Howard," Gus said evenly. "You've ruined my prospects with this lovely lady. I hope you're happy."

"I'll be happy when we're on the other side of the court of inquiry."

"You're concerned I'll accuse you of killing Nick? And Victor? And Bernard?" Gus said. "Emma died of fever, but those three deaths are tougher to explain."

"Ah, but you're forgetting the curse," Perkins said.

"Your talk of a curse worked with your crew," Jo said. "And with the townspeople. But I doubt it will sway a judge."

Perkins swung his pistol from Amity to Gus. "Then I'll say Gus killed them all. When he trapped me under this building and threatened my life, too, I had no choice but to shoot him."

"Ah, but don't forget, Mr. Perkins," Amity said. "We two ladies are witnesses."

"You are sensible women. You see that I must respond to a threat. And should you tell the judge any different and suffer misfortune down the line, well, there's that curse again."

Jo squared her shoulders. "I don't take kindly to threats, Mr. Perkins. Neither does Amity."

"And what do you intend to do about it? Go to Chief Bailey? He's unimpressed by you and your little newspaper, you know. I doubt he'd lift a finger to help." Perkins cocked his gun, still pointed at Gus. "No, the only solution lies with Gus here. He's already proven himself capable of mutiny. Should questions be raised tomorrow about those men dying, he'd best stand ready to take the blame."

"If I do that, you'll leave these women alone?" Gus said.

"So long as they refrain from stirring up trouble. And once the inquiry's over, I want you out of here on the next steamer." Perkins' hollow laughter echoed among the pilings. "If they don't arrest you first, that is. For my part, I intend to stick around and find that gold."

"I expect you'll find it," Jo said. "Whatever else may be said about you, Mr. Perkins, you're a clever man. You get rid of your adversaries by whatever means necessary. You should have been the *Iona*'s captain, not Nicholas Watson."

"Quite true," he said. "Now, if we're all in agreement about what happens in court tomorrow, we can go our separate ways for the evening and be no worse for the wear."

"I've no problem with that," Jo said. "As I made clear, I've suspected Mr. Leighton all along,"

"And I am seeing him in a new light," Amity said.

"What about you, Gus?"

"I know when I'm bested." Gus raised his hands in a gesture of surrender. "Three against one."

"I'm glad we've reached an understanding." Perkins lowered his pistol. "Now let's get out of here before that blasted watchman comes snooping around. You lead the way, Miss Felch." He waved the pistol toward the sawdust mounds. "Gus will follow. Miss Elliott and I will bring up the rear."

Jo picked her way through the mud. Night was coming on fast, a curtain of darkness descending all around. But once she ducked from beneath the building, she could still see clearly enough to follow her own footsteps back the way she'd come. Soon they'd be on the boardwalk, where she hoped Perkins would holster his pistol.

Rising with the tide, the mill pond's waters lapped gently at its edges. Ahead, she saw a flicker of shadow, a small dark shape that darted from behind the sawdust. In a sliver of light, she recognized the gleam in his eye. Pablo.

Her heart sank. He must have followed her and Gus here. She glanced back at Perkins. His drawn pistol was pointed straight at Amity's back.

Slowing her steps, she gestured for Pablo to get back. From a nearby stack of logs came the sound of movement. She glanced that direction but saw nothing. A rat, probably. Maybe a pair of them.

She crept forward, praying Pablo had the sense to stay hidden.

"Get moving," Perkins barked from behind her.

She picked up her pace. *Stay there, Pablo. Stay there.*

She was nearly past the mound when a figure emerged from behind it. A figure far too big to be Pablo. Directly in front of her stood Bob Melbourne. He had his pistol pointed at Perkins. "Drop the gun!" he said.

Amity screamed. Jo dove toward the pile of sawdust, hoping to dodge the trajectory of any bullets that went flying. She landed softly, tiny particles of wood dispersing into the dusk.

A shot rang out. Gus lunged toward Amity. With a splash, they tumbled into the pond.

Perkins clutched his arm. "Bastard!" he yelled.

"I said drop the weapon." Melbourne eased forward, his gun still trained on Perkins. "Else it's more than your arm that will suffer."

Perkins tossed his pistol to the ground. It landed with a soft thud. "There's the man you're after." He pointed with his good arm toward the pond. Treading water, Amity was clinging to Gus. "Stole my gold. And he's a murderer too."

Melbourne strode toward him. "Well, isn't that curious? Only moments ago, I overheard Miss Felch saying you'd gotten rid of your adversaries by any means necessary. You didn't deny it. And as I understand it, some from your ship have died under suspicious circumstances."

Perkins's face contorted with an ugliness Jo hadn't seen there before. "They deserved it. Every one of them."

"Setting the world right, are you?" Melbourne wrenched Perkins' arms behind his back. Blood trickled down his shirtsleeve as the handcuffs clicked shut. "I'm interested to hear how you managed it. You can tell me all about it down at the station."

Like a wounded animal, Perkins flitted his gaze from Jo to Amity and Gus. "A curse on you. All of you," he said as Melbourne dragged him forward.

"That curse has certainly been convenient," Jo said. "Can't fault your hanging onto it."

She watched as he trudged beside Melbourne into the dusk. At the pond's edge, Gus helped Amity out of the water.

Pablo emerged from the other side of the sawdust. "Are you all right, Miss Felch?"

"I'm quite well, thank you." With her hands, she brushed sawdust from her skirt, from her sleeves, from her hair. "But Effie must be worried sick over you, Pablo. However did you find us?"

He glanced down at his feet, then back at her. "You came here to find a bad man. A very bad man."

"A bad man who could have hurt you. You were smart to fetch Officer Melbourne. Going back to the police station can't have been easy." She tousled his hair. "You're a brave lad, Pablo."

# CHAPTER THIRTY-TWO

## Josephine ~ 1889

In the courtroom gallery, the benches were filled with onlookers. Those with a stake in the shipping industry had professional reasons for wanting to hear how the court ruled in the matter of the wrecked ship *Iona*. Others were simply curious, the proceedings being the main attraction in Astoria that day.

Jo suspected that among this group were some who'd held onto items they'd taken from the wreck. Depending on how the court ruled, a few might feel compelled to return what they'd taken. Others, she knew, would not be swayed regardless of how the court ruled. Greed was a powerful motivator.

She sat in the front row, with Noah on one side of her and Amity on the other. Next to Amity sat Gus, and next to him, Pablo. Effie sat beside the boy, her arm circling his shoulder.

On the bench behind them sat Arthur, Roger, and Douglas. All three looked freshly bathed. Their clothes, though threadbare in spots, looked to be cleaned and pressed. Their landlady must have seen to that.

Behind them sat Olin Stein with his notepad and pencil. Earlier, Jo had overheard him talking with the crew members about Howard Perkins' arrest. The men had said little. Even from jail, Perkins had power over them. Or perhaps it was only the curse that kept them quiet out of fear that his bad luck would spill onto them. Once that sort of thinking took hold, it could be hard to undo.

Jo's notepad and pencil were on her lap. She'd make notes, of course. But how much she decided to put into print would depend on what happened at the hearing.

She scratched behind her ear. A small clump of sawdust fell from her hair and landed on Noah's trousers. He brushed it away.

"Sorry," she whispered. "I thought I'd got that all out in the bath."

"No matter." His hand flitted over a tendril of hair that had escaped her topknot. "Trees and tresses go together."

The door at the front of the courtroom opened, and the judge entered. "All rise," said the bailiff. This wasn't the county judge, but a federal official who'd come from Portland, the federal courts having constitutional jurisdiction over matters governed by maritime law.

A tall man with graying sideburns, the judge took his seat behind the bench. Shuffling ensued as the observers took their seats. He pounded his gavel. "This court is now in session concerning the wrecked ship *Iona*." Looking over the top of his glasses, he shuffled through a stack of papers. "I see that the captain, one Nicholas Watson, is deceased. And the first mate is..." Frowning, he looked up from his papers. "Currently being held at the county jail on kidnapping charges."

Gus rose to his feet. "I was second mate aboard the *Iona*. If I may, sir, I'd like to explain."

"Under the circumstances, I suppose you'll have to do. Approach the bench." The judge motioned him forward.

Gus moved to the front of the courtroom. He stood tall, his hands clasped in front of him.

"Name," the judge said.

"Gus Leighton. Second officer aboard the *Iona*."

The judge extracted another paper from his stack. "I see from the underwriter's report that the vessel was registered to Miss Emma Craig."

"Emma Watson." Roger rose from his seat. "Captain and her was married."

Forehead furrowed, the judge scanned the paper. "Captain Watson had a wife. Recently deceased, it says here."

"That's right," Roger said. "Emma took sick out of Manzanillo. Died at sea."

The judge glanced again at the paper. "The deceased wife is Catherine Watson. She died last month in Gloucester, Massachusetts."

Murmuring rippled through the courtroom at the scandal of Captain Watson having had a wife back home while sailing with Emma.

Roger shook his head. "That can't be right. Emma was his wife."

Gus turned to him. "It's true, Roger. Captain Watson had a wife back in Gloucester. He intended to divorce her, but her health was failing. He didn't feel he could leave her. But he was in love with Emma, so they decided they'd sail as if they were married, in hopes they one day would be."

White-faced, Roger sat down. "Had no idea," he said.

"Me neither," Douglas said.

"Order!" The judge pounded his gavel. "Now we've sorted through that, let's come back round to the ship and its contents. This report says items were taken from the *Iona*. By local beachcombers, I presume. Have these items been recovered, Mr. Leighton?"

"Some were, after a notice ran in the paper." Gus glanced at Jo. "The crew took what's theirs, and the police are holding the rest pending this court's ruling."

"Any items of notable value still missing?" the judge asked.

Gus hesitated. "None that I can say for certain."

"And you say the crew has claimed their belongings?"

"To my knowledge, they have," Gus said. "It's only those items belonging to the deceased that may be unaccounted for."

The judge nodded. "Hearing no objections, the court instructs the police to inventory said items and attempt notification of the families of the deceased. Any items left unclaimed ninety days from notification shall be sold at auction. That brings us to the vessel. This report says she was in ballast when she foundered. Is that correct, Mr. Leighton?"

"That's right. The *Iona* was in ballast, headed to Portland to pick up a load of lumber."

"No cargo value, then. As for the schooner, I see an insured value of one hundred thousand dollars. That's a large amount. When I see figures like that, my concern is intentional grounding with the intent of collecting on the insurance."

"I understand your concern, your Honor. But I assure you, there was nothing suspicious about how she wrecked. A fierce storm blew in. In the waves, the ballast shifted. Try as we might, we couldn't right her. I should also note that with the captain and Emma both deceased, there was no one aboard who stood to benefit from a claim on the insurance."

The judge drummed his fingers. "The *Iona* foundered in a storm, and the call went out to abandon ship."

"That's right, your Honor. It was every man for himself. Thanks to the valiant efforts of some here in this courtroom, all were saved except for Bernard Ainsworth."

"Ship abandoned," the judge said. "Salvors prevail."

Jo heard the shuffling of feet behind her. "Excuse me, excuse me. Story to file."

She turned to see Olin Stein racing toward the exit. No doubt he wanted the *Gazette* to break the news that anyone could keep what they found from the *Iona*—even the vessel itself. With the ship abandoned, the insurers would get nothing.

The door clicked shut behind Olin. Adjusting his glasses, the judge turned over another paper. "Ah, but there was one left aboard the vessel. Goes by the name of..." Squinting, he held the paper close to his face. "Queenie. A dog. The underwriter's agent reports she was aboard the ship even after the call to abandon."

Muffled laughter filled the courtroom.

"With all due respect, your Honor, I wouldn't count Queenie as part of the crew," Gus said.

"Doesn't have to be part of the crew. A cat found aboard a ship has been enough to satisfy a previous court that the vessel was not abandoned. And so the court amends its ruling." The judge struck his gavel. "Because the *Iona* was not entirely abandoned, items of value, including the vessel itself, shall be retained by the insurers against any claims they pay out."

Whispers overtook the courtroom. A dog! Who'd have thought?

Gus cleared his throat. "If I may, your Honor. Before you adjourn these proceedings, I wish to bring evidence of misconduct aboard the *Iona*. There is reason to believe her first mate, Howard Perkins, killed three men while we were at sea."

Gasps came from the gallery. "That's a serious charge, Mr. Leighton," the judge said.

"I realize that, sir. I wouldn't bring it without cause."

The judge's eyes narrowed. "I hope this isn't a case of your settling some grievance against the first mate by making frivolous accusations."

"It isn't, your Honor. I'm prepared to come before the court with facts that will prove my accusation is both serious and substantiated. Including Mr. Perkins' admission of wrongdoing, made before witnesses."

"And these witnesses are prepared to testify?"

Jo stood. "I am, your Honor."

"As am I." Amity rose beside her.

"Very well." The judge fingered his sideburns. "First Officer Howard Perkins is hereby remanded to stand before this court on charges of misconduct aboard the *Iona*. His trial shall be convened at the earliest possible date following adjudication of charges pending against him in this county. As a British citizen, he is entitled to assistance from the British consul in Portland. The court so ruling, this session is adjourned." He banged his gavel again.

The spectators rose. As he exited the room, conversation erupted all around.

Amity took Gus's hand. "You were perfect," she said.

Arthur came up behind them. "You've got proof that Mr. Perkins killed Captain Watson?"

Gus nodded. "He all but admitted it last night."

"And we have an empty rat poison container that Pablo says Perkins tossed in the chain locker after the captain fell ill," Jo said.

Douglas patted Pablo on the back. "Smart lad."

Standing next to the boy, Effie beamed. "I'm forever telling him that."

"As steward, Victor probably noticed the poison was missing," Gus said.

"Kept close tabs on his inventory," Roger said.

"Victor must have intended to go to the police in San Francisco," Jo said. "Only Perkins got to him first."

"And made it look like an accident." Douglas shook his head. "Good thing the boy held onto that container."

"He also kept that wicked man from getting the poor woman's gold," Effie said. "Tell them, Pablo."

Shyly, the boy stepped forward. He looked from one person to the next, the men who'd crewed the boat he'd sailed on, the strangers who'd taken him in. "I saw Mr. Perkins. Through the..." He glanced at Jo.

"The skylight," she said.

He nodded. "Mr. Perkins, he put money...gold money...in his...satchel." He smiled, clearly pleased he'd remembered the word.

"And you knew it wasn't his," Noah said. He'd helped draw the story out of Pablo last night. "So, when he wasn't looking, you moved the gold out of the satchel."

"And replaced it with weights from the anchor locker," Amity said.

Arthur gave a low whistle. "Gold. No wonder Mr. Perkins wanted me to find that satchel."

"I know you heard men bragging in the saloon about what they'd found," Jo said. "All the same, I don't understand why you did his bidding. Did he promise to give you something in return?"

Arthur shook his head. "He said if I didn't, he was going to go to the police and tell them I was the one who stabbed Bernard. Since I'm a..." Color rose in his face as his voice trailed off.

Gus set a hand on his shoulder. "That's all in the past, Art."

"When Bernard's body washed up on shore, Perkins had to pin the murder on someone else," Jo said. "You were an easy target."

"He told me the boy must have stabbed Bernard," Roger said.

"And that's why you came by our house looking for him?" Jo said.

Roger nodded. "Mr. Perkins was hopping mad about you getting the kid sprung from jail. He wanted me to nab him and haul him back to the station. Said it was the only way to get justice for Bernard. He knew we was close, Bernard and me."

Douglas scratched the side of his head, mussing his well-oiled hair. "What I don't get is if there was gold in that satchel, where is it now?"

The boy eyed Effie. She nodded. "It's all right. You can tell now. No harm will come of it."

"The money...I put it...in Miss Emma's shoes."

"Her shoes?" Gus shook his head.

"The gold belonged to Emma." Effie jutted her chin. "Pablo gave it back to her the best he knew how."

Douglas turned to Jo. "You print that in your paper, folks'll be elbow to elbow at the waterfront, searching for shoes."

"Fat chance," Arthur said. "Gold don't float."

"Strange that Mr. Perkins didn't grab that satchel when the ship started to founder," Roger said.

"And climb the rigging with it?" Gus said. "That would've been a trick, all right."

"And here I thought it was all the curse," Douglas said.

"A curse is like any other wrong-headed idea you get in your head," Jo said. "It can blind you to the truth. Even the truth about who you can trust."

Amity smiled. "Well said."

"I should hope so." Jo looped arms with Noah. "I am in the word business, you know."

# CHAPTER THIRTY-THREE

## Olivia ~ Present Day

I t's torture, waiting for Jason to call. Olivia reminds herself that the results from the mug Jimmy handled might not come in till tomorrow. Or there might be no results at all, her suspicions nothing more than the result of an overactive imagination.

But if that's the case, why is he planning to leave town? And why has he told her before saying anything to Finn or Jillian? She knows she should be glad. Whatever else happens, Finn's going to be extricated from this mess. She will be too. The building will remain unencumbered, and with any luck, there will be no lasting damage to her relationship with Finn.

That's her hope. Her worry is that with Jimmy, she's dealing with somebody who's one step ahead of her. Someone with an agenda she can't figure out.

She tries to pass the time reading, but the distraction fails. She can't keep her mind on the story. So, she goes downstairs, Micki padding along behind her. At the computer, she busies herself with entering inventory into the database she's setting up.

Now and then, she glances up at the clock. Two. Two-thirty. Three o'clock. Jason's shift has begun. Her phone stays silent. Three-thirty. Four. Four-thirty. Give it up, she tells herself. There's always tomorrow.

At 4:46, her mobile rings.

"Jason here," he says when she picks up, reiterating what she already knows from her caller ID. "You were right to be suspicious. Jimmy Stone's real name is Lars Christiansen. He dropped off the radar after charges were filed against him for murder."

Olivia gasps. "Murder."

"Of a cop, no less. Some sort of shootout in Puerto Rico over an admiralty violation."

"Having to do with a shipwreck, I'll bet."

"Looks that way. Illegal disruption of a protected area. Police confronted him and some other folks. Someone got trigger-happy, likely Mr. Christiansen. I also found a civil suit filed by a bunch of investors over some sort of business venture he ran. Deep Sea Innovations, it was called. According to the complaint, the only innovation was how quickly he disappeared with their money."

"Wow." She sinks into a chair.

"I also ran a check on the woman you said is with him."

"Jillian Woodhull."

"Yup. Something of a messy divorce case between her and Andrew Woodhull, grandson to Marianne Woodhull, the lady you said runs the Seaworthy Institute. Or ran it. There's a legal filing concerning her mental capacity."

"I wonder if Jillian forged her name on the permit they're using."

"Or persuaded Marianne to sign it when she lacked the legal capacity to do so. We've alerted the state authorities who issued that permit. They'll look into it."

"Will you arrest Jimmy?"

"That was the plan. But when we asked at the motel where you told me they were staying, the clerk said they checked out this morning."

A sinking feeling takes hold in her stomach. As she feared, Jimmy is one step ahead of her. If only she'd acted sooner.

"No vehicle, apparently," Jason continues. "So we can't track them that way, even if we had the resources for it, which we don't. I put a notice out to all the usual places—state police, US customs, that sort of thing. But I have to tell you, given how well he's slipped by so far, there's a good chance he's already on his way to swindle someone else."

He promises to fill her in on any developments. She hangs up. Micki comes over from where she's been lying on the rug and rubs herself around Olivia's ankles. Absently, Olivia reaches down to pet her.

"Gone," she says. "Just like he said."

She should be glad. But worry niggles at her. She grabs her phone and dials Naomi.

"What's up?" Naomi says. In the background, Olivia hears the whir of a washing machine on the spin cycle. Naomi spends Sunday afternoons at the laundromat.

"I was just wondering," she says. "Did Jimmy say anything to Finn about them leaving town?"

"Not that he's mentioned to me." On Naomi's end, the machine rattles to a stop. "All he could talk about this morning was what they found last night. Guess they don't need that equipment after all."

"They found the gold?" She tries to square this with what Hanna told her about the shoes.

"Yup. Supposedly, Jimmy spotted it with that submarine thingy. He says tonight they'll bring up the goods. Where'd you get the idea they were leaving?"

"Jimmy told me last night. He said it was my fault, that I'd ruined everything."

"That's ridiculous."

"And now Jason Reynolds says they've checked out of their motel."

"That doesn't make sense. Not after what they found. And how would Jason know anyway?"

"I brought him Jimmy's mug from the Dockside last night. He lifted fingerprints and ran them through a database. Jimmy's real name is Lars Christiansen. He's wanted for killing a cop in Puerto Rico."

There's a beat of silence on Naomi's end. "Killing a cop," she repeats.

"That's not all. A bunch of investors have filed a lawsuit claiming Jimmy—I mean Lars—swindled them out of their money."

"Yikes," Naomi says. "So you think he figured out Jason was onto him, and they skipped town without the gold?"

"Possibly. Or maybe Jimmy intended to leave anyway, like he told me. He could've just made that up about finding the gold, to rub it in."

Naomi sighs. "I'd better track down Finn and let him know. It won't be pretty."

"And how are you going to explain to him how you know all this? That I put the police on Jimmy's tail?"

"Oh. Right."

"It's better if Finn finds out on his own. What time has he been going out?"

"Ten o'clock. Why?"

"Just curious." Olivia doesn't want to drag Naomi any deeper into this than she already is.

"Poor Finn. He was really counting on a share of that gold. But even if it's there, he can't bring it up without Jimmy. I keep trying to tell him life's not all about what you can acquire. But he can't seem to grasp that."

"He had it hard when he was young," Olivia says. "He's still trying to prove something to himself."

They hang up. Olivia tries phoning Jason. But the dispatcher says the officers are all tied up with a suicide attempt on the Megler Bridge. Unless it's life-and-death, she advises checking back in a few hours.

A few hours. Olivia takes a short break for dinner, then goes back to entering titles into the database. It's a good distraction. Naomi will be impressed at the progress she's making.

But in the back of her mind, Olivia knows what she has to do. If there's any chance Jimmy and Jillian are still around, she can't let them get away. Or worse yet, let any harm come to Finn. Jimmy—she still thinks of him as Jimmy—has killed one man over undersea treasure. He could easily kill another. Because besides Jimmy and Jillian, Finn is the only one who knows the *Iona*'s location. The only one who knows where the gold is, if it exists.

At a little past nine, she tries one more time to reach Jason, but the officers are still at the bridge. She silences her phone, puts on her warmest jacket, and heads for the marina. When she gets there, the security guard waves her through. She's been here enough with Finn that the guard probably thinks they're family.

The docks are deserted. Gentle waves lap at the pilings. A change in the wind, a weather system moving in, and conditions can quickly go from mild to treacherous.

She stops in front of Finn's boat. It's older than he is, but it's his pride and joy. He shows it off to anyone willing to step aboard. A combination commercial fishing boat with aluminum top house and bulwarks, it's good for seining, crabbing, trolling, and longlines. Between the fo'c'sle, the topside, and the day bunk in the top house, it sleeps nine people, not that Finn ever brings that many aboard. The fish hold is bigger than he needs, too, with the way fishing is going these days.

She checks her watch. Nine thirty-five. She climbs aboard the boat, steadying herself as it rocks gently. Skirting the tophouse, she edges around to the stern. From here, she'll be able to hear who's coming without being seen.

She pulls her jacket tight and stomps her boots to warm her feet, wishing she'd opted for her warmer pair instead of these slip-ons. She gazes up at the stars, searching for the constellations she used to find with her grandma when they'd sit outside at Cape Cod on warm summer nights. Orion. Pegasus. Leo. Cassiopeia. All anchored by Polaris, the North Star, the earliest way for seafarers to get their bearings, find their way home.

Voices get her attention. Finn and Jimmy, bantering. Jillian's crystal laughter.

Quickly, Olivia scoots to the port side. She grabs hold of a metal ring on the deck, she lifts the cover to the fish hold, and climbs inside. Curling into a ball, she pulls the cover over her. She gags on the smell of fish, so thick that no amount of hosing down could ever erase it.

She won't have to stand it for long, she tells herself. Just long enough to figure out what Jimmy's up to.

The boat rocks with the weight of them coming aboard. Even Jimmy seems in a good mood. Either he doesn't know that the police are onto him, or he thinks he's got the upper hand with them.

Finn fires up the motors. The boat putt-putts away from the dock, then picks up speed as they hit the river. In Olivia's hiding place, the engine noise is louder than she anticipated. She struggles to catch snippets of conversation. From what she can tell, they're focused on what they'll do when they get to the site. Confirm where Jimmy made last night's find. Dive down after the treasure. Bring it up. They speak of the ocean's bottom where they'll be diving, sandy and hard. They discuss the currents, the tide.

"Tie off!" Finn yells.

Olivia's body jolts upward, like she's on one of those fair rides she hates, with its sudden dips and whirls. Her head thunks against the fish hold's lid. Amid the pain, she feels the lid raise and lower. Just as suddenly, she is jerked back toward the floor. Water sloshes in around the lid's edges, soaking her.

Like a bucking bronco, the boat tilts, whirls, dips. She's thrown up and down. Head throbbing, she lifts the front of her jacket, a ridiculous attempt to protect her phone, tucked in an inside pocket, from the surging water.

The boat quivers and shakes. Thrust backwards, she body-slams against the side of the hold. The bar. They're crossing the bar. Finn has done this hundreds of times. Thousands, probably. She'll be safe. She just has to grit her teeth and hang on. They'll be over it soon.

And they are. As suddenly as the jolting began, it quits. The boat regains its rhythm. Slap, slap, slap, pushing through the waves. She hears voices again. Footsteps. She twists, trying to get at her phone, thinking she should time how far it is from the bar to wherever they're headed, but in the confines of the hold, she can't work the zipper of her inner pocket.

From above, there's the sound of boots clomping close. The lid rises, exposing her to the night air. Jimmy's face looms. "Well, well, well." He grabs her arm and yanks her out of the hold. "Looks like we've got us a stowaway."

Finn sticks his head out from the tophouse. "Olivia. What are you doing here?"

"Turn back, Finn," she says. "Keep going, and there will only be trouble."

Jimmy's grip tightens. "Already got ourselves plenty of that. Told you to mind your own business. But no, you had to go sticking your nose where it doesn't belong."

"Let go of her, Jimmy." Jillian steps toward them. "You're just making things worse."

"Can't get much worse, can it? She's trying to run us off so she can have the gold to herself. Next thing you know, she'll have the police on our tail."

"Police." Finn comes out of the tophouse. "Why would they care what we're up to?"

"Because he's wanted for murder," Olivia says. "And cheating investors."

Jimmy's face twists into something dark, ugly. Jillian reaches for him. "No, Jimmy. Don't—"

Her words are lost. Jimmy lunges at Olivia. Shoves her hard. She braces herself, trying to keep her footing, but there's nothing to hang onto. He shoves her again.

"Leave her—" Finn's voice is the last thing she hears as she plunges into the water. She comes up sputtering. Dark waves lap around her. Her arms and legs move wildly, panic prickling every inch of her skin.

"Life ring!" Finn yells.

A splash as something hits the water on the starboard side. "Gone." Jimmy laughs.

Olivia struggles to keep her head above water. Gasps for breath and gets a mouthful of saltwater.

"Bastard!" The dark, hulking shape of Finn lunges at Jimmy.

A glint of steel in the moonlight. Jimmy's got a gun, pointed at Finn. "Stand down," he says. "Stand down, and no one gets hurt."

"Stop," Jillian sobs. "Stop this madness."

Calm, Olivia tells herself. Calm. The difference between life and death, the diving instructor said.

She catches her breath. Wills her limbs to quit flailing. Treads water. Smooth. Even. But she's cold. So cold. Can't last long at this temperature, the instructor said. Not without a wetsuit. Ten minutes? Five? Her mind feels fuzzy around the edges. Too fuzzy to remember. Too fuzzy to care.

The voices on the boat fade into the background. Maybe it's drifting away. Maybe she's the one drifting. The currents. The currents. Too strong to fight. Go along with them. See where you land.

She blinks. A bright light illuminates a circle around her. Heaven opening its gates, welcoming her in. Stay or go. Go or stay. She's not sure she has a choice.

In the distance, more voices. Calling and calling and calling her name. Can't they see she's tired? So tired.

Her eyelids close. Her limbs relax. Not so cold after all. The waves, gentle and lapping, cocoon her. All she has to do is let go.

Splash. Splash. Splash. An arm comes around each of her armpits, pulling her close. Ethan, she thinks. He's come for her. She relaxes into his chest. "You...you found me," she sputters.

"It's what we do." A man's voice. Not Ethan. But she'll go with him, she thinks through the fog in her brain. She'll go wherever he takes her.

He wraps his arm over her chest. Pulls her onto her back, and she's floating, floating toward the light.

# Chapter Thirty-Four

## Olivia ~ Present Day

It's going to take some time, but Olivia is determined to get over the trauma of nearly drowning. Back at the Italian restaurant with Ethan, she even manages to joke about the Coast Guard swimmer who rescued her.

"I thought it was you at first," she says. "But he was so young and strong and handsome, and I realized I was mistaken."

He laughs. Then his face sobers. "I'm just glad they got there when they did."

"Naomi gets the credit for that. She knows me too well. Knew I wouldn't ask what time Finn was going out unless I intended to do something about it."

"Which was rather foolish, I have to say. And also brave."

"I couldn't stand the thought of Jimmy getting away. And I was afraid he'd hurt Finn since he knew where the wreck was."

"Naomi was smart to contact Jason when you didn't answer your phone. Thank heavens Jason took it seriously and got the Coasties involved."

"I curse my mobile sometimes. But I doubt Jason would have acted if Naomi hadn't shown him where I was with her FindMe app."

"For which I'm exceedingly grateful. But I don't get why she had you on that app in the first place. You two always keep tabs on each other?"

She laughs. "Not at all. We went to that big book expo last month, and Naomi insisted it would help us keep up with each other. And it was handy, I have to admit."

"Handy and lifesaving. Although I honestly don't see why Jimmy felt the need to do you in. You didn't know where the wreck was."

"I guess he got it in his head that I was plotting to run Jimmy and Jillian off so Finn and I could go after the gold together."

"The gold that doesn't exist?" Ethan says.

"Those Finnish families might not have gotten all of it," Olivia says. "Rich ladies have lots of shoes."

"I hope you don't intend to go searching for them."

"Not a chance. That's up to Glen now. I put him in touch with Finn. He's going to allocate some grant money toward hiring Finn to take him out to the site. His group will make a proper search for artifacts from the *Iona*."

"Jimmy Stone must be fuming."

"I'm sure he is, from his prison cell. I expect Jillian regrets ever getting involved with him. She's got a lot to answer for herself. Helping him hide from the law. Obtaining that permit under questionable circumstances. She may face charges too."

"Could be she'll turn state's evidence," he says. "Hey, I told the diving instructor about you keeping calm in the water. She's impressed."

"I'll bet she is, after the way I panicked in the pool."

Ethan raises his wine glass. "They say practice makes perfect. Here's to learning as we go."

She raises hers. "And to Queenie."

They clink glasses, then sip from them. Redolent of cherries and oak, the wine tickles her tongue and warms her throat. One of life's simple pleasures, not to be overlooked.

"And who's Queenie again?" he asks.

"The dog that never abandoned ship. That's what the judge ruled, anyhow. I sent Glen a copy of the Evening Register article about it. Hopefully that will keep people like Jimmy from ever bothering that wreck again."

"Four paws, changing history. I like it."

"Me too. Though without Josephine Felch's newspaper, that detail might have been forgotten. The court records were lost in a fire, and when I went back to the library and checked the competing newspaper, I found an inaccurate report on the ruling. They printed a small correction a few days later, noting that the judge amended his ruling after their reporter left the courtroom. But the correction would have been easy to miss."

"Then here's to Josephine Felch," he says, and they clink glasses again.

"To Josephine," she repeats. "May our paths keep crossing."

# Author's Note

I'm lucky to live on Oregon's North Coast, near Clatsop Spit, which used to be called Clatsop Sands. The waters there are known as the Graveyard of the Pacific because of the estimated two thousand ships that have wrecked there, with hundreds of lives lost.

As described in this book, these treacherous waters result from a collision between the outflowing Columbia River and the incoming currents and tides of the Pacific in an area called the Columbia Bar. Bar pilots who keep up to date on the literal shifting sands guide big boats over the bar. Jetties north and south of the bar have mitigated the hazards somewhat, but large tides and big storms still generate life-threatening conditions.

Though long out of print, James A. Gibbs' *Pacific Graveyard* contains well-researched accounts of noteworthy wrecks in this region. In Astoria, the Columbia River Maritime Museum educates visitors on many fascinating aspects of the Columbia, including shipwrecks. The museum also hosts an annual shipwreck conference.

This book is a work of fiction, so any resemblance of the characters to real present-day people is coincidence. For authenticity, I drew details from actual historical events where I can, though I alter these facts to fit the story. In constructing my account of the fictional ship *Iona*, I drew from accounts of the "cursed ship" *Melanope*, which was owned by the captain's mistress and abandoned at sea during a storm in 1906. The vessel's remains were later salvaged off the mouth of the Columbia.

For details of the rescue, I've drawn from accounts of the *Admiral*, which ran into the South Jetty in 1912. A locomotive was used to transport rescuers to the wreck, and two of the survivors were found stumbling along the train tracks. Other wrecks I've mentioned are also real, including the "beeswax" wreck near Neahkanie Mountain, the wreck of the *Peter Iredale*, and the ghost ship *Mindora* (though the *Mindora*'s misfortunes occurred earlier in the century).

Because of the hazards of the Columbia Bar, the federal government opened the Point Adams lifesaving station on Clatsop Spit (Sands) in 1889; for this book, I have it opening earlier. I modeled the cannery at Point Adams after one that opened on the spit several years later. Locals did come out to salvage items from shipwrecks, and rescued sailors did sometimes stay in the area, taking up with local women.

Fire did not actually destroy Oregon's 1889 federal court records, but there were plenty of courthouse fires around the state during that era, including ones in Yamhill and Tillamook, towns not far from Astoria. In 1883, fire also destroyed Astoria's Clatsop Mill, which I used as a model for the mill in this story.

Readers may be surprised to learn that in the Victorian era, women did own newspapers. So-called girl reporters, also known as "petticoat detectives," exposed many of society's ills. Though they sensationalized some stories, they also blazed a trail for today's investigative journalists.

Thankfully, I've never personally endured a near-drowning. For my account of Jillian's experience, I used details from one of James Delgado's dives near the mouth of the Columbia, as he recounts in *Adventures of a Sea Hunter*.

Subscribers to my bimonthly newsletters are the first to learn about my newest books, including more Tidewater Chronicles mysteries featuring Jo and Olivia. In my newsletter, I also share deals and discounts. When you sign up at , you'll get a free novella to download.

Thanks for reading!

Vanessa Lind

P.S. Yes, scalloped cheese was really a side dish during the Gilded Age.

Book endings are bittersweet, aren't they? You get attached to characters and their world. When the book ends, you're left wanting more. That's why I enjoy writing series.

Want to know more about how Ingrid met Sam and became part of the bookshop? I've got a free novella telling that story, exclusive to newsletter subscribers. If that intrigues you, here's the download link: https://BookHip.com/MMGQXTJ

And if you find you're getting attached, don't worry. You can follow the characters you love through all the dual timeline mysteries in The Tidewater Chronicles.

Happy reading!

Vanessa Lind

www.vanessalind.com